DOWNWARD

Bethan White

First published 2016 worldwide by
T Squared Books.
www.tsquaredbooks.co.uk

Copyright ©2016 Bethan White

ISBN: 978-0-9954521-0-7

T SQUARED BOOKS

This book is dedicated to all who travel with a black dog at their side.

Lightning Crashes

*

It all seemed very strange. Every day was different; that was one of the things that stopped being a lettings agent boring him to death. Actually, the only thing, but perhaps one thing was enough. It could be worse. He could be emptying bins. He could be teaching thirty snotty-nosed kids who despised him. He could be … but right now, being a lettings agent was a bit confusing. He couldn't get the lights to work in this stupid house, for one thing. He had told the landlord over and over about making sure the bulbs all worked, that the wiring had been checked, but click, click – the switches just weren't working. And this stupid couple he was showing round. Every time he turned his back, they wandered off. He had found her in the cupboard last time, just standing there, staring at the wall. He was going to recommend they didn't let to these two. They didn't seem to have all their sandwiches at their picnic.

He turned to speak to the husband, boyfriend, whatever the hell he was. And he'd gone. *Again.* But sitting there, looking up at him with that manic grin they sometimes seemed to have, was a black Labrador. Labrador cross, perhaps. It was certainly a big bugger. Well, that was a clincher. This house was strictly no pets. The landlord was absolutely adamant about that. He might be a total moron when it came to making the house habitable and attractive to potential clients, but he wouldn't be shifted on pets.

This dog seemed quite well behaved, though. It just sat there, panting softly, rolling its big, brown eyes.

'Sorry, boy,' he said. 'I don't carry dog treats on viewings.'

The dog looked at him, dolefully.

'There's rarely the call.' He looked down at it. Was that a tooth starting to show at the corner of the animal's mouth? Was that rumbling noise the beginnings of a growl? Where the bloody hell were that dim couple? Standing in the cupboard like some kind of vegetables, bringing a bloody dog when there were no pets allowed, disappearing *again*.

'Hello?' he called. Had this hall always had this echo? 'Hello? Are you there? Your dog is getting a bit …' yes, that was a growl and now he could see all of its teeth. It was bigger as well. Could dogs grow like that? *Should* dogs grow like that? It was rearing up now, its breath hot and rank, its mouth wide to take his throat in just one bite, to shake him, and shake him, and shake him, until …

'Chris! For God's sake, what is it?'

He sat up sharply, drenched in sweat, heart racing. Where was the house, the couple, the dog? He looked round, eyes wild. 'There … there was a dog. A big, black dog.'

Megan put a soft hand on his chest and pushed him back down onto the pillow. She pushed his hair back from his sticky forehead, soothing him as if he were Kyle, climbing into bed with them, confused and crumpled from a bad dream. 'There's no dog.'

He nodded, but with less conviction now that reality was biting. 'There was. A Labrador or some such thing. Big. Black. Teeth.' He half-heartedly mimed a vicious mouth, snapping his teeth at her, smiling.

'Perhaps it was a Labradoodle,' she said. 'A cockerpoo.'

'A sprocker.' His smile faded. 'It was scary, though, Megs. It was so real. So ordinary. I was showing this dim couple round a house and the lights wouldn't come on. Then, this dog suddenly appeared and … it was friendly, then it went for my throat.' His eyes were wide as he relived it.

She leant forward and kissed his forehead. 'Babe,' she said, quietly, 'it's just that dream. You know, that dream you have?'

'I've had this dream before.' There was a slight query in his voice. Every time, she thought, every time he wakes up wild-eyed and sweating from the dream of the dog and every time he has forgotten it is the same old, same old. But it was real to him, there was no getting away from it, and when she had had a quiet word with the GP, he had just said it would go away when Chris settled down at work, when he felt more secure, when the baby was born. There was always a holy grail in view, the time when Chris would stop dreaming of the dog. But here they were. He had had two promotions, he was doing well as far as she could see at work. They had never been closer, their relationship was steady as a rock. And if the sex was less amazing, well … that's how it went, wasn't it? That's what her sister had said anyway, and no one's marriage was sounder than hers. Samantha of course said the opposite, but then, that was Sam. Always with the glossiest boyfriend, the latest clothes. But she didn't have a three year old. Or a man who woke up sweating and babbling about a dog he could never remember seeing before …

She kissed him again. 'Yes, sweetie. You have had the dream before. But what do we always say?'

He smiled, remembering. 'It's only a dream. And as long as it doesn't leave poo on the carpet, no worries.'

She tapped his nose with her finger and smiled. Eventually, he came out of it. But somehow, in the back of her mind, that black dog sat, waiting patiently, for its moment to come. She shivered.

'Cold?' he said, holding out the covers. 'Come in for a cuddle.'

She looked longingly at the cave, with his naked body tempting her to stay. But she had heard the stirrings that meant that Kyle was waking up and long experience had taught her that ten minutes well spent now, coaxing him out of sleep and into wakefulness instead of letting him wake on his own and fly into a panic, would be time she would never regret. So she swung her legs out of the bed with a smile and went to the door.

'It's okay, Kyle,' he heard her say as she opened his door. 'Mummy's here.'

3

Chris closed his eyes and listened to her voice, soothing her son, bringing him back to the world of day from the dark of night. He let her sing-song voice wash over him, sending him back to sleep. To where the black dog always lurked, ready to go for his throat.

Breakfast was the same as always. Megan ran the house on military lines almost, routine being what kept her menfolk on what passed for the straight and narrow. The apple didn't fall far from the tree and Kyle was like his father in almost every way, looks, temperament and the tendency to completely lose the plot if things went a little bit to the right or left of centre. So breakfast was always the same. Two Weetabix with cold milk, no sugar for the big one, Readybrek with a spoonful of jam for the little. She would have a slice of toast when Chris had gone to work and Kyle was intent on his millionth rewatch of Tree Fu Tom. One thing about having a child wedded to routine was that you knew exactly what he would want to be doing at any second of any day. She had worried he might be on some Spectrum somewhere, but the GP had reassured her, just as he had reassured her about Chris; normal, just perhaps a little fragile. She watched them eat, in from the outside to the middle, turn the bowl round a quarter of a rotation and begin again. She sighed, but quietly so they didn't hear. She just hoped that doctor knew what he was on about. Some days, she wondered.

Chris Rowan sometimes wondered who he was. He also wondered whether other people had the same kind of thoughts, but he had been brought up by parents who, though very loving, had not really encouraged that kind of conversation. His father was dead, but his mother was still very much around, busy, bustling, never still for a minute. She worked tirelessly for the church of which her new husband was vicar and although Chris sometimes wondered whether her air of spirituality was perhaps a disguise she had adopted when she first met Mike, everyone else seemed to think it was genuine, so who was he to say? But he couldn't even picture a conversation with her that began, 'Mum, do you ever look in the mirror and ask "why am I me?"' She would tut, smile, give him a hug which didn't involve any more than a quick arm around the shoulder. No kiss, no understanding murmur, nothing like he had seen Megan give to Kyle a million times a day. And Megan – the dreams were bad enough; if he told her he wasn't sure who he was sometimes, she would worry even more.

But at work, he knew who he was. No one very important or interesting and sometimes, he knew, he was 'that bastard agent' when he had to tell people that the landlord had chosen another would-be tenant, but by and large, he was next down in the pecking order from the boss. And if he would never actually *be* the boss, that was fine. It was a living. Just.

'Chris!'

'Dave!'

He and Dave Stanley greeted each other exactly the same way every morning. Kyle would have approved.

'Are you snowed under today?' This was another common starter for ten and it usually meant that there was a problem house or flat to show. There was one that was hanging around like a bad smell – could it be, perhaps, that rather unusual odour in the kitchen, that mixture of very old kipper and brussels sprouts? Chris and almost everyone else in the office had shown the house to what seemed like every DINK couple in town, but no dice. The desperation was beginning to show. The last time it had been shared with anyone it was by the office junior and she had come up with the great idea of the coffee bean under the grill. She had nearly burned the house down and now the kitchen smelt of old kipper, brussels sprouts, coffee grounds and burning. But the question had to be answered.

'I was going to catch up on some calls later this morning. I have a viewing at nine thirty,' he glanced at his watch and grimaced; time was whizzing by this morning, 'and then I'm showing a couple round about four properties in the afternoon. If they fall in love with the first one, I will be free later.'

'Brilliant! That sounds as if it might work. Unless you want to add forty-three to their list.' No one even bothered to use the road name any more. Forty-three was all it needed to move a cloud over anyone's sun. 'The landord's getting a bit testy.'

'Dave. Do me a favour. This is a top of the range couple. They won't want to have anything to do with forty-three. And if the landlord's getting testy, he should do something about that smell.'

'Don't think I haven't told him that, Chris, about a hundred times.' Dave was getting on his dignity, never a good place for everyone else in the office. 'If you're too busy, I can always …'

'No, no.' It was always a good idea to head Dave off at the pass when he went all hangdog. If he went out on a gig himself two things would happen – it wouldn't get let and no one would be allowed to forget it for the next six months. 'I can do it. Do you have someone in mind for it?'

'Yes. It's not ideal, to be honest. It's a woman on her own, but earning well as far as I can tell from the application. She intends to live there herself at first, then take on a housemate. She's from here originally but has only just moved back after years away, apparently. Abroad. Somewhere, dunno.' Dave was riffling through papers on his desk. Although it was only five past nine on a Monday morning, it already looked like a bombsite. 'What if you show the couple number forty-three if they don't plump for anything else? If all else fails, it might make them feel more kindly towards one of the others. Then, if they hate it …'

'Which they will,' Chris couldn't help adding.

'Show it to this woman. Shall I tell her five o'clock?'

That would mean getting home late. Kyle's tea would be late. His bath would be late. Bedtime would be never …

'Chris? Five?'

He snapped to. 'Sorry, Dave. Just restructuring my evening. Yes, tell her five. But also tell her someone else is viewing it. Who knows, the Dinkies might be as mad as trees and actually like the dump.'

'Stranger things have happened, sure enough.' Dave Stanley was not an unreasonable boss and he knew he asked a lot sometimes. But the salaries here were a good bit above the other letting agents in town and he paid a decent commission on an ad hoc basis when they shifted somewhere totally crap like number forty-three. So Chris might be in for a nice surprise in his pay this month, if he pulled out all the stops. He clapped him on the back and dropped heavily into his chair, looking hopelessly at the paperwork. 'I've got her mobile number somewhere.'

From his left, an arm stretched out and his secretary's hand, conveniently placed on the end of it, twitched a file to one side. A scarlet-tipped finger pointed silently.

'Oh, there it is. Thanks, Jacintha. I knew it was somewhere.'

The girl shook her head, her asymmetric bob swinging. Chris could never really balance her looks – ditzy as all get out with always at least one eye hidden behind bizarre hair – with her efficiency. She looked as if she didn't know what was going on yet in fact she knew *everything*. Gossip in the office said she was a girl with a mission and that mission was to be running the office inside a year. And sometimes it was true she had the look of someone who might be planning a palace coup – but nothing to worry about, surely. Chris ignored his gut feeling and picked up his day's folders. He wouldn't be back in the office now until tomorrow with any luck, so Jacintha and her plotting needn't bother him overmuch.

The door was still swinging and he didn't hear her say to the room in general, 'Is Chris all right? He looks a little stressed, don't you think?'

No one answered; she hadn't expected them to. But, in her experience, little seeds just occasionally grew into the bindweed that brought the tall poppy to its knees.

The viewing at nine thirty turned into a viewing at almost ten. Chris had planned his timing to allow for walking there and the walk had ended up as a trot. The day was warm and humid and he could feel the sweat pooling and cooling in the small of his back as he approached the rather acid-faced couple waiting for him outside the house they were due to view. They had had all the time in the world to spot the negatives – too near the road; within yelling distance of the local primary; weeds on the drive. Chris thanked his lucky stars the neighbours were away – their camper van was often parked outside and did little to enhance the view. Nevertheless, he pinned on his best smile and walked the last few paces with his hand extended.

'Mr and Mrs Pugh,' he said, stifling a grin as it suddenly dawned on him that with a name like that, they would probably love number forty-three. 'I'm so sorry to keep you waiting. I …'

The husband spoke. His voice sounded as though it cost him either extreme effort or a lot of money he was unwilling to spend. 'Mr Rowling, I presume?'

'Rowan.'

The woman looked at him, disbelievingly. 'I'm sure the letter said Rowling.'

He widened his smile. 'A typo, perhaps,' he said. He extended an arm up the short drive of 'Dunroamin'. 'Shall we?'

The woman looked mulish and stood firm on the pavement. 'Do you have identification?' she asked. 'One hears such things. Malcolm?'

Her husband looked hard at Chris, as though with more attention he might discover his real identity. When that failed, he nodded. 'My wife is quite right, Mr Rowling,' he said. '*Do* you have any identification?'

'Rowan,' Chris said, tiredly, reaching for his wallet. His driving licence said Christopher Rowan, so what good would it be? He handed it over and husband and wife bent their heads over it as though it were holy writ. The woman raised her head sharply and Chris would later swear he saw whiskers twitch around her shrewish mouth.

'It says here you are Christopher Rowan,' she accused him.

'Yes,' he said, still just about smiling. 'That's who I am.'

'But the letter said Rowling. Because Malcolm and I laughed about it, didn't we, Malcolm, saying I wonder if he's any relation to that JRR Rowling.'

'JK. JK Rowling.' This was getting very surreal.

'Who's that?'

Chris decided on a change of plan. 'Do you have the letter with you?' he asked, politely.

'Of course.' Malcolm Pugh brandished a file he had had clamped under his arm. 'Maureen always files and keeps all correspondence. We don't have E Mail or any of that nonsense. Good old paper and ink always does for us, doesn't it, Maureen?'

She nodded, setting a fat curl on the top of her head bouncing. Chris knew he would have to keep his eyes off it or he would become mesmerised. Things were odd enough without him going into a hypnotic trance. 'Good old paper and ink, always does for us, yes.' She tapped the file. 'It's all in here.'

'May I see the letter?' he asked.

Malcolm Pugh leaned the file on the garden wall and flicked the catches. Inside, all was filed in alphabetical order, little tags separating the pages. He muttered as he walked his fingers through the categories. 'Complaints … hmm … legal action … hmm … here we are, Lettings. Let me see … yes, here it is.' He held it out, but didn't let go. Chris craned round to read it.

'Dear Mr and Mrs … yes, time, date – there we are, look.' He hardly managed to keep the glee out of his voice. 'Mr C Rowan will meet you at the property on …'

Pugh snatched it back and looked at it. Then he reached into the breast pocket of his jacket, brought out some glasses and put them on. He peered again. He then held the letter out to his wife, who did the same, the only difference being that her glasses were in a handbag. Without another word, he shoved the letter back into the file and snapped it closed. The couple looked at each other and gave one small nod, the complicit agreement of a marriage too long to be measured in mere years; this went back lifetimes. 'The original said Rowling,' the wife said, sniffing. 'I know that because I said to Malcolm, didn't I, Malcolm, I wonder if …'

'Shall we look around?' Chris knew if he didn't jump in quickly he would be standing on the pavement all day, the day of the groundhog, that is.

The two looked the house up and down as if it had just made an off colour remark and gave the smallest of tandem nods. Chris led them to the front door and smoothly slotted the key in. He had shown this house before, to the previous tenants and indeed the ones before and the ones before that. No one stayed here long. The landlord's requirements were at the edge of legality, with so little allowed it was almost like being in prison. No redecorating. No pictures to be hung on any wall whatsoever. No children. No pets. No unmarried couples. And probably, as Clint Eastwood admonished Clyde the orang-utan, no farting, no spitting, no picking your ass. Although Chris had to agree, he was with him there.

He opened the door on the dingy hall, with wallpaper which had once, long ago, been bang on trend. The fake dado level was marked with a rose-spattered frieze, the wall below it a dark claret and darker claret regency stripe. The carpet was protected by a plastic runner. The stairs went up to the right, to a landing which was, as they would soon discover, as dingy as the hall. He waited for the usual reaction, which was always a variation on 'it's horrible, but it's vacant and we can afford it; how bad can it be?'

'Oh, Malcolm,' Maureen breathed. 'Isn't it lovely?'

Chris had to fight the urge to clean out his ear with his little finger. He turned to her, and made an effort to sound unsurprised. 'Pardon?' he said.

Maureen Pugh gave him the full benefit of her outrage. 'Excuse *me*,' she hissed. 'I was *speaking* to my *husband*!'

Then, as if no one had spoken, Malcolm Pugh agreed with his wife. 'It is lovely, Maureen,' he announced in his strange, distant voice. 'Very homey.'

'There are quite a few restrictions as to redecoration,' Chris felt it incumbent upon him to point out.

They looked at him uncomprehending.

'You can't redecorate this property,' he said. 'Nor can you ...'

Maureeen Pugh fluttered her eyelids as her eyes rolled up in her head. For a moment, Chris thought she might be about to have a fit, but no – she was merely astonished. 'Why would we want to, Mr Row*ling*?' she asked. 'It's just perfect as it is.'

'It is? I mean, it *is*, isn't it? Well, I'll wait for you down here while you have a look around, shall I?' he said, stepping out into the porch.

They trotted up the stairs and he could hear them twittering to each other as they went from room to room. Downstairs, they went into paroxysms of joy at the dark brown painted kitchen, at the rose-trellised lounge and the dadoed dining room. He was not surprised when they came back to him and offered to sign, then and there, on the dotted line. He fought down his natural inclination to ask them if they were sure. They had come home, in a very real sense. A dowdy, dingy couple had found their dream home, one as dowdy and dingy as they.

As Malcolm Pugh filled in the forms, as behoofed him as the man of the house, Chris tried to make small talk with the wife, but got nowhere. All she would say was that Malcolm – or Mr Pugh as she referred to him always to anyone who was not actually the man himself – had received a very substantial promotion at work and he had been moved to the head office. Of what, Chris couldn't tell – no doubt the forms would help. She herself had always been a homemaker, although they had never been Blessed. He assumed that could mean that they had no children but with these two it was hard to say for sure. They rented because all property was theft. He hadn't had them down for closet communists, but still waters perhaps ran deep.

After what seemed an insanely long time, the forms were filled in. Maureen whispered in her husband's ear and he looked at her proudly, as if she had just produced a rabbit from her knickers.

'My wife was asking when can we move in?' he said.

Chris put the forms into his case without looking at them. 'We have to check your references, Mr Pugh, especially since you are new to your job. Then we have to take a deposit, which I believe in the case of this property is one and a half month's rent. We also need a month in advance. That comes to …' he paused to do the sum in his head, '… two thousand six hundred and twenty five pounds. In addition, there is our non-refundable fee for doing the credit checks and so on, another …'

'*How* much?' Maureen Pugh hissed. '*How* much?'

'Two thousand …' Chris began.

'Outrageous!' her husband chimed in. 'For this? One thousand and fifty pounds a month for this hole?'

'I thought it was perfect,' Chris felt it fair to say.

'We like it, yes. But that rent is daylight robbery!'

'Do you want to proceed with this?' Chris was at the end of his tether. He could feel a headache coming on; he almost wished for the weird couple and the dog. 'Because if not …'

The two Pughs looked at each other for a long while, their mouths moving slightly, soundlessly. Every now and again, one of them would glance covertly at him, as though checking he was still there. Eventually, the Man of the House spoke. 'We'll take it, but I will be speaking to your superior about this rent.'

'Mr Stanley doesn't set the rents,' Chris said, ushering them out and ostentatiously double-locking the door. 'The landlord sets them, with advice from us if required. And this *is* a three bedroomed house; very sought after.'

The Pughs sniffed and walked, stiff-legged, down the road without a backward glance. Chris looked up at the house, drab and down-at heel in its very unique Thirties way. And he felt very sorry for it. He even whispered, 'Sorry,' before looking around, making sure no one had seen him. This morning had been bad enough already – to be seen apologising to a house would put the tin lid on it.

Despite the borderline insanity of the Pughs, he had some time on his hands and decided he would drop their paperwork in before setting off again with the Dinkies. He got back to the office and walked into an atmosphere you could cut with a knife. Every head turned towards him and Jacintha gave him a wintry smile. Dave Stanley's desk was empty.

'Hello, Chris,' she said. 'Dave asked me to tell you to pop into the board room when you got in.'

'Okay.' It couldn't be anything he'd done. He hadn't been anywhere except with the Pughs. He pushed open the door to the board room, to see Dave Stanley sitting at one end of the table, with a file in front of him. 'Dave? Can I help you?'

'Ah, Chris.' Stanley's voice oozed false bonhomie. 'Come in. Take a pew.'

Chris flinched.

'I've … um … I've had rather an odd phone call this morning, from a Mr … what's his name, now …' he flicked open the front of the file, 'Pugh.' He looked up and then realised why the word seemed familiar. 'Oh. Pew. Pugh. No pun intended. Now, Mr Pugh has told me …'

Chris was still standing in the doorway but now came in and sat down, halfway along the table. 'Don't tell me. I was late. The rent is too high …'

'Were you late? He didn't mention that. No, he said that you gave them a false name and behaved very oddly.'

'Gave them a false name?' Chris was incredulous. 'They thought my name was Rowling.'

'Ah, now, that sounds right. It says here …' and he ran his finger over the page, 'yes, it says here "He told us his name was Rowling." Can you explain that, Chris?'

Chris massaged his temples and bowed his head. He spoke quietly, because to raise his voice would risk vomiting. He didn't get heads like this very often, but he was on his way to an absolute doozie now. '*They* said that my name was Rowling. They showed me a letter which of course said Rowan, but then they more or less … well, I got the impression that they were almost accusing me of switching it somehow. They were …' He stopped. 'And how did I behave oddly? They looked around and all I did was wait at the bottom of the stairs. Well, the porch, if I'm honest. That hall at Dunroamin always gives me the willies.'

'Apparently,' and Dave looked down at the file, although he was clearly not reading any more, 'apparently, you looked up Mrs Pugh's skirt and made a lewd remark. Mr Pugh wasn't prepared to say what it was you said. Can you recall? Perhaps explain a misunderstanding?' Dave looked expectant.

'Of course I bloody can't!' Chris risked throwing up as he almost shouted. 'She has to be one of the most unattractive women on the face of the planet. If hers was the last skirt in the world, I wouldn't give it a second look. They're making it up!'

Stanley made a note, then tapped his pen a couple of times against his pursed lips. 'Chris, I won't pretend I'm not disappointed. I made my apologies on your behalf to the Pughs, and offered them a discount off the rent, which they graciously accepted. It means we get hardly anything for the property ourselves – that landlord isn't likely to agree to it so it will have to come off our commission, but I suppose you win some, you lose some. But it worries me that you make a judgement call on the attractiveness of the woman as to whether you would look up her skirt, and that will be on your permanent record. I won't actually give you a written warning, because I do feel that perhaps you misread the Pughs. The jack the lad attitude you sometimes display doesn't suit everyone. However,' he leaned forward and pushed himself upright, pocketing his pen, 'let's say no more about it. I have the mobile number for your extra client this evening on Jacintha's desk. She will give it to you on your way out.' He looked up at the clock. 'Just time for a bite of lunch before your appointments. Perhaps you should have something. You look a bit pale. Low blood sugar, perhaps.'

Chris had so much to say. Bugger the blood sugar, which was fine. Well done to the Pughs, who had bagged their discount. He didn't look up skirts of any woman – who looked up skirts these days? There was far more than a shadowy hint of knicker on show on any High Street, anywhere, night or day. But he settled for, 'Thanks, Dave. I'll bring the paperwork from this afternoon in tomorrow, if that's all right with you. It'll be a bit late after I've shown forty-three.'

'Fair enough.' Dave Stanley wasn't a man to let bad words fester and had forgotten the Pugh incident almost entirely by the time he resumed his place behind his desk. 'See you tomorrow, then.'

Jacintha's ears pricked up. So, Rowan was being sent home. In disgrace, hopefully. She had never liked the little prat. She handed him a piece of paper, without a word. Best not to be seen hobnobbing with the man in disgrace.

'Thanks,' Chris muttered, and went out, being careful to slam the door behind him. As he stood outside, with twenty five minutes before his afternoon appointment, his phone warbled in his pocket.

'Hello?'

'Chris? Where are you?'

'Megs? Um … outside the office. Why?'

'It's Monday. We always have lunch on Monday.'

She had a small part-time job in a local beauty spa, more to give her mother a chance to look after Kyle than for any other reason, though the money was handy. Monday lunch was as near to a date as they ever got these days.

'Oh, look, Megs … I'm sorry. Today isn't going too well, to be honest. I had the couple from hell this morning and they've …'

'Well, don't worry, then.' The phrase was friendly, but the voice wasn't.

'Look, babe, I didn't mean to …'

'No. You're busy. That's fine. I'll see you tonight.'

He put a hand to his head. It was absolutely hammering. 'Look, Megs, I …'

But she had gone.

Chris had painkillers from the doctor for when he got one of his heads.

There had been talk of scans and investigations but a migraine was a migraine and he had had them all his life, so he passed on all that. He had tried everything, from cooling patches to top-strength tablets and he had come to the conclusion that nothing really worked. The patches in fact made things worse as they gave him a rash and also made him look a prat, walking around with a big white patch on his head. But right now, anything would be better than the hammering right over his left eye, so he popped into his local pharmacy, which had the additional bonus of being run by a guy he had gone to school with.

'Chris, mate, how …?' The pharmacist stopped himself from asking how his old mate was. He clearly felt like shit. 'Headache?'

Chris nodded, so slightly it hardly showed. He pressed his fingers to his forehead and grimaced, leaning on the counter. 'Mark,' he said, quietly, 'I've got less than half an hour before I need to show a couple round four houses. What have you got?'

'Driving?'

'Mmm.' Again, the minute nod.

'That limits me a bit, but … hang on.'

Chris had his eyes closed, but he heard the door squeak that showed that Mark had disappeared into his little sanctum where he did his dispensing; hopefully he would come up with something miraculous, but by this time a couple of paracetamols would do as long as they hit the spot. The door squeaked again.

'Chris? Do you want to sit down?'

A tiny shake of the head.

'Okay. Well, drink this. I think it will do the business. I'll warn you it tastes pretty vile.'

Chris didn't care what it tasted like and just tossed it back. It hit his tonsils in a viscous wave which had more than a hint of the farmyard about it, backed with chilli, garlic and something he never wanted to meet again. 'What the …?'

'That will be the asafoetida, mainly,' Mark said, with a smile. 'There's some other stuff in there as well, mainly herbal but I think I'll keep the recipe to myself, if that's okay. The … um … non-herbal bit is a trick I keep up my sleeve for very special friends.' He looked at Chris, watching his eyes closely. 'How's it going?'

Chris blinked once, twice and moved his neck experimentally. The stiffness was going and the hammering above his eye had gone already. 'Blimey, Mark,' he said, grinning. 'What the hell *was* that?'

'As I said,' his friend told him, 'I think I'll keep that to myself, if you don't mind. It's just a little trick I learned when I was training.' He lowered his voice. 'A bit frowned on, if you catch my drift. Let me give you something to help if it comes back, but I don't think it will. But next time, take something as soon as you get the first symptom. Do you get these often?'

'Now and again.' Chris pocketed the pack of Advil and rummaged in his pocket for some money, which Mark waved away. 'Stress-related, I suppose you could say. It's been a hell of a day already and more to come.'

'Well, take it easy,' his friend said. He had known Chris since infant school and he knew he was always a bit tightly wound. But if his magic potion didn't sort that out, nothing would. It wasn't strictly illegal but on the other hand, it wasn't strictly legal, either. Nothing you couldn't pick up outside any club, anywhere. 'Drive carefully. I wouldn't want you to end up having a blood test for a few hours, if that's okay with you.'

Chris opened his eyes wide. 'God, Mark! What was in that stuff?'

'Like I say, nothing to worry about. Just something to relax you. And it has taken your headache away, hasn't it?'

Chris nodded. 'Yes. Not a sign.'

'There you are then. Them as asks no questions, isn't told a lie ...'

'So watch the wall, my darling, while the gentlemen go by.' They had had a teacher who managed to squeeze a bit of Rudyard Kipling into any lesson and everyone he had taught could have gone on Mastermind on the subject with no preparation whatsoever. Chris turned and met the startled eye of an old lady who had come up behind him on rubber-soled feet. He thought he would leave the explanation to Mark; he didn't want his headache back, after all. 'Thanks,' he said, raising a hand and felt rather than saw the old dear's eyes follow him from the shop.

The Dinky couple were not waiting on the pavement when he got to the first house, which gave him time to go in and open the front and back doors to let some air in. The day wasn't great for showing, because hot and humid weather meant that the homes all seemed a little fusty on first sniff. The slight breeze the door-opening created helped a little but he was already dreading forty-three. But not as much as he had been that morning. In fact, he was feeling great. A small, warning synapse in his head was trying to tell him that he shouldn't be quite this laid back after a migraine, but he just pushed it away. After the way his day had gone so far, it was a relief to feel this good. He went upstairs to check the rooms. This house was nice but pricey – if these two didn't take it, it might be time to bring the rent down a touch. It needed all the TLC he could give it to make it look its best and he had just run his hankie around the basin to get rid of the spiders' webs across the plughole when he heard someone downstairs.

'Coooeee. Mr Rowan?' At least they had his name right. 'Mr Rowan?'

'Up here,' he called back. 'Hang on, I'll be right down.' He stuffed his webby handkerchief into his pocket and went down the stairs, treading as lightly as he could on the fourth step; it gave an ominous crack sometimes and he didn't need that right now.

The couple were standing in the hall, looking around in a friendly, uncritical way. The husband was like something off an underwear advert, all glossy hair, smooth cheek and hidden pecs. She was the same, but more so; except for the pecs, perhaps. She had other assets instead. The afternoon was looking up.

'Mr and Mrs Mitchells?'

'That's right. But please, call us Matt and Polly. Mr and Mrs Mitchells are my mum and dad as far as we're concerned.' He smiled, his teeth as perfect as the rest of him.

'I won't show you round,' Chris said, although walking around in the waft of gentle perfume Polly gave off with every move would have been nice. 'Everything is in very good order, I think you'll find. The house is let unfurnished, but the few small pieces that are here are yours to use if you want or we will remove them to storage if you'd rather. The white goods are included.'

The perfect pair walked off in the direction of the kitchen and

Chris could hear them murmuring to each other, cupboards opening and closing. Then their voices got more distant as they went out into the back garden. The garden was one of this property's little secrets, secluded, tidy, low maintenance – in fact no maintenance, as a non-negotiable weekly gardener was included in the rent. They passed him in the hall and went upstairs, where more cupboard-opening went on. Mr Perfect even flushed the loo – perfect and pernickety, a combination which would usually get right up Chris's nose but wasn't bothering him at all this afternoon for some reason.

They came back down the stairs, the wife giving a little start when the stair sounded behind her like a gunshot in her ear.

'What do you think?' Chris asked hopefully. If they took this one he would have a few hours to kill and he could go and get Megs some flowers. Some chocolates, even. Spoil her a bit.

'We like it, Chris. But we'd still like to see the others, if they're still available. This is perfect as far as storage goes and of course the garden is lovely. But it's the location in general, isn't it, darling?' Polly turned to her husband and flashed him a look of such intensity that Chris felt himself get a little hot. He suddenly had a flash of his dream of the night before but this couple wouldn't be standing staring at the wall in a cupboard, he didn't think. He made a mental note to knock first if they were in a room with the door shut. 'And I can't remember what the details said about pets,' she went on. 'Are pets allowed?'

'What pet do you have?' Chris asked, sweat prickling under his arms. Say 'black lab' and he would be out of there like a rat up a pipe.

'A cat,' she said. 'Older, well trained, no trouble.'

'Cats are fine at all the properties you are viewing today,' he said. 'They all have cat flaps even, as memory serves.'

Her face lit up. 'Oh, that's lovely. We couldn't do without Mortimer, could we, darling?'

Her husband gave her a peck on the cheek but didn't reply. Chris had the feeling that Matt could do without Mortimer only too easily.

'Well,' Chris tried not to sound too like a used car salesman, 'shall we go on to the next property? It's a little smaller than this, but is in a very quiet road and backs on to a small park. Ideal for Mortimer, I would imagine. Would you like to come in my car? I could drop you back here later.'

'That would be perfect.' Polly seemed to do most of the talking. 'It will save looking for spaces. Do the other houses have a drive, Chris?'

There was something about the way she said his name that made Chris putty in her hands. The houses did all have drives as a matter of fact, but if they hadn't, he would willingly have dug one with his teeth.

House number two was too small. House number three was too big. But house number four was just right. Feeling a little like Goldilocks, Chris pulled the final front door shut behind him and gave them the relevant paperwork, to be dropped in to the office the next morning. They would need guarantors – although they looked all glossy perfection he was a part-time model (surprise, surprise) and she worked in an office. Rent wouldn't be a problem, they assured him, but it would sometimes be paid by her mum and dad. He didn't care if it was paid by the Aga Khan as long as it hit the agency account on the right day, but he just smiled encouragingly and drove them back to their car, which he now saw was a rather elderly Clio with one bashed in wing. He felt a little better seeing that. His car might be a company car, but it was immaculate and he had never had so much as a near miss in his life. Matt Mitchells might look like a film star, but he was clearly a crap driver as well as a rubbish breadwinner. Chris was humming happily to himself as he drew up outside number forty three.

He was about half an hour early, which was a bonus. He could go in and open the doors and windows, try to get rid of that awful smell. He could have kicked himself for not getting an air freshener spray at Mark's pharmacy. They had some little pocket-sized Febreze canisters on the counter, no doubt aimed at the town's student population trying to damp down the smell of trainers before going out on the pull. Never mind, too late now. His mother had always said that running the cold tap in a room would freshen the air, but he had never found it worked. Striking a match was supposed to work as well, or was that just in the loo? It was a bit immaterial, as he didn't have any matches with him. He tried the tap thing anyway – who knew, sometimes these old wives' tales had something in them. There was a faint whiff of chlorine as the water ran, but still the sprouts and old fish prevailed.

It was probably because the tap was running that he didn't hear the woman come in. Or it could have been Mark's Marvellous Medicine. Whichever, he jumped a mile when she tapped him on the shoulder.

It would have all been too much if the woman standing there had been even more beautiful, even more fragrant than Polly Mitchells. She wasn't, but she wasn't at all bad. She was also vaguely familiar. He held out his hand. 'Chris Rowan,' he said, smiling his best rental agent's smile. 'Miss Taylor?'

She looked at him with a quizzical smile, one eyebrow raised. 'Please call me Louise,' she said. 'I'm a little early. Is that all right?'

Chris smiled again and edged out into the room. She had come up rather close and had him trapped up against the sink. He didn't like having his space invaded and he could feel the heat off her body all down the front of his. He found it both vaguely erotic and a little threatening. The weather had grown more thundery over the course of the afternoon and there was a strange stillness in the air. Even the birds had gone quiet, as though they were listening out for a distant storm.

'Early is good,' he said. 'I like early.'

'Yes,' she said. 'I remember that.'

'Pardon?' He opened his eyes wide and turned to face her. 'What did you say?'

'Early. You're an early morning kind of guy, as I recall. Although it was just the once, so it may have been an aberration.' Her face was straight, she was giving away no clues. She laughed, not very pleasantly. 'You don't remember me, I can tell.'

'You are kind of familiar,' he said, thinking furiously. 'I thought I knew you as soon as you walked in.'

'Was that in the Biblical sense?' she asked. 'Or from the checkout in Asda?'

'What?'

'Never mind. Let's set the record straight. We met at a company dinner, back when you worked for …'

'I remember!' He clicked his fingers. 'We went to that restaurant where the food was so rubbish we all got absolutely bladdered. And we …' He stopped.

'Indeed we did. Four times, in fact. I was impressed. I remember wondering if you were that good when you were pissed, what would you be like sober.'

He laughed uncertainly. 'Nothing like as good, I would imagine,' he said. 'Too inhibited by half.'

'Well, it's nice you remember me,' she said, a little tartly. 'You lost my number, I expect.'

'Umm …'

'Don't answer that, Chris. It's best we just put this behind us, don't you think?'

He didn't like the use of the 'we' and 'us'. We and us was him and Megan, not this woman he had shagged after a works' do. But she was a client now, and so he didn't walk out, which his gut was telling him to do.

'There's a bit of an odd smell in here, don't you think?' She was suddenly all business. 'Kippers, is it?' She sniffed again. 'Sprouts?'

'We're having it investigated,' he said, lying shamelessly.

'Hmm. I hope so. Would you like to show me round?'

'I find most clients prefer to wander round by themselves.'

'I prefer to be shown round,' she said, firmly. 'Then I can ask questions as they come to me. That way nothing gets missed.'

He shrugged. 'Okay,' he said. He did, after all, know this house almost as well as he knew his own. He'd certainly been in it often enough. 'Let's start in here, since we're …'

'Here.'

'Exactly. Well, as you see, the kitchen isn't absolutely new, but it is in good order, with all white goods included. There is a small utility room off to the rear and I know previous tenants have used it for a freezer, which isn't included in the fitted items. The back garden is well-kept at the moment and there is a clause in the contract requiring it is kept in a neat condition. Which isn't to say,' he said, turning to her, 'that we expect you to be Capability Brown or anything. It just means the landlord likes the lawn mown regularly, that kind of thing.'

She nodded, but said nothing. He could feel her eyes burning into him whenever he turned his back, so he ushered her ahead of him, to stop the staring. His Capability Brown crack usually got at least a smile, but from this woman – nothing.

Into the lounge and at least here the smell was less all-pervading. A desperate colleague had put a bowl of potpourri on the mantelpiece on some far distant showing and it lent its own faint, musty aroma to the mix. But the room was large and light and the woman nodded, looked out of the window and stepped back, looking at the open plan stairs that went up one wall, expecting him to lead the way.

A thought occurred to him. 'Why have you come to us?' he asked. 'Why don't you get something through …?'

'I don't work there any more,' she said. 'I left. After our little dalliance, in fact. I wasn't well.'

His heart lurched. What was she not well with? Nothing catching, surely. He would have to see if he could find out. But, wait … Megan had had all kinds of tests when she had Kyle. If he had given her anything, they would know, wouldn't they? The thoughts might as well have been on a rolling LED sign above his head.

'Nothing catching,' she said, her voice harsh. 'I had a breakdown, if you must know. But I work for a nice place now. The GP practice in the High Street. Do you know it?'

'We go there.' He didn't know why he found all this a little threatening, but he did.

'Really? I don't have much to do with patients. I am the practice manager, bill paying, HR, that kind of thing.'

He smiled. 'Interesting.'

'Yes.' It was not really an answer, just something to say. 'It pays well, I'll give it that.'

'Ah. Right, shall we go up?' He ushered her ahead. He really, *really* didn't want her behind him. She stepped onto the bottom stair and turned to him, but didn't speak. This was really awkward. He was beginning to think he should just give her the key and leave her to lock up. She had worked as an agent, after all. If she couldn't turn a key, it would be a sad thing. She went up the stairs, testing each tread as she went. He waited at the bottom until she was well ahead of him and got the full view of her rather nice arse as she stamped on each step. A nice little jiggle, not too much, not too little. He compared it to Mrs Pugh and also to Polly Mitchells and gave it an eight, with Pugh equalling zero, Mitchells ten. He gave a little chuckle to himself. This wasn't so bad.

The landing was long and dark, with the bedrooms at one end and at both sides. The bathroom was in a dead end behind them. It wasn't very big, but there was a small ensuite in the end bedroom, so it would suit two people sharing okay. She turned and went in, checking the bath for worn enamel, the loo for limescale, the sink for cracks. It passed muster and she went through into the bedrooms, one by one. He hung back. She seemed to have found her pace and the smell up here was hardly noticeable, so he didn't need to talk it up. If there was one thing that could sell number forty three to a potential tenant, it was the master bedroom, which was big, airy and had a stunning view. It was just a shame that so few people got round to coming upstairs. Most of them did a runner after the kitchen.

She went into the biggest bedroom and he could hear the usual doors opening and closing. What was it with women and fitted wardrobes? What did they expect to find in there? A small shiver went through him. The dream cast a long shadow.

'Chris?' She seemed to have got over her earlier snit. This sounded more positive – perhaps forty three was let at last. 'Chris? Could you come here a minute, please?'

Bugger. What was it now? Damp on the ceiling? Woodlice under the carpet? He pushed open the bedroom door and couldn't see her for a minute. 'Louise?' The name came naturally. Miss Taylor would be a bit too formal, after what they had apparently shared.

'In here.' She was in the small ensuite. 'Hang on, it's too small for two. I'll come out.'

He walked over to the window and looked out. The view was lovely. The house looked out over the Downs and although this meant it was out of the centre, it still had good access to public transport. He stopped himself; he was even enjoying the view like a letting agent now. He really had to get out more. He leaned his head on the glass but it wasn't much cooler than the hot, humid air in the room. If only the thunder storm would come, freshen things up a bit.

Again, he didn't hear her come up behind him. It was just her hand touching his that let him know she was there at all. He tried to turn round, but she held his left arm firmly with her left hand and pulled his right hand round behind him. His breath caught in his throat and he felt a hammering in his head, not his headache coming back, but the hammering that comes with panic and the feeling of impending doom. He had heard the phrase 'rabbit in the headlights' but he hadn't understood what that felt like until now.

He could feel her heat against him, but this wasn't like downstairs. This was different and he thought he knew why. He looked into the window, trying to see a reflection, but although the distant sky was dark with thunderhead clouds, he couldn't see the room behind him at all. She was pulling his hand and he pulled back but something inside him stopped him trying too hard. Finally, with the inevitability of a train crash, his fingers met, not her workaday suit but wetness and he knew she was standing behind him, pressing against him now, without a stitch of clothing.

His throat was tight and dry. When he spoke, it sounded like someone else. 'Louise,' he croaked. 'Please ... I don't do this kind of thing any more.' It wasn't what he wanted to say, but it was all that came to mind.

'What? Never?' She pressed his fingers tighter against her. 'I don't believe that, Chris.'

He turned, against the pressure of her body, against her clutching hand. 'No,' he said, holding her arms and pushing her away. 'Never. Except in my bed at home. With my lovely partner, Megan. With my son asleep across the landing. So, please, get dressed. I won't ever mention this to anyone, so don't worry.' He didn't like the wild look in her eye. But another part of him liked the rest of her very much.

She hadn't missed his eyes flicking down her body and she relaxed into his grip. She said nothing, just stood there, letting him admire her; she kept herself in shape and didn't mind his scrutiny. She let the moments pass, her eyes downcast. Then she chose her moment. 'I don't mind who you tell, Chris,' she said. 'I'll tell people as well, of course. How you took me upstairs in an empty house and ripped my clothes off. How you had a hard-on you couldn't control. I won't say you raped me, that wouldn't be fair. Shall we settle on "took advantage"? I think that sounds alright, don't you? Because you *do* have a hard on, Chris, don't you? Why don't we do something about it, because you certainly can't go outside like that. It literally is showing through your clothes.'

He knew that. He wanted … not this woman, although she looked the part and was certainly ready for it. He wanted … he wanted it to thunder. He wanted his head to stop spinning. He wanted his cock to go down and leave him alone …

She looked up at him, smiling.

He bent his head and kissed her, hard, and she melted into his arms as if she had never been away.

The black dog, already enormous, was growing bigger. Could dogs grow like that? *Should* dogs grow like that? It was rearing up now, its breath hot and rank, its mouth wide to take his throat in just one bite, to shake him, and shake him, and shake him, until …

The peal of thunder woke him and for a long moment he couldn't work out where he was. It was dark, but not the dark of night, just the dark that comes with the mother and father of all storms. He looked around and saw that the window was lighter against the dark of the room, with thin threads of sun coming through the clouds. He was lying on the floor, on his own clothes, his jacket under his head. He couldn't remember anything for a minute, then it came flooding back in a torrent that made him groan aloud. Louise. Naked. Under him, over him, God alone knew what she hadn't done. He hadn't remembered her being quite that limber when they had had their one night stand. How he had let himself be conned into this, he couldn't imagine. Because he *had* been conned, that much he was sure of.

He turned his watch to the window. Seven o'clock. Oh, God! How was he going to explain this away? He rolled over onto his hands and knees and got up, gingerly. He remembered biting. He went into the ensuite and switched on the light over the mirror. There didn't seem to be any marks, at least. He stepped back further to get a longer view and nearly threw up in horror. There, low on his stomach, was the biggest bite mark he had ever seen. It pulled no punches. It couldn't be hidden. It was there, like the mark of Cain. Stupidly, helplessly, he rubbed at it but it wasn't going anywhere. As someone who never wore pyjamas and indeed often wandered the house naked, this was going to be hard to explain. Harder to explain than getting home as late as this. He splashed cold water on his face and got dressed hurriedly. He'd think of something. He would *have* to think of something. He clattered down the stairs and out to the car and drove through the teeming rain towards his home, his home with Megs and Kyle. He was almost crying in panic. But he was a salesman. He would sort it out. He would say he had walked into a desk. A doorknob. Something. He would tell her about Mark and his potion. Yes, that was it. He felt woozy and fell over. Hurt himself that way. He felt better. He smoothed down his hair and started to hum something that sounded pretty much like Pink Floyd from his side of things. It was all going to be fine.

And for a few days it was. The bruise was kissed better and then some. He was given a freshly made plate of pasta, all was forgiven. Megan was sorry she had sniped at him at lunchtime, she hadn't known about his headache, poor baby. Mark was an idiot, she had a good mind to report him.

And then she found the lipstick on his underpants and another brick fell out of the wall.

Let Her Cry

*

The phone rang and rang. Where was she? Megan didn't ring her mother like most women in her position would – what would be the point? All she would get was that smug little silence, the silence that said, 'I told you so. Your father and I never liked him anyway. Come home, dear, and let's put it all behind us.' Then it would start about Kyle, had she thought of taking him to see someone. He seemed bright enough – and here the dreaded 'I suppose' would creep in, along with 'of course, we love him to bits, but …' – perhaps a child psychologist? Bearing in mind his father's …

So, no. Not her mother. Sam was always her first port of call. Had always been her first port of call, ever since school. Sam was one of the cool kids, always with the right clothes, the right hair, the right everything except attitude; Megan's mother hadn't liked her much either. Come to think of it, Megan thought, as Sam's phone went to voicemail, that was probably why their friendship was so strong.

'Sam …' She paused. How did you begin a conversation like this? 'Sam. I just found lipstick on my child's father's boxers' just somehow didn't sound right. 'Sam,' she said, trying to keep her voice level, 'I need to talk to you about something. Can you ring me back when you get …'

'Megs?' Sam's voice broke in. 'Whatever's the matter?'

Megan should have known she couldn't fool Sam, but she tried all the same. 'No, I'm fine. I just thought … we hadn't seen each other lately and I thought …'

'Rubbish. What's he done?'

Megan tried for a laugh. 'Don't be silly.'

She heard Sam expel an angry breath through her nose. She had had that habit since they were girls and it used to get her more detentions than enough at school. But now, it just meant she was on the warpath and watch out. 'Megan,' Sam said. 'This is me, okay? I can tell you're upset. I know you are not playing away from home. I know only a man can make you sound like that. Therefore, it's Chris. So, I repeat, Megs, what's he done?'

And still Megan couldn't tell her. Her mouth just wouldn't make the sounds. She found herself sobbing into the phone as she leaned her head against the back of the settee. She could feel the texture of the fabric, she could feel the warmth of the sun on her shoulder, she could hear the birds outside. Everything from outside was working okay; it was just inside she was broken. From a far distance, as though from another planet, she heard a voice and the voice said, 'Stay there. I'm on my way.'

Stay there? She had no choice. Somehow, her legs weren't working any more. She gave an involuntary jerk – Kyle! Then she remembered; today was his playgroup day. Morning, anyway. He didn't enjoy it, the other children seemed to make him edgy, but she took him anyway, every Thursday, come hell or high water. His life was going to be full of people, most of whom would not be to his taste, but that was life, after all. Her heart broke every time she walked away, but sometimes, you had to be cruel to be kind. She decided to have a wallow in it all and the tears flowed like rain and she was still huddled into the settee cushion, her face swollen with weeping, when Sam burst into the room, all Marc Jacobs, from the skin out. There was something about Samantha Cormack that put most women's teeth on edge – perfection on that level can be very wearing. But she took Megan in her arms, not caring where the snot and tears might land and that was why, when all was said and done, she was the person Megan had turned to for the past fifteen years and counting.

Eventually, it was time to move into the kitchen and have a cup of coffee. Noses were wiped, eyes were dried and soon, coffee was made and enhanced with a little something to keep the cold out – not that the weather warranted that, but the cold inside is sometimes the hardest to beat – Samantha cut to the chase.

'I've heard random blubberings from you before,' she said, with a smile which didn't reach her eyes, 'but this is something on another level entirely. I know he hasn't missed your birthday, your anniversary, any of the usual, so – what is it?'

Megan looked into her coffee in silence.

Samantha managed people all day long; it was what she had been born for, she often felt. So she could work a silence with pinpoint precision. When the time was right, not a second more, not a second less, she asked the sixty four thousand dollar question. 'So, he's having an affair, is he?'

Megan's shoulders went up defensively and she folded her arms across her body, shielding herself from hurt. She nodded, a tiny movement of the head which looked almost like a trick of the light.

'Someone at work?' Sam had seen it so often, though she had always avoided it herself. She never crapped on her own doorstep – as mantras went, it could do with some polishing, but it worked for her.

This time, Megan's left shoulder went up in a little shrug. 'Dunno,' she said, sounding like Kyle.

'So,' Samantha sat back and raised her hand, ready to count off the points on her fingers. 'Yes, he's having an affair. You don't know who with. Or, therefore, presumably, how long it's been going on.' She looked across the table at Megan, whose eyes were beginning to brim again. 'Is that right?'

A tiny nod again, with lips set in a line.

'Megs,' her friend leaned forward this time and reached both hands across the table. 'How in God's name have you got yourself in this state if you don't know for sure? You don't know who. You don't know when. You don't know for how long … for all you know, there could be a completely innocent explanation. In fact, what made you think it in the first place? You know he works weird hours sometimes – surely, it can't be that.'

Megan patted her friend's hand and put her own into her pocket. Samantha rolled her eyes. Not another hankie, surely? How many tears did the woman have left unshed? But no. Not a hankie – a pair of Calvin Klein's, a little frayed as to the elastic and perhaps not in the first flush of whiteness, but unremarkable.

'These look like Chris's,' Sam pointed out. 'I was expecting something frillier.'

Megan looked up, her eyes harder now, not so tear-filled. 'I know what you mean. No, I didn't find some alien knickers in his pocket, nor the classic receipt or credit card bill. I found this.' She unfolded the boxers and pointed. There, unmistakeable and unrefutable, was a smear of lipstick, ringing the fly.

For the first time in many years, perhaps even ever, Sam was speechless. She had put aside her mild prejudice against Chris. After all, no one is ever good enough for a best friend, right? But this … what could she say to this? She looked up to meet Megan's eyes and she felt her own begin to swim. Megan was a mother, a wife in all but the legal shenanigans, and yet there she sat, looking just like the little girl lost and scared in the cloakroom all those years ago. Sam got up and walked around the table and stood protectively over Megan. If Chris had walked in then, she would have gone for him, tooth and nail, for what he had done. But he wasn't there, so instead, she just crooned to her friend, trying to take away the pain. 'The bastard,' she said. 'The bastard.' Then, again when the time was right, she stood up and stepped back so she could look Megan in the eye. 'It's over with you two, yes?'

'There's Kyle,' Megan said, folding up the CKs and putting them back in her pocket.

Samantha didn't really do kids and Kyle was no exception. But even so, she knew that when you had them, you tried that bit harder. But surely, kids or no kids, there were some things it was hard to rise above. 'Yes, but …'

Megan stood up and took the mugs over to the sink. With her back to Sam, she gave her decision. It was easier to say it to the little back garden, with the rose struggling up the back fence, limp in the heat. 'I'll ask him for an explanation. If …'

'An explanation?' Samantha was aghast. 'What kind of explanation can there possibly be for lipstick on his underpants? On a collar, possibly. A grateful client. A secretary's birthday do. But it would have to be a bloody great letting opportunity to make anyone that grateful, wouldn't it? Megan – you're off your head if you let him get away with this!'

'He had a migraine.'

'And?'

'What do you mean? He gets really bad heads …'

'Having a headache means you *don't* have sex. Not that you do. Unless when he has a headache he doesn't want to actually do the shagging, he just likes a nice comforting blow job.'

Megan looked at her friend, startled. For all her attitude, Sam didn't usually talk like that.

'Don't give me the Bambi look,' Samantha snapped. 'You knew what you'd have to do the minute you saw that lipstick. There are things you can forgive and there are things you can't. And this, you can't. Do you really want Kyle to be brought up by someone who comes home from work after having a quickie? Where's the respect? You deserve more.'

'But … where will I go?'

'Go? You don't need to *go* anywhere. He's the one that goes.'

'We can hardly afford this place as it is. If he has to find somewhere else … well, we'll go under.'

'Stop it with the "we",' Samantha advised her. 'There is no "we" any more. Unless you mean you and Kyle. The sooner you sort this, the better, Megs.'

'I'll talk to him when he gets home tonight.'

'What? With Kyle here? You know how …' she just stopped herself from saying 'needy' '… time-consuming Kyle can be. I can just picture the scene. By the time he's in bed, you're both shattered and then it will all be too late. You'll go to bed, he'll probably want …'

Megan held up her hand. 'Okay. Okay. You've made your point. I'll ring Mum to pick up Kyle. She won't mind an extra afternoon with him, I don't expect.' She knew as she said it that she would have to deal with the inquisition afterwards, but this situation wasn't going to end without at least some gloating from her mother, so why worry about that now? 'I'll go round to the office and get him on his own.'

'You'd do that?' Samantha was impressed.

'I think I have to, don't I?'

'What if it's someone there? The lipstick donor?'

'Well, that's perfect, isn't it? I can stand and watch when the shit hits the fan.'

Samantha walked through into the lounge and picked up her keys and bag where she had dumped them on her way in. 'Well, let me know how it goes, Megs.' She held her friend close in a hug and whispered in her ear, as though Chris was in the room, smirking, covered in lipstick kisses. 'Keep strong, you deserve better than this.' Then, before the crying started again, she left.

Thursday was Chris's day in the office. When things were very busy he occasionally got called upon to do a showing, but after the flurry of Monday, the week had been fairly quiet. Mr and Mrs Perfect had passed the credit check by a whisker, but they had signed on the dotted line and everything was going ahead. By an unspoken agreement, the Pughs had been passed on to Jacintha to handle – to Chris's amusement she seemed to think this was a good thing, but he was sure she would soon learn that the Pughs came at a price. Louise Taylor had also signed on the dotted line for number forty-three; stranger things had happened, according to Dave Stanley. He didn't know the half of it!

Although the office policy was to keep things open-plan – the result of a long-ago team-building exercise – there were small rooms that anyone could use if they were wrestling with how to make a crappy house in a rundown neighbourhood seem more like Versailles. Choosing the images for the website could be a mission and quiet and peace sometimes helped. So it was perhaps a good thing that Chris's task for that Thursday midday was precisely that – making a silk purse out of the pig's ear that was number ninety-two, Falklands Close. It seemed that every single picture included a red flag; whether it was peeling wallpaper or the corner of next door's trampoline, this house needed serious talking-up before it could go on the market as a let. He had just managed an expert crop, leaving in the feature fireplace but removing the damp patch over the window, when there was a tap on his door.

'Yes?' He was surprised. Knocking first was not something that generally happened at Stanley Lettings.

Jacintha stepped into the office, a plastic smile on her plastic face. 'Your … wife …' Did he imagine the question mark or was this just another annoying manifestation of her constant moronic interrogative? 'Is outside. Wants a word, apparently.'

He leapt up, his heart in his mouth. 'Kyle?' he said, almost as an involuntary reaction, like closing your eyes when you sneeze.

'No.' Megan had pushed Jacintha aside. 'No, it's not Kyle.' In a deft movement that surprised even her, she managed to get Jacintha back over the threshold and slam the door in her face. 'It's you.'

A cold hand closed around Chris's heart and gave it a warning squeeze. He hadn't had that many relationships before he met Megan. If he were to be scrupulously honest, he had never had anything worthy of the name before her. And yet, breakups had been very traumatic – no one likes to get the bum's rush. He didn't speak – he didn't want to condemn himself without at least hearing what she had to say. It might not be … That. He still couldn't give last Monday night's experience a name or even a face; if he kept it in the cupboard, it might yet go away.

'Have you nothing to say?' she said.

'I don't know what *to* say,' he replied. 'I don't know what you're here to say to me, so how can I answer?'

She sighed and sat down, across the desk, like a client. The distance might work for him or against him. The next few moments would tell. 'I want to ask you what happened on Monday,' she said.

The hand squeezed tighter. Somewhere in the corner of the room, behind him, in the shadow of the filing cabinet, a dog shifted, its chain rattling against its black coat.

'Monday?' If only he could make some time, some time to think.

'Yes. Monday. The day you came home at gone seven, with a bruise you got from falling over. The day you had a migraine and got some special medicine from Mark that made you woozy. The day you got a nice blow job from someone.'

The hand squeezed so tightly he could hardly breathe. 'The day I got a *what*?' He couldn't even remember that bit. At least, not clearly. 'I don't …'

'Remember?' Her eyes and voice were cold. She reached into her bag and pulled out the Calvin Kleins. 'She wears red lipstick, if that helps to narrow it down at all.'

The underpants, as she threw them across the desk, skittered over the polished surface and slid off onto the floor. He didn't bend down to retrieve them and neither did she. Something was wrong here. Louise didn't wear red lipstick, but he could hardly say that now.

'Chris!' Her voice was almost a howl. 'Say something!'

'What can I say? You've made up your mind. No matter what I say, you won't believe me. I would imagine you've already passed it by Sam?'

Her eyes flickered downwards. 'No.'

'Yes, you have. You don't do anything without passing it by Sam. I would imagine that Kyle was planned with Sam long before he was planned with me.' He watched her and knew he was right. 'So, you've shown her the evidence, as I think we should call it, and you've delivered the verdict. Guilty as charged, I would imagine. Am I right?' She didn't need to speak. 'Yes, I thought so. So, what's the sentence? Move all my things out by the weekend? Never darken your door again? Have Kyle every other weekend to take to the zoo?'

Her eyes filled with tears as she looked at him, speechless.

'Well, I'll allocute, shall I? If it's good enough for *Law and Order*, I guess it's good enough for me. Yes, I did have sex with someone on Monday. She made all the running and I was under the influence of whatever Mark had given me so I gave in. He told me to drive carefully; he didn't tell me to stay away from psychopathic women bearing a grudge.'

'So, you're blaming Mark, now?' Her eyes were wide with disbelief.

'No, no, of course not.' He shook his head. 'He wasn't to know … Look, it's a long story and it begins before we even met. There was this woman, we had a one night stand and she turned up on Monday as a client …'

'She must have been a hell of a lay.'

'Pardon?'

'A one night stand more than five years ago and as soon as you clap eyes on her again you're at it like weasels.'

'No, it wasn't like that. I didn't even recognise her.'

Megan muttered something and reached down for her bag.

'Sorry. What did you say? I didn't catch …'

She stood up. Speaking clearly and looking him in the face, she said, 'I said that you are not who I thought you were. I thought you were a decent man who loved his family – that's me, by the way, me and Kyle – and worked hard to protect and care for them. To me, that means not shagging any slag who crosses his path.' She turned to leave then thought better of it. 'Where did you do it, by the way? Just to complete the picture, you know.'

He licked his lips, which were dry as dust and put a hand to his chest, where the hand was squeezing and releasing, squeezing and releasing, just enough to let him live. 'Number forty-three.'

'Oh, the smelly house!' They had often laughed about the smell in the kitchen and just whispering 'forty three' when they encountered a whiff anywhere could reduce them to hysteria. Had once reduced them to hysteria; he didn't need the snicker of the black dog in the corner to know that everything that was once him and Megs was now to always be in the past tense. 'That's marvellous and makes me feel so much better. I suppose you did it in the kitchen.'

'No. The bedroom.' He said it before he engaged his brain. Of course she didn't want to know where he did it, as she charmingly phrased it. Mentioning the kitchen was one last, one very last ditch attempt to bond back with her, to share the laugh, however hollow. And he had just blown it.

She went to the door and opened it, then paused, one foot still in the room, one foot still in the place where he could win her back. But the pause was so fleeting, the pain in his heart so intense, that he couldn't speak and the moment was lost. She didn't turn, she didn't raise her voice, but he heard the word as clear as crystal, ringing through the heavy air from her lips to his brain, with nothing in between to prevent it.

'Goodbye.'

It was a while before he felt able to leave the room which now smelled sour with loss and fear. His colleagues were not the most empathetic people in the world – they were, after all, letting agents – but there was something in Megan's walk, the set of her mouth, the line of her shoulder, that told them that nothing good would come of interrupting Chris that day. He would come out when he was good and ready, should that day ever dawn.

He opened the door and walked into the main office, which immediately fell silent. Even the landlord haranguing David Stanley about an unreasonable repair bill lowered his voice. It was what Chris and Megs had always called an Attenborough moment, when the wildebeest sense a cheetah, the chimpanzee the snake and silence falls over the veldt or forest. They could sense a wounded animal in their midst and did the civilised version of cutting him out and throwing him to the wolves. The shoulders went up, the voices went down and he walked out of the door into the street without a single person speaking a word to him. If it hadn't been for the black dog, he would have been all alone in the world.

'Mum?' For the second time that day, Megan bit the bullet and phoned her mother to ask her a favour. This was a biggie, one she had never asked before and she wasn't sure what the answer would be.

'Hello, dear. It's Mummy, Kyle.' There was silence for a moment. 'He's watching the television, Megan. We were just wondering when you would be coming to pick him up.' She lowered her voice. 'I don't think he had a very good morning this morning.'

That at least made two of them.

'I think some of the children there are a bit too boisterous for him. Anyway, when are you planning to get here, dear, because I need to go shopping some time today. We're out of milk, nearly.'

Megan knew that they would be no such thing. Her mother ran her kitchen like she ran her life – like clockwork. A place for everything, everything in its place and woe betide any foodstuff that let itself run out. There would be hell to pay.

'Mum,' she tried hard to keep the wobble out of her voice, 'I wondered if you could hang on to Kyle for today.'

'Oh, dear, I really don't … till when?'

'Tomorrow, really. Probably tomorrow. Or Monday, if you could manage it. I … I need some time, Mum, I …' It was no good – the tears were back and this time they weren't planning to go away.

'Megan, dear,' how did the woman manage to make that sound like an admonishment? 'Are you all right? Are you ill?' Then, the razorblade crept into the voice. 'It's *Chris*, isn't it? What's he done now?'

'That's not fair, Mum. He has never …'

'Hmmph. I knew it. He's having an affair, isn't he? Your father and I never liked him. He's …'

'Mum. Not now. Not the usual. I just need a few days to sort myself out.'

'But we've never had Kyle overnight before. I don't even know what he likes for breakfast.'

'Readybrek with a spoonful of jam.'

'So bad for his teeth, dear.'

'Don't try and change it, Mum. Just do it, for a couple of days, please. Strawberry. The other meals don't matter so much, but breakfast has to be that and no deviation.'

'What about clothes?'

'He'll be all right with what he's got on now for tomorrow. I'll drop some more in, but not when he's there. Let me know when you're going out and I'll leave them on the step.'

'Megan?' Her mother's voice was shrill. 'Has he *hit* you?'

'God, no! Whyever do you think that?'

'Well, you clearly don't want to be seen.' Her mother's outrage was palpable, even over the phone. 'I'm assuming you have … marks.'

Sometimes she hated this woman more than anyone in the world. More, even, than the anonymous one-night-stand that had wrecked her life so thoroughly. 'No, Mum,' she said, her voice tired and flat, 'no marks.' She rang off and stood with her forehead against the cool of the wall. A broken heart, now; that left no marks that anyone could see, but the scars were there, for ever.

Waitrose was packed. Kyle was cranky, not happy about being pulled away from the television and also scared, in the wordless, subliminal way children have; it doesn't have to be monsters under the bed, the world has enough in it to scare them without that. And his grandmother was behaving strangely. And where was his Mummy? His Daddy? His lip began to tremble and a tear rolled down his cheek.

'Hello, Margaret.' A shrill voice was suddenly just inches from his ear, a huge nose looming above his face. 'Is this little Kyle? What a sweetie. Oh, crying, pet? Aww, Margaret, poor little chap.'

Margaret Harris had hoped to get to the shops and back before Kyle began to kick off. He was his father's child all right. A lovely face that pulled you in and made you love him, then as mad as a box of frogs underneath. He needed to be Seen by Someone and now that things would be changing, she would make it her business … And now, to put the finishing touches on a rather trying day, there was this woman, what was her name? Sylv? Sheila? This woman, anyway, butting in and making Kyle cry.

'He's had a tiring day, Sandra.' Yes, that was it, Sandra.

'Stella.'

Whatever. 'He doesn't really like playgroup but today's his day, so … well, routine is important, isn't it?'

'Oh, mine just ran a bit wild, I suppose,' the large-nosed woman said, a tad complacently. 'We didn't really believe in routine.'

Margaret's smile was acid. She knew what was coming next.

'And it did them no harm. Two doctors and a university lecturer, so we can't complain. But what's wrong with this little one, eh? Tom,' she called over her shoulder, 'come and get Kyle some ear money.'

Ear money? Margaret Harris could hardly contain her annoyance. But along came Tom, as ill-co-ordinated in both movement and clothing as his wife. Standing together, they looked like an unmade kingsize.

'Oh, here we go,' the man said and, with a flourish, produced a ten pence coin from behind Kyle's ear.

The child's face lit up and he smiled up at the man. 'More,' he said.

'Here you are,' there was a click and another coin appeared, then another and another. Soon, Kyle was crowing with laughter, tears forgotten.

'They're a joy, aren't they?' the annoying woman said. 'We don't see ours half often enough.'

Margaret Harris smiled grimly. Stella's perfect children had also managed to pop out six perfect grandchildren, all an appropriate time after their marriage to perfect sons-in-law. She could feel her jaw clenching.

'And how is Megan?'

And suddenly, it all poured out. She hadn't meant it to, but it was sitting on her tongue and she couldn't help it. How Megan was having problems at home, she was a victim of domestic abuse – here, Margaret dropped her voice and spoke the words silently, looking as she did so, disconcertingly like her own mother had when saying 'sex' and 'pregnant' – and was afraid to come out because she was so badly beaten about the head. How Chris was always a worry to them, how they were glad it was all over, how it wasn't going to be easy for them …

Stella's face was a picture. That had shut her up. Even the ear money seemed to have dried up for now. 'But, Margaret, that's terrible. Is Megan all right? Has she spoken to the police?' She tugged her husband's sleeve. 'Tom, Tom, did you hear that?'

'Now then,' her husband said, calmly, giving the ear money to Kyle, who clutched it close. 'Don't push yourself forward, Stell.'

'It's just that I volunteer, you see,' she said. 'At a women's shelter. Megan could get help there. She should at least Speak to Someone. Look,' she rummaged in her bag, 'I've got a leaflet. Give her this.'

Margaret Harris could suddenly hear the juggernaut approaching that her gossip had unleashed. If she wasn't careful, this could crush her and her newly-fragile family. Ignoring Kyle's cries at being separated from the ear money man, she snatched the leaflet, turned the trolley and, as far as she could in a packed supermarket, legged it.

Stella and Tom looked at one another. 'Classic displacement,' she said, with all the knowledge of someone who has a psychologist in the family. 'More going on there than meets the eye. Mind you, I never liked her.'

Her husband looked at her fondly. He didn't like her worrying. 'Her Megan's bloke works at the letting agents down the road from here,' he said. 'Dave Stanley comes to my Lodge – I'll have a word.'

She put a hand on his chest – such a kind man, a husband in a million. 'Thank you, Tom,' she said. Keeping up the niceties of politeness was what kept a marriage fresh, in their opinion. 'I think that would be a good idea.' And, bathed in the golden light of a job well done, they made their way to the organic section.

The pavements seemed extra hard that afternoon as Chris trudged around the town. He passed he didn't know how many houses with boards outside and he ignored them all; previously, he would have been making notes of who had what on the market but, looking down the long tunnel of fear and despair, he saw nothing but the approaching train. Sometimes, his heart would lurch and he would imagine that everything would be all right. Megan would forgive him and they could put all this behind them, make a fresh start, somewhere new, maybe. Another baby, even – he knew that everyone said that children couldn't mend a broken marriage, but it might work. A little girl – that would be nice.

He turned into the park, but avoided the children's play area – if he saw a boy who even slightly resembled Kyle, he knew he would break down. He went down to the lakeside, avoiding the smears of goose shit on the edge. There had been a petition up recently to stop the projected cull of the Canada geese, but he hadn't signed; he had spent too many afternoons scraping their leavings out of the treads of Kyle's trainers to want to do that. His eyes began to well up with self-pitying tears. This would be where he would come, with his boy, on his one afternoon a fortnight. Better find somewhere else, before he made a fool of himself.

He didn't even know he had gone home until he found himself putting his key in the door. A thought flashed through his mind that perhaps he wasn't allowed here – but he dismissed it as stupid talk. Of course he was allowed. He hadn't hurt anyone, hadn't broken any laws. He had just … well, what had he just? He had had the misjudgement, years before, to take a madwoman to bed for the night. That couldn't be allowed to colour the rest of his life, surely? He would tell Megan the whole story, leaving nothing out. He had been a bit of a player, back in the day. He often didn't remember their names in the morning, let alone years later – phone numbers were for wimps. He never rang them back. But now, he didn't do that kind of thing. Megan and Kyle had changed all that. He put the keys down quietly on the hall table and called Megan's name. There was no reply and yet the house clearly wasn't empty. It didn't have the feel of an empty house and he should know – he could sum up an atmosphere in seconds. So why had he allowed this to happen? He just couldn't explain it; Mark's Marvellous Medicine would only stretch so far as an excuse.

'Yes?' Megan's voice came from the lounge. 'Chris? Is that you?'

'Of course it is,' he said, walking through. 'I didn't know where to go. I just needed to come home.'

She sat silently, with her back to him, not moving or, it seemed to him, breathing. Then, very slowly, she turned her head and as soon as she saw his expression, bereft, beyond broken, her resolve crumbled and she ran into his arms.

'Oh, baby,' she whispered into his hair as she held him tight. 'We can work it out, can't we?'

'We have to,' he said. 'We just have to.'

They rocked there, holding each other, murmuring, kissing, oblivious to the ticking of the falling plaster on the fragile wall around them and the stirring of a big, black dog, hiding in the shadows.

Across town, a door swung open and heads turned to see the big man come in and stand, surveying the room. A blonde secretary, her asymmetric bob swinging, left her desk and approached.

'Can I help?'

'Yes.' His smile was open and infectious. 'I'd like to speak to David Stanley, please. Just tell him it's Tom.'

Mad World

*

For the rest of his life, Chris would list the days that followed his return to Megan that sad Thursday as the best he had ever spent. They both loved Kyle dearly but to have him at his grandmother's for a day or so was bliss. No waking up in panic. No picking over food to make sure he knew what it was. No demands. Just the two of them, slobbing around in pyjamas until they got dressed to go out for a nice, grown-up drink and dinner – yes, it truly was bliss. And when they went to get him back on the Sunday evening, the way he jumped into their arms, laughing and yelling with the sheer joy of having them back, well, that was bliss too. The black dog seemed to have scarpered – by that night, Chris had stopped looking for it in dark corners and listening for its growl, always just under the threshold of his hearing.

Then Monday struck like a thunderbolt. Chris pushed open the door to the agency and felt the chill; he almost could sense the frost forming on his hairline as his sweat ran cold. Jacintha, a false sad face pinned on over her secret gloating, leaned forward. Her whisper was as fake as her expression.

'Dave said would you go straight through,' she said, cocking her head on one side like a rueful sparrow.

Chris didn't acknowledge her. The feeling in the pit of his stomach, heavy and yet liquid, took up all his attention. He went through into the board room, where Dave Stanley sat at one end of the cheap table. He had a file in front of him and when he heard the door go he flinched slightly but didn't look up. Chris pulled out a chair, deliberately scraping it on the floor. That should get him; it was like nails down a blackboard.

His boss looked up, as though he had only just realised he was there. 'Ah, Chris, thanks for stepping through. I'm sorry to make it all look so serious,' he made that irritating quote sign in the air and Chris wanted to punch him for that alone, 'but I think we need to talk things through. Last week brought quite a lot of things to my attention and I know you would rather talk them over than … umm …' He ran out of steam.

'Dave,' Chris said. 'Can you just cut to the chase? If it's my day off on Friday, I did ring in and I am owed …'

Dave Stanley had his hand in the air. 'No, no, nothing wrong with that. We all need a day now and then. No, it's something a little more serious.' Stanley's face changed almost as though he had thrown a switch. He had chosen, from his limited repertoire, the Concerned Boss Who Has A Difficult Job Ahead expression. 'I had a visitor on Thursday, just before we closed. A Tom Maddox.'

Chris thought for a moment. He hadn't shown a house to anyone called Maddox and as far as he could remember, their landlord list didn't include that name either. 'Sorry, I have no idea who that is.'

'Really?' Dave Stanley risked raising an eyebrow although he was aware it made him look rather brainless; more like Roger Moore than Gregory Peck, both serious exponents of eyebrow work when it came to expressing extreme emotion.

A little more thought but the answer was the same. 'No. Sorry. Who is he?' A thought dawned. 'Nothing to do with that bloody woman, is he?'

'I don't know. Is he?'

Stanley was really beginning to piss Chris off. He didn't have the strength to get mad, he felt as though his clothes – no, his actual *skin* – had become lead. 'Dave, can we cut this out, please? I don't need the third degree right now. I have some personal stuff going on at home, so I just need to know what's going on *here* and get back to work. Is this or is this not about Maureen Pugh?'

'Who?' David Stanley couldn't keep names in his head without a face to go with them and happily he had avoided having to make the connection in the case of Mrs Pugh.

'I'll take that as a no, then,' Chris said. 'So, what is it about?'

'Tom Maddox is a friend of mine, from the Lodge.' It wasn't often Dave came out with the fact that he was a Mason; unless he was recruiting. 'He met your mother-in-law …'

'She's not really my mother-in-law,' Chris felt he had to add.

'You know what I mean. Megan's mother. Anyway, he met her in the supermarket …'

'Better say Waitrose,' Chris said. 'She wouldn't like you to think she shopped anywhere low rent.'

Again, the eyebrow. 'I see.' Antagonistic; interesting. 'Well, Tom and his wife were shopping and met … Megan's mother …'

'Margaret.'

'Margaret, then. Where was I?'

'In Waitrose.'

'Yes, met her and Kyle. Apparently, Megan had asked her to have him because … well, in a nutshell, Chris, she was unable to pick him up from nursery because she didn't want to be seen in public after you had knocked her about.'

Dave finally had Chris's attention. 'Pardon?' He sat back, totally wordless beyond that one. 'Megan had told her this?'

'I don't have the details of the conversation, Chris. Just the gist.'

'The *gist*. You have the *gist* of a conversation that Margaret had with some random bloke and his wife in a posh supermarket and you call me in for a bollocking?'

'Bollocking?' Stanley was on the defensive now. 'I don't think that this would count as a bollocking, Chris.'

'We're getting there, though, aren't we?' he countered. 'Has it not occurred to you that you all saw Megan, in this very building, on Thursday? Did you notice a split lip? Black eyes? Sling? Crutch?'

'That's very specific, Chris.' Like everyone caught on the back foot, Stanley sought refuge in attack. 'Is that what she has, sometimes?'

Chris Rowan had finally had enough. His leaden skin sloughed off, leaving him in his Superman costume, albeit invisible. 'Dave,' he said, in a quiet, flat voice that sounded as though it came from a distant planet, 'Dave, I always knew you were an arsehole. But how much of an arsehole, I realise now I had no idea. How can you think I knock Megan about because her bloody mother rambled to some bloody stupid...' He stood up and took a step back, knocking over the chair. Stanley flinched and for a moment, Chris felt the power. Then the lead skin was back and he felt the fight go out of him. 'I do not hit Megan. I don't even kill the spiders in the bath. I don't lust after random women I show round homes, as you laughingly call them. I just want to come here, do my job, go home to my lovely family, without all this *shit!*' The last word was shouted and every head in the outer office swivelled towards the sound as though they were on wires.

'There's no need to raise your voice, Chris.' Stanley realised, possibly a touch too late, that he had not been following the protocol as set out in his most recent people-managing online training module.

Chris lowered his voice so that even he could hardly hear it. It sounded like someone else, someone he had known once. The black dog pricked up his ears; his master's voice. 'I don't know why you called me in here, Mr Stanley,' he said. If the stupid idiot couldn't conduct a disciplinary hearing properly, he would have to do it for him. Let's keep things formal, shall we, Mr Stanley? 'I don't know how my hitting my partner, not that I do, has anything to do with work. I don't know what this Maddox person knows about it – as I understand it, Megan's mother told him a story in Waitrose which has grown out of all sense and reason into a ... what? A complaint?'

Stanley inclined his head. 'I suppose we could call it that, yes,' he said. His voice was also tight.

'How can someone who isn't a client complain about me? I think this exceeds all management protocol that I have ever heard of.'

'It isn't just this, Chris, though, is it? There's that thing last week of you looking up that woman's skirt. And ...'

'And?'

'Well, Jacintha and I ... walked into work together this morning

...' Chris was triumphant. So, the rumours were true, '... and she told me that when you worked for your last employers, one of your colleagues from another branch had a nervous breakdown because of your treatment of her.'

'What?' Had that bitch Louise Taylor been putting the knife in here as well?

'You had had a relationship, apparently, and it all ...'

'A relationship?' Chris was gobsmacked. 'It was a one nighter. It meant nothing at all.'

'That saddens me, Chris.' Stanley was remembering his Empathy Training. 'I thought you were better than that.'

'It was years ago. I was young, so was she. We were pissed ...'

Just a shake of the head said all Stanley had to say.

'And what about you and Jacintha? You think we haven't noticed? You think your *wife* hasn't noticed?'

Dave Stanley was on his feet, spluttering. Chris had never seen anyone actually splutter with rage before and it was intriguing. 'How *dare* you?' he said, finally. 'Jacintha could be my daughter!'

And this was where Chris Rowan made his fatal mistake. As he mulled it over, long and often, in the dark hours of his future, he knew it was a mistake. But at the time, he just couldn't help it. He shrugged, and said, 'Well, you said it, Dave, not me.'

The spluttering stopped and a white tenseness appeared around his boss's mouth, another feature new to Chris. 'Get out. I have given you enough rope and now you've hung yourself.'

'Hanged.'

'What?'

'Hanged myself. People get hanged. Pictures get hung.'

'You supercilious bastard,' Stanley spat. 'Nobody here can stand you because of your bloody jumped up ways, do you know that? None of us are surprised that you've turned out to be an abusive sex maniac. Just get out. I'll pay you three months in lieu, but I never want to see you in here again. Is that clear?'

'What? You're sacking me because some old git believed what that mad cow Margaret Harris said to him in a supermarket?'

'No. I'm sacking you because you're a fucking liability. You might be able to rent out houses I wouldn't put a pig in, but you're a menace. All the girls in the office say they don't like the way you look at them. You're creepy, Chris, that's what you are and that, among other things, is why you're fired. Now, get out and don't speak to anyone on the way.'

'But …'

'Check your contract, I should,' Stanley said, but he was already sitting down again and didn't look up. 'Be grateful you get your three months in lieu. I'm not bound to pay it.'

Chris stood there, almost beyond moving. He had just been sacked, for the first time in his life, and it was scary. He hardly dare look down in case he was literally rather than metaphorically standing on a cliff edge with nothing below but the distant baying of black dogs, circling the rocks below, baying and howling, eager for his life.

He walked through the outer office, not looking right or left. He had tunnel vision anyway, with the panic, and wasn't sure how he would react if anyone spoke to him. He was on the pavement, in a daze, when he felt a hand on his arm. With exaggerated care, he turned and saw one of the part-timers standing there, a look of concern on her face.

'Chris?' she said, from an immense distance away. 'Are you all right?'

He nodded, then put his hand to his head. Somehow he wasn't sure whether he was making the right movements. Everything was disjointed and weird. That was it; this was all a dream and he'd wake up soon. 'Fine,' he said, but he couldn't hear his own voice.

'No, no you're not,' the woman said. He realised to his horror that he couldn't remember her name. Couldn't actually even remember if he had ever known it. 'We don't really know each other very well,' she said. 'My name's Cassie, I'm only in on Mondays and Wednesdays. But I've noticed how you haven't looked well these past few … well, months, actually. Someone in my family suffers from depression too, so I suppose …'

'I don't get depression!' His voice came out much louder than he had meant it to and people turned to stare.

Cassie smiled. She had a nice smile; she reminded him a lot of his sister. 'No, of course not. But you're not well, are you? Everything been getting on top of you, I expect. You've got a little one, I understand. How old is he now?'

'Three. Kyle's three.'

'A lot of work, a three year old. And this job can be very stressful.' Her voice was starting to get through without the cottonwool muffling and he looked at her instead of through her. 'Would you like to go and get a coffee?'

'But …' he gestured in the general direction of the office.

'Oh, don't worry about them. I don't. If they don't like it, they can lump it. Sometimes people have to come first. So … coffee?'

Making up his mind was very difficult, suddenly. He wasn't sure whether he was even going to be able to put one foot in front of the other, let alone decide between a million different coffees. He wanted to shake his head, but even that was a choice too far. She took his hesitation for consent.

'Great. Look, don't let's do the Starbucks Costa Nero route; let's go to a nice greasy spoon; there's one down the road, look. Come on.' She took his arm and towed him along behind her. She was just a little thing, but very determined. 'I know a coffee can't solve everything, but it goes a long way down that road, I think. Is it today that your other half works?'

However did she know that? He nodded.

'Well, while we're having a drink, why don't you text her? Arrange to meet for lunch. You need to talk this through. And then, we can have a good old chat.' She stopped towing him for a while and turned him around to face her. Just a little, middle-aged woman in a grey suit, nothing special. But he could feel the care coming off her in waves. A tear coursed down his cheek and without hesitation she reached up and wiped it away. 'That's a good start,' she said, kindly and returned to the towing technique. 'You've had a bitch of a day; let's see if we can put at least some of it right. You don't want the black dog to get you.'

He stopped as though she had shot him. 'Black dog? How do you know about the dog?' Who had been talking? What was happening?

She looked at him fixedly. 'It's the best analogy I've heard for depression. Winston Churchill used to refer to it in his diaries. Some people feel it is something less … well, less *alive*, a blanket, fog, something like that. But for others, it's more malevolent, more living and out to get them. Depression …'

'… which I don't have …'

'… which you *do* have, Chris, trust me on this, depression takes people all kinds of ways. You just need to recognize it and learn to deal with it. Not snap out of it. Not work your way out of it. Just deal with it and don't let it win. Mental illness is no slur …'

He pulled away from her. Who was this woman to speak to him like this? Calling him mental? 'I don't think coffee is a good idea, not today, Cassie. I don't want to …' He was snarling at her, though he couldn't hear it. 'Just because your brother or somebody gets a bit down in the mouth now and then you think you can talk to me about mental illness. Well, I don't get depression. I've just had a bad day, like you say. I'll be fine. New job. New house, maybe. We'll move, that's it. Somewhere new. So, you can take your mental illness chat somewhere else and I feel sorry, Cassie, to be honest, I feel sorry for whatever poor bugger in your family suffers from whatever it is, because you'll talk the hind leg off him, I should think.' And he stormed off down the road, shoulders set, legs stiff with anger and pain.

She watched him go and this time the tear she wiped away was her own. 'No, Chris,' she whispered, 'no, I won't talk anyone's hind leg off. Because I don't talk to myself.' And with a sigh, she turned back to the office, the black dog wagging its tail behind her.

Chris had gone out so quietly that it was a few minutes before David Stanley felt he could look up. As soon as he saw he was alone, he buzzed through to his secretary and asked her to come in.

She came into the room, blonde hair swinging. It had a pink strand in it which in some lights he found attractive but this morning just thought looked bloody silly. She held a file under one arm but it was empty. She slid onto the desk and put his hand on one of her thighs. She gave a little wriggle but today it had no effect. She leaned forward so her top gaped open; she knew he liked that.

'Oh, for fuck's sake, Jacintha,' he said, pushing her off his desk none too gently. 'Can you just give it a rest? I actually wanted you to send an email for me, not to come and … well, I want you to send an email.'

'Sorry, I'm sure,' she said, sniffing. 'What would you like this email to say and who is it to, *sir*?'

He had known it was a mistake, the first time he had gone back with this little tart to her flat. She was on the make, he knew that much, and she didn't find him remotely attractive; why the hell should she? He wasn't going to see forty again, forty-five if he was being honest, and even his nearest and dearest would never say he was handsome. On some people a smattering of grey hair looked distinguished. On him, it just looked old. So he had started touching it up with a dye and now he was stuck with it. But chest hair doesn't lie, so he had started having waxes. He had got the wolf of incipient middle age by the ears and he was afraid to let it go. If he knew one thing for certain about Jacintha, it was that she was a malicious little madam and he didn't want his occasional failure in the sack all round the office by nightfall, so he pinned on a smile and reached for her hand.

'Sorry,' he said, pulling her onto his lap and shoving a hand up her skirt, more for the look of the thing than anything else. 'I've got a lot on my mind today.'

She wriggled down onto his hand and immediately threw her head back in paroxysms. Surely, he thought, that had to be fake? No one had a hair trigger as quick as that. His missus could take hours. He left his hand there out of politeness and waited for her to stop gasping. Could he be the only one in this room who could hear commonsense come through the door, bringing clean, fresh air with her? It was quite a relief to know this was all over – although he knew she wouldn't go quietly. Still, sufficient unto the day is the evil thereof, as his old granny used to say …

When he was sure he had her attention, he said, 'It's just a quick email to Chris. I was … hasty, this morning and I really didn't mean half of what I said. Nor did he, I suspect. I just want an email, from the general office address, you know, enquiries@, that one. Say that I … no, don't use my name, just leave it vague. Something like having considered the situation, the company has decided to give him one more chance, in view of his service thus far … blah, blah, you know the kind of thing.'

With a final squirm, she got up and tugged down her skirt. But not too much. This was one secret she needed the whole office to know about – otherwise the gutless bastard would never leave his wife. She left enough evidence around, the woman must be blind or stupid. Little did Jacintha know that the current Mrs Stanley had caught her husband in just the way Jacintha was trying now and was up to all her little wiles. Also, she knew where the business bodies were buried and she had two kids to add to the mix. Oh, no, Mrs Stanley the Second had no fears from potential Mrs Stanley the Third.

'When do you want me to send it?' The last thing Jacintha wanted was Chris Rowan back in the office. The man could let a hole in the ground to even the most discerning tenant – without him around, she might get to show what she could do. Apart from wriggle and gasp, that was.

But Dave Stanley wasn't concentrating any more. He had dumped his problem – *two* problems, in fact – and it was not in his nature to dwell. 'Oh, let him sweat for a while. Send it when you've got a minute, later on.'

Jacintha's smile as she left the office was triumphant. She had given her man a good time – as she saw it – and also had permission to send the email when she had a minute. And who could say when that might be? This year, next year, sometime, never …

Megan had gone to work but hadn't been there five minutes, or so it seemed, before her mother was on the phone. Kyle was being cranky at being with her again; Megan had clearly spooked him by her abandonment over the weekend – she wasn't sure at this point whether her mother meant her leaving Kyle with her for a day or so or her possible behaviour alone with Chris overnight – and she really couldn't cope. Besides which, they needed to talk.

Megan's heart sank. She hadn't felt like coming in to work that morning, but once there she embraced it as a time out of the mad world she seemed to be inhabiting these days. The spa was an oasis of calm anyway – or at least, that's what the advertising said – but she was really looking forward to a nice busy day, plenty to occupy her mind, stop it going round in fruitless circles. She stood her ground. So Kyle was cranky; what three year old wasn't? She would pick him up on her way home, as usual. Meanwhile, had her mother tried bribery? It wasn't big, it wasn't clever, but with a three year old in a snit it was often all that worked. She put down the phone and was aware that someone was standing in front of her. She pinned on her best smile.

'Good morning,' she said. 'Can I help you?'

'I was wondering if I could make an appointment for a massage,' the woman said. 'I have a lot going on in my life at the moment and I really need to destress – I'd heard that you are the best in town.'

'That's very good to hear,' Megan said with a smile, bringing up the appointments on the screen. Mondays were often booked solid but today the woman was in luck. One of the alternative therapists was just back from maternity leave and she hadn't built her client list right back up yet. 'I can fit you in with Mandy in … well, now, actually. She has a cancellation.' She always thought that sounded better than 'nothing to do'. 'I just need to check she is in fact available – if you'd like to take a seat over there, I'll just check with her for you.'

The woman didn't move, just stood there, looking at Megan's name tag. 'Megan Harris,' she said. 'That sounds familiar. I wonder if we were at school together.'

Megan doubted it – this woman could give her six years, easily. But she was a client, so it seemed rude to point it out. 'It's a rather ordinary name,' she said, pleasantly.

'Perhaps. I'll remember, I'm sure,' the woman said. 'Would you like my name? It's Louise Taylor.'

Chris walked and walked, without knowing where he was going. It wasn't so much a case of trying to get somewhere as trying to get away from somewhere else. And even that was receding into a hazy distance. His phone rang and it brought him down to earth with a bump. He was standing on the bank of the river where it went through the park, but he wasn't in the goose shit bit, happily. He shook his head and answered the call.

'Chris?'

'Hello, babe. How're you doing?'

'I'm at work.'

'Well, that's one of us, at least.'

That brought her up short. 'Where are you, then? Showing?'

'We'll talk later. Are you up for lunch?'

There was a pause. Too long, really, for just a lull. 'I don't want to see you in public today, no. But we do … need to talk.' She hated using her mother's overworked phrase, but somehow nothing else quite fitted the bill.

He sighed. Surely, they had talked it out and talked it out all over the weekend. 'What do we need to talk about now? I thought we …'

'A new client came in today. She had some time to kill before her therapist was ready.'

Chris was puzzled. He held the phone away from his ear and looked at it, as though the answer to his confusion might be written there, but no. 'Sorry, babe. Have I missed a line or two? What's she got to do with us having to talk?'

Again, there was a pause. Then, the bombshell. Or, if not a bombshell a piece of small ordnance which made a breach in the wall and let the darkness in. 'We got chatting. Not a very nice woman, I didn't think. A bit strange. Wore too much makeup, for one thing. Very bright lipstick.'

The black dog dropped a ball, dark as night, heavy as a black hole, at his feet and looked up at him, panting.

'Her name was Louise. Louise Taylor. Apparently, she's a friend of yours.'

Sound of Silence

*

It was only when he found himself walking down the street with an overnight bag in his hand that Chris Rowan realised he had no friends. Not just no good friends, mates from way back, blokes he went to preschool with, no – he just had no real friends at all. Mark the pharmacist, the only one he was still vaguely in touch with, had, inadvertently, started this spiral of chaos, so he didn't really count, not any more. He didn't even have the usual raft of fake ones on Facebook; he had decided within a few days of starting his profile that life was too short to spend hours telling people he had just had a cup of tea and discovering that they had all just done the same. The shock of his sudden thought was so severe it made him stop dead in his tracks. He half-turned, back to the little, over-mortgaged house he had just left, back to the only place he felt even moderately safe, but he knew that would do no good. It didn't matter that he had left Megan standing in the hall, blind with tears and sorrow. She didn't want him to go, he knew that. But also he knew that she couldn't let him stay. He ran the conversation – if sobbed, screamed, whispered words of despair could be called a conversation – through his mind as he walked, every footfall sounding like soil thumping on the coffin of his life.

They had met back at the house. She clearly didn't want to meet in anywhere public and all he wanted was to hunker down in familiar surroundings. Like Kyle, he didn't like challenge or change at the best of times and this could hardly count as the best of any time. He had never known a week like it for emotional ups and downs and felt as if he had been through a wringer. His chest hurt from the tension and he felt as though he was carrying a bowling ball in the pit of his stomach. His head was light and his eyes were on a timer set a few seconds after reality, causing a halo of light to form around everyday objects as he looked around. It was such an extraordinary feeling he couldn't leave it alone and his eyes darted everywhere, checking it was still happening, dreading it, yet loving it. Could it still be a dream? He shook his head; no – all his dreams had a dog in them. But not in a good way.

Megan was calm. But again, not in a good way. She had driven back to the house and had parked her car carefully. He had been watching from the lounge window and he saw her go through her usual ritual, turn off the engine, check once more she was out of gear, reach for the handbag, check for errant mascara in the rear view, check once more she was out of gear, look round the car interior just in case there was … well, he'd never really known what she was looking for but it clearly wasn't there, because she got out and closed the door, bending to look just one last time. God, he loved that woman.

He hadn't locked the door so she was inside in minutes, standing in front of him, uncertain, trembling. He could see now that everything wasn't normal. Her makeup had clearly been fixed over tears, her mouth was trembling even before either of them spoke. They were so close together in the little room, full of the detritus of a family life: Kyle's lego box under the window; Megan's slippers, kicked off anyhow that morning, toes pointed inwards, the backs trodden down; Chris had dropped the Sunday supplement beside his chair the night before and there it still lay, TV page for Monday uppermost. They were planning to watch *The Walking Dead*, to see which of their favourite characters had been killed off this time. They *had* been planning to watch it …

'Megs …'

'Chris …'

Neither of them had the strength to say anything else. There was at the same time too much and too little to say. He had been sacked, but somehow her problems still took precedence. He was at the disadvantage that he had no idea what Louise Taylor had told Megan. He didn't want to meet that trouble halfway, so, lacking anything else to do, he just sat down in his usual chair. He had no choice; his legs had ceased to hold him up. He wanted to be sick.

'What are you going to do about the job?' Megan broke the ice, her voice tight and quiet with the effort to be civil.

'I don't know,' he said, because he didn't. 'I need to check my contract.'

'Couldn't you apologise?'

He blinked. 'What for? For beating you up? For lusting over some raddled old bat on the stairs? I didn't do either of those things.'

Her smile was small, cold and cynical. 'No, that's true. But you did screw a client in an empty house.' Her words fell like stones.

'Megs, I …'

'She was very specific,' she said, still with no inflection. 'In fact, she was so specific – and, as you probably recall, she has a certain charisma and a particularly penetrating voice – she was so specific I had to take her into a back room. People were beginning to stare.'

She waited for him to say something, but he couldn't. There seemed to be something stuck in his throat and he could scarcely breathe, let alone speak.

She gave a little laugh, cold and lonely, like an echo in a night-street, a reminder of what they had once had. 'Apparently,' she said, 'there are quite a few things I have been leaving out of our sex life – which is leaving you very unsatisfied, by the way – that you just adore. For example, I had no idea you liked …'

'Stop!' He found the strength to stand. He went over to where she sat, huddled back in one corner of the sofa and fell to his knees in front of her. He didn't miss the fact that she flinched. 'Stop.' This time his voice was gentle, soft and far away. 'I don't know this woman. We talked it all over, only yesterday we were talking it all over. How can you still be worrying about her? I love *you*.'

'Louise …'

'Don't!'

'I have to use her name, Chris. I can't call her "that woman" forever. She is a real person now, not just some ghost in our machine.'

He bowed his head, resting his forehead on her knee and she pushed him away, but gently.

'Louise told me that you said otherwise. Don't worry, I didn't believe her; I know you love me. But … she says you have known each other for years …'

'I *met* her years ago, yes. That's not like *knowing* someone for years, though, is it?'

'She knew everything, though. She knew about where your mum works, she knew about when we moved here, how Kyle was three weeks early and didn't make a sound when he was born … she can't have found out all that stuff unless … well, unless you've been telling her. When you meet. For sex, she says. Do you know,' she dashed a tear away, 'do you know what she said?' She dropped her voice into a lower key, the rather husky tone that Louise Taylor spoke in. 'She said, "Oh, don't worry, Megan. It's purely physical for me. I don't want Chris full time, though I could have him if I wanted him. I just want him for his body. And that's what he wants of me."' She went back to her normal tone. 'And, do you know, that might have been okay.' She found a smile from somewhere. 'But … but, you know, Chris, it's *not* okay! She's older than me, she's fatter, she's …'

'That's not an issue,' he said, raising his head. 'I don't care who's older, fatter, younger, all that. I only want *you*. I haven't seen Louise Taylor for years, not before last week. I don't even *like* the bloody woman!'

'Doesn't that make it worse? Doesn't that just prove her point?'

Suddenly, Chris had had enough. He was arguing, he realised, about a relationship with a woman which didn't exist. He was justifying behaviour which he had not indulged in. It had to stop and of course, the pit of his stomach told him, it would never stop. If they got over this blip, there would be another blip along the road, and another, and another, and yet another, like evil speed humps, slowing their lives down for ever and ever. He stood up and looked down at her, tear sodden, curled in her corner. 'Do you want me to go?'

She bowed her head and the seconds passed like years until she finally nodded.

'Right. I won't argue with that.' He turned for the door, then paused. 'I don't know how we'll sort the money out. I appear to be unemployed. But something will come along, doubtless. Perhaps you could go and live with your mother for a while.' He enjoyed twisting that knife. 'I happen to know that the market is very buoyant for this kind of house; it won't linger long once you put it up for sale. I don't want anything if there should be a profit. I'm not sure when I will be in a position to give you anything for Kyle.'

She twisted round and looked at him over the back of the settee. 'You seem to have the finances all sorted.'

He shrugged, but turned away. He knew that a shrug didn't go with the expression in his eyes. 'I'm an estate agent,' he said. 'I can't help it.' He waited for her to say something, to stop him, but the avalanche was too far down the mountainside by now and was carrying all before it.

And so now, here he was, walking down the road with a couple of shirts and a change or two of underwear in a bag and precious little else. He didn't look down, but he knew the black dog was pacing at his side, tongue lolling, tail wagging, waiting for the next bit of excitement to begin. The adrenalin which had flooded his body while he was with Megan was receding and in its place was the bitter bile of fear. He had never been homeless in his life. He had gone from his mother's house to a shared flat to his home with Megan without so much as a night on a sofa in between. He had met a lot of people who had no home; of course he had – he was a letting agent, after all. He had helped them find somewhere, if he could, but as he walked, a list of reasons he couldn't help them came unbidden into his head, churned out by his hindbrain in time to his heavy tread. No job. No partner. No money. No references. He tried to keep the last reason at bay, but eventually, he said it out loud. 'No hope.'

Megan sat on the settee, huddled in the corner like a frightened child. She still couldn't believe quite what she had done. She had thrown out the only man she had ever really loved, the only man she wanted to start a family with, the father of her child because some mad woman – she had to be mad, surely, to talk the way she had done with no fear of being overheard – had told her … and that was where her sensible self shut down and the child took over. She had said some things which had made Megan's scalp crawl with middle-class loathing. Self-loathing, more specifically. This woman had delved into the innermost parts of her lack of confidence and had exposed it, like a cadaver on a medical school slab. There was no possibility that she had not slept with Chris, not once, not twice, but many times over the years. And the pillow talk had clearly been very specific. All the things she thought he disliked, had no need for in bed or elsewhere, apparently, these were all the things he craved the most. She blushed again, all by herself in her corner of the settee.

She had almost – to her amazement – dropped into the sleep of the emotionally exhausted, when she was woken by the phone. She almost managed a smile as she looked at the clock. He had managed to hold out for almost half an hour!

'Chris?' She snatched the phone up and held it to her ear with both hands, snuggling down further to wait for his loving answer.

There was a pause. 'No, it's Sam. Is everything all right? You sound a bit … I don't know … fragile.'

The trouble with having a friend like Sam, Megan had decided years ago, was that dissembling was pointless. She had x-ray eyes, she always said and they could see into a person's soul. 'No …' she decided to give it a go anyway, 'No, everything's fine. I was just expecting it to be Chris, that's all. We …'

'Don't give me all that bullshit, Megan.' Sam was crisp and businesslike. 'You haven't taken my calls all week, not since I was round at yours. I've heard … let's call them rumours, shall we, about Chris. If you don't know about them, it's time you did.'

Megan felt a tear roll down her cheek. 'I've heard them,' she murmured.

'You have?'

She didn't need Skype to see her friend's eyebrows disappear under her fringe in disbelief. 'Yes.'

'What? The one about him and that woman? In the house?'

Megan was tired. She was tired to her very bones and she had had enough, even of Sam. 'Yes.' Her voice was flat. 'Yes. The one about him fucking Louise Taylor's brains out on the bedroom floor. Yes, the one about him doing precisely that, minus the bedroom floor detail, for years, from before he met me and since at every opportunity. Yes …'

It took a lot to shut Samantha Cormack up but this time she had nothing to say.

'Yes. I know. And yes, I know he's lost his job. And yes …' her voice fell to a whisper. To say it out loud would be to make it real. 'He's gone.'

Sam spoke finally, and they were the only words Megan wanted to hear, though not from her. 'I'm on my way.'

Chris pushed open the door of the little café halfway across town and as he did so, several clichés crossed his mind. One was that he remembered nothing of how he had got there. He had crossed roads, negotiated people on the pavement, possibly even spoken to the odd one or two, but since shutting his ex-front door, he had hardly any memory. The other was that he had run home to mummy. He had never seen himself as quite that person, but it seemed that he was, indeed, a mummy's boy after all. It just remained to be seen how much of a boy's mummy his mother was, when push came to shove.

It wasn't often Chris looked at his mother without her knowing he was there. It was a shock to him to see her looking tired; mothers are immortal, everyone knows that. But she looked pale and a little flustered, with a queue at the counter and no other help in sight. She was smiling – she was always smiling – and he could hear her clipped tones making small talk as she sliced cake and made another pot of coffee. The little café was run as a charity by her husband's church and they didn't have too much in the way of hi-tech coffee making equipment but looking at her now, that was probably just as well. He took a step forward and something about his movement caught her mother-radar and she looked straight into his eyes. And knew.

It only took a second for her to ping into action mode. 'Oh, Chris! Darling! Thank goodness you're here. Sally has had to shoot off

– crisis with the children, I think. Can you grab a pinny and give me a hand.' She beamed around the room and raised her voice a little. 'Don't worry, anyone still waiting for toasties and other goodies. My son has arrived; the Seventh Cavalry.' She focused her smile more directly on her son and it pulled him in like a tractor beam in *Star Trek*. 'Come on, Chris. Spit spot.' He and his sister had loved Mary Poppins books as children and his mother had never forgotten.

He put his bag down at the end of the counter and ducked under the flap. It had a dodgy catch and it was best not to put it through its paces too often. He had never forgotten the day when he had brought Megan round, showing off his girlfriend to his mother and Megs had leaned on it and had crashed to the ground, complete with a Victoria sponge and a plate of brownies. Sarah Green had fallen in love with the girl then and there as she lay there, licking cream and jam off her fingers. All she had said was 'Mmm. Yummy.' He shook himself to get rid of the memory.

'Right, mum,' he said, tying on Sally's discarded pinny. 'What first?'

She gave him an absentminded hug and he realised with a lurch how little she was, how frail her arm felt around his waist. She wasn't old, of course she wasn't. But somehow nothing felt very permanent today. 'Can you make two cheese and onion toasties for those ladies over there … no, wait. I'll do those. If you could do the coffees, teas, cakes for a minute, then we can draw breath. It's really busy today.'

The next hour passed in a whirl of slicing, pouring and giving the wrong thing to the right people, or vice versa. Then, suddenly, everyone was gone. The place looked like a bomb had hit it, with chairs all anyhow and crumbs to further order. Sarah Green didn't stand on ceremony at the Chat Café; she knew almost every one of her customers by name and more. She knew their little joys and sorrows – she was that kind of woman. Or at least, she was that kind of woman when it came to customers; with her family, as Chris and Claire could both attest, not so much. Chris was nearly mad with frustration as she went around the room, straightening, wiping, replacing sugar packets and depleted paper napkins. He managed to keep it under control until she reached for the hoover; that was a step too far.

'Mum! Will you just sit down for a minute? Please?'

She looked at him, startled. 'But, darling, I must just …'

'No, no, you mustn't. A few crumbs on the floor will wait a while. We need to talk.'

She sat down, gingerly, on the edge of a chair and smiled uncertainly at him. Then, she jumped up again. 'Coffee?' she said, brightly. That would stave it off for a minute or two.

'Mum. Sit. Please. I need to talk to you. If you would rather I go back to the vicarage and wait, that's fine. But we have to talk.'

She subsided back into her chair and sat waiting, shoulders tense. A small smile played around her mouth. She didn't know what was coming. She *feared* what was coming, but until he told her, it wasn't real. That policy had served her well all her life and she wasn't about to let go of it here, today, in the face of who-knew-what. She took a deep breath and broadened the smile. 'All right, dear. What would you like to tell me?'

There was no way to wrap this up in any conversational cotton wool. 'Megan and I have split up.' It sounded bald and cold but this was the best way with his mother, he knew. Dress up a statement even a little and she would hang on to the good bit and ignore the bad. Even when his father was dying, on the very day he actually died, she was talking about how well he looked, how he was planning a round of golf. So, straight from the hip was best. And even so, she made the best of it.

'Oh, darling!' she said, leaning back in her chair, her hands on the table. 'Every couple has their ups and downs. Even your father and I …'

'This is for keeps, mum,' he said. 'There … well, things have been said that can't be unsaid. She believes that I have been having an affair and she won't forgive me.'

His mother's silence was like a well, sucking in all sound and so the ticking of the thermostat under the coffee pot, the traffic outside, all became unnaturally loud. She was known in the church as a good listener but this was to give her unwarranted praise; she usually said nothing because she had no idea what to say. Before her husband died, she had had no faith except that a cup of sweet tea would heal all ills. And if it didn't, then just ignoring it would make most things go away.

After that, everyone was simply on their own; she had exhausted her repertoire. But then, when her grief over his death was still a little raw scab, to be picked at now and then when she was alone, Mike Green had come along, a white knight in shining armour. He had enclosed her in loving arms and made the lingering nasty bits go away and there was just one fly in this healing ointment; he was a vicar, and not just any old vicar. He was a vicar who lived up to his Christian tenets in literally everything he did. She often told him he was too good for her and when she said it, she meant it. He hadn't asked her to share his faith, all he asked was that she looked as though she did. She had assured him that she had let Jesus into her life and the look of joy on his face had cut her to the quick – she wore her Christianity like a coat she could take off one day; for him, it was like his skin. But, it worked and if he knew she had doubts, he never said so and as for her, she relied on her old belief, that what you don't know, won't hurt you.

'Chris, darling, I'm sure you will work it out.' Her words came out like a tickertape machine; response 4B subsection iv.

'I don't think so, Mum. It's … well, it's complicated.'

Her eyes went wide. 'Don't tell me you actually *are* having an affair, Chris! How could you? That lovely little boy. Megan. I just don't understand you.'

He sighed. Why was it always his fault? Ever since he was a child, it was always his fault. If his friends came round and one of them so much as snagged a nail, it was always his fault. One time, and it had rankled for years, one of his friends – could it even have been Mark? – had eaten a cake she was saving for tea and *he* had been sent to bed and Mark – yes, it definitely had been Mark – had been taken out with Claire for a cream tea, because there was nothing in the house to eat. And there were loads of other …

'Chris! Are you listening to me? I said, who is she?'

'Who is she who?'

'Who are you having an affair with?' She lowered her voice on the word 'affair' as though a Christian café was not quite the place to say such a thing out loud. 'Is it that little bit of trash in your office? She's no better than she should be.'

'Jacintha? No, she's having it away with Dave.'

'Chris! How can you be so flippant? He's married, isn't he? With children?'

'Yes, yes, he is. But it isn't exactly a novelty, Mum. People are having affairs left, right and centre.' He sighed when he saw her expression. 'But not me. It was all a misunderstanding.'

She straightened up and brushed an invisible crumb from the table, pursing her mouth. 'I don't see how an affair can be a misunderstanding, Christopher.'

Oh, oh – his full name. So, that was how it was going to be, was it? He squared his shoulders. He wasn't going to tell her the gory details, but there was going to be no option. 'Mum, I made a mistake. One mistake. I had a migraine …'

'I didn't think you still had those.'

Ah, now the Gestapo tactics. 'Now and again. Anyway, Mark …'

'I didn't think you still saw Mark.'

'Sorry? Oh, sometimes, in the shop. Anyway, I went to Mark and he gave me something for my head and it made me … well, it clouded my judgement for a while. And I was showing …' Suddenly, it was all too much and he stood up. 'Look, Mum, I can't do this. I was going to ask if I could stay with you and Mike for a few days, just while I get myself sorted. But it obviously isn't going to work …'

She jumped up and went round the table to put her arms around him. To anyone passing, it would look like a hug, but in fact there was no warmth in it. She was using Vicar's Wife 3A, subsection ix. 'Of course you must come and stay with us, darling. Mike will be delighted. We just don't see enough of you.'

He put his arms around her loosely. Grateful Son 2A, subsection desperate. 'Will Mike be okay with me being there?'

'Of course he will.' The pause was minimal, but in his heightened state he felt it as though it lasted hours.

'As long as you're sure …'

There was no pause this time, because she didn't know what to say. She had the option of a lie or having him walk out of the door. Silence was, as always, her best response. He bent his head and rested his cheek on the top of her head. How had he got to this? Where was it all going, apart from to hell in a handcart?

Ain't no sunshine

*

It wasn't until he had put his bag down on the spare bed, that Chris cried. He wasn't sure that he was even crying about leaving Megan, although that was clearly what they called on *Criminal Minds* the 'stressor'. He was crying for his whole life, for his old bedroom in the house his mother had sold when she married Mike. He and his sister had spent their entire childhoods in that house. Their height charts were still there in pen on the kitchen door frame; his parents had only stopped measuring them when Chris got taller than his father, the joke being that no one could reach up to make the mark any more. He had remembered that day. It was the first day he had looked, properly looked at his dad and seen how old and ill he was looking, how his breaths were snatched, how the whites of his eyes were pale yellow, how he only looked plump because his stomach was distended through what turned out to be a terminal cancer.

He couldn't blame his mother from moving on, but he and Claire had begged her not to sell the house. She didn't need the money and they both needed a place to rest their heads. Claire wasn't married then, he wasn't yet with Megan; they could have shared it, stayed in their old rooms, with the familiar. Just until they didn't need it any more. If that day ever came.

So now, instead of putting down his bag on his old bed, in his old room, with his childhood all around him from the teddy on the bookshelf to the Power Rangers on the wallpaper, here he was in the guest room at the vicarage. It was decorated to offend no-one, with muted beige the main component of the colour scheme. There were twin beds, each with a matching muted beige duvet and one flat pillow. There was a dressing table which had been given a coat of muted beige chalk paint and been finished with a plate glass top, to save wear and tear. There was a fitted wardrobe. There was a single vase in the middle of the dressing table top, a bunch of dusty lavender sticking stiffly out of its gold-edged fluted top. The lavender was the most colourful thing in the room and the whole atmosphere screamed charity shop – there was even a hint of that musty, fusty, long-neglected smell, under the worn-out perfume of the dried flowers.

There was a tap on the door and Mike Green put his head around it. Chris turned away and surreptitiously wiped his eyes. He heard his bag being lifted and carefully placed on the floor. His stepfather muttered, in his soft, careful voice, 'No luggage on the bed, old chap, if that's all right with you? We have to think of the next … person who will be sleeping here, don't we? Is everything all right in here? Only, your mother was wondering, are you coming down to tea?'

Did the man ever make a statement? Did he always talk in questions? Oh, God … oh, sorry, not God, oh, bugger … oh, sorry, not bugger … even in his head, Chris was being careful. He would have to find somewhere else, quick, or he would be as mad as a hatter. He turned, pinning on a smile. 'Sorry about the bag, Mike. Didn't think. I'll be down in a minute.'

The vicar stepped forward and leaned in to pat Chris on the shoulder. At no time did any part of his body except his hand come any nearer than two feet away. If Mike Green had a failing – and he always said, self-deprecatingly, that he had many, whilst believing he had none – it was that he was not a natural hugger. A manly pat was best in the circumstances, particularly as his stepson was clearly upset. Best not make it worse with displays of affection. 'I'll tell her you're on your way down, then, shall I?' He looked at Chris, eyebrows raised in anticipation.

'I'll be right down, yes.' Chris nodded and the hand was removed and the vicar was on his way downstairs.

'He's on his way,' Chris heard him carol as he turned the bend in the stairs. 'Just washing his hands.'

Chris snorted and almost smiled. Oh, God – he allowed himself that indulgence with the vicar a stairsworth of space away – how was he going to bear even a night in this house, with its lavender and no cases on the bed and washing your hands a euphemism for everything from breaking your heart to having a shit. His inner teenager rose up inside him and for a moment he felt like trashing the room, but he settled for putting his bag back in the centre of the left hand bed's duvet.

But, before he went downstairs, he washed his hands.

Megan had stopped trying to compete with Sam about one hour after they first met. She had never believed it, no matter how often Chris had told her, but she was actually much prettier than Samantha, with a much better skin, brighter eyes, glossier, curlier hair. She saw Sam through the rose-coloured specs that Sam managed to subliminally place on every nose and so she didn't see that the make-up was covering old acne scars, that the eyes owed more to clever shadow and a lot of work in the salon than to nature and that even Sam had now forgotten what colour her hair really was. But, old habits die hard and so she washed her face, brushed her hair and changed her top before Sam was knocking on the door.

As soon as Sam walked in, it seemed as though things were already getting better. It was as though the sun had broken through the clouds as she enveloped Megan in her arms. Neither woman spoke as they rocked gently together; it was as though the years fell away and they were back in the girl's changing room, with Megan weeping after another bout of bullying, Sam comforting her before going off to sort the bullies out. And now, just like then, when the hugging finally had to stop, so Sam was on the attack.

They went into the kitchen, as always, and were soon leaning against the worktop, coffee in hand. Sam always said that their coffee said all that needed to be said about them. She took hers black and vicious, as strong as you like, no sugar. Meg liked hers with milk and sugar and if she was honest, she preferred a nice hot chocolate to coffee any day. They cradled their mugs and looked at each other, waiting for the first one to make a move. Naturally, it was Sam.

'He's a bastard, Megs. You've done the right thing.'

As far as either of those statements went, Megan wasn't sure she could totally agree with either, so she sipped her coffee and looked at Sam over the rim of her mug.

'No, seriously. You should hear what that woman Louise Thingie …'

'Taylor. Louise Taylor.'

'Right. You should hear what she's saying.'

'I have.' Megan said it so quietly it was a wonder Sam heard and Megan wasn't at all sure she meant to say it out loud at all.

'What? You've spoken to her? Directly?'

'She came into the spa. Pretended she wanted to make an appointment and then proceeded to tell me everything. In very, very glorious Technicolor.'

Sam was hard to shock, but for once Megan had managed it. 'I can't believe she did that! What a cow!'

'Yes,' Megan said. 'And that's why I am beginning to wonder if I over reacted in chucking Chris out.'

Sam slammed her coffee down. 'Are you crazy? Of course you had to chuck him out. He's been at it with this … this …'

'Cow. Yes, exactly. Look, Sam, I know you've never really liked Chris …'

'He's not good enough for you, Megs, that's all …'

'Has anybody been? Have you *ever* liked even one of my boyfriends?'

Sam looked stunned. Had it always been that obvious? 'I just want you to be happy,' she said, not answering the question.

'That's no answer. Just tell me one of my boyfriends you liked. One where you encouraged me to go out with him. Just one. That's all I want to hear.'

'I liked that Whatsisface … you know the one, the accountant.'

'Oh.' Megan drew out the syllable, cynically. 'I know the one you mean. The one with halitosis and the row of pens in his top pocket. The one who took me out for a Chinese and used a calculator to work out my share of the bill. As I recall, he didn't forget to allow for the fact that I had eaten four of the prawn toasts to his two. So, he was perfect for me, was he?'

'I didn't say he was perfect ...'

'Good. Because as I recall we got pissed the next night and laughed about him until you were sick.' Megan put down her coffee mug on the draining board and moved round to stand next to Samantha. Sam was taller than Megan, just the right height for her shoulder to be handy for crying on and she leaned against her now. 'I know you want the best for me. I still think Chris is that best. The more I think about this woman ...'

'Who he shagged silly on a bedroom floor and all points west,' Sam pointed out.

'Yes, as the story goes.'

'Story! Come on, Megs. It's no story. He clearly did it.'

Megan straightened up. 'You say that as if she just lay there like a log. She was part of this too, Sam. What if she ... I don't know. What if she made all the running? What if she was in cahoots with Mark, got him to give Chris something that would, I don't know, make him lose his inhibitions or something?'

'God, Megs? A *conspiracy*? How did we get here?'

Megan shrugged and moved away again, picking up her mug and taking another sip. 'You're probably right,' she said, in a voice flat with pain. 'Let's change the subject for a minute, shall we?'

'But ...'

'Yes. I know you want to pick at it till it bleeds. But I don't want to talk about it any more. I've got Kyle to pick up soon. In fact, I should have done it earlier; Mum is getting a bit arsey.'

'She *loves* him,' Sam said, in a knee jerk reaction. Grannies love grandchildren. It was probably written down somewhere, with all the other rules like mothers being immortal and chocolate being good for you as long as it's the expensive sort.

'Mmm.' Megan couldn't bring herself to deny it, but she wasn't sure enough of it being true to agree. 'She finds him a bit ... difficult.'

'Of course he's difficult,' Sam said. 'He's three. And a boy. According to those at work who've got kids, that just goes with the territory.'

Megan had to speak as she found. She adored Kyle with every fibre of her being, but she couldn't help noticing he wasn't quite like all the other kids at playgroup. 'He is tricky, Sam,' she said. 'He hates change. He hates …' Suddenly, the facts hit her like a wall. 'How is he going to cope with Chris not here?'

Sam was in a cleft stick. No, she didn't like Chris. No, she didn't really like Kyle much either, he struck her as a whingeing little shit, all snot and trauma at the slightest provocation. But she disliked Megan's mother more than either of them; she was the cause of all Megan's insecurity from the cradle, if she were to make an educated guess. Sam's own mother was chaotic, often three sheets in the wind, had had more men in her life than most women owned shoes and yet here was Sam, as normal as could be expected, allowing for life's other little ups and downs. Whereas Megan, from a steady, neat home which would make any social worker applaud, was as damaged as a woman could be and still walk upright. Life was a bitch, you could say that for it. She settled for a smile and a non-committal 'mmm'.

Before Sam was pinned down to a more complete answer, which would have had to be based on the fact that Chris barely seemed to know who he was most of the time, let alone be close to the kid, she was saved by the bell.

Megan raced to the door as though she had wings on her heels and Sam's heart broke for her. If it was Chris, back with his tail between his legs and with the nous not to use his key, it was bad news. If it wasn't Chris, it was bad news. In fact, it was even worse news. It was Margaret Harris and Kyle.

Megan's mother swept into the house, shepherding Kyle ahead of her as if he were some kind of pushalong toy on wheels. She nodded to Sam. 'Sam.'

'Mrs Harris.' For all that she had spent a good amount of her adolescence in the woman's house, Sam could still only find it in her heart to be barely civil.

'I thought you might be here.' Margaret Harris was a past mistress of the unspoken undertow in any statement and Sam didn't miss this one. She wasn't ready to leave Megan yet. They hadn't really talked things through, practical things that needed to be said. Like, how was she going to survive, financially? She was near the wind as it was; with nothing coming in apart from child benefit and the pittance from her job, Sam couldn't see her managing on her own for long. And going back to this cold woman was not an option. But it was clear that Margaret Harris thought the kitchen was too full of people to the tune of one, so she drained her mug and left, pausing in the hall to give Megan one last hug.

Hands washed and grace said, Chris sat down at the vicarage kitchen table and looked out down the dark tunnel in front of his eyes at what it held. There was cake, there were sandwiches, there was even, God forbid, little triangles of toast spread with anchovy paste. What *was* this meal? It was three o'clock in the afternoon, for God's … heaven's … Chris's head already hurt with the effort of keeping his thoughts as Mike would like to find them.

'Tuck in, darling,' his mother said, brightly. 'You need feeding up. You're too thin. Mike and I were saying, weren't we, when you were over with … erm … were over last. You're too thin.'

Please, Chris thought, please, will you use Megan's name? Will you say the word 'Kyle'? I'm not an invalid. They're not dead. Out loud, he said, 'I'm comfy this size, thanks, Mum. I was a bit chunky before, don't you think?' But to keep her quiet, he took one of everything on the table. The anchovy paste was just as disgusting as he remembered it, but washed down with a mouthful of tea and a bit of lemon drizzle cake he managed to swallow it without gagging.

'Your mother is a marvellous cook, isn't she, Chris?' Chris wondered what it was about vicar's voices. Did they have lessons in that tone? He sounded as though he was announcing the first lesson, not complimenting his wife on the spread. And, to be fair, it was amazing.

'Do you do this every day, Mum?' he asked. 'I should think you get fed up with cake at the café.'

'Well, not *every* day, dear,' she said, with a vicar's wifely smile. 'I did put on a bit of a spread for you, to welcome you to our home.' She and her husband exchanged a secret glance that swept the table like a lighthouse beam. 'We want you to stay as long as you want to. Until you feel …'

She stopped, but Chris knew she almost said 'better'. He bit back his riposte. 'Less separated'; 'less unemployed'; 'less' he had to face it, 'less bloody suicidally unhappy'? He settled for the banal. 'Thanks, Mum, Mike. It's good of you.' He bit into the lemon drizzle and was almost sick. Suddenly, all the food tasted of forced good humour, it had the taint of the good deed well done. He wanted something bitter, something that matched his mood of dark despair. Something he could feed the dog.

'I *thought* Sam would be here,' Megan's mother told her as she came into the lounge with a cup of tea, following Megan and Kyle. Megan, kneeling at the Lego box with her son didn't bother to reply. Most of her mother's statements didn't need an answer. 'She's always here when anything goes wrong. Like a storm crow, she is. There's never a crisis but what …'

Megan kissed the top of Kyle's head and murmured to him, then pushed herself wearily to her feet and went and sat down opposite her mother. 'Mum,' she said, in a voice worn out by much repetition. 'Sam is my best friend. I mean, probably, my *only* friend. She isn't just here for the bad things. We have girls' nights in, we have girls' nights *out*. She has bad times too, you know. When she breaks up with someone …'

Her mother snorted, but she ignored it.

'… I'm there for her. I wanted her to come and to be quite honest, I am rather angry that you drove her away.' Her voice showed the strain of speaking like that to her mother. All her life she had had to be careful what she said or retribution would be swift. Her mother had never struck her, not even tapped the back of her legs, but her tongue could lash like a whip and, although there was little enough to begin with, her love would be withdrawn until further notice. And of course, she wasn't disappointed this time.

'My goodness, Megan. I'm only speaking as I find.' Margaret Harris was the epitome of hurt and outrage. 'I do what I can, goodness knows. I take your child for days on end – and, frankly, Megan, he isn't easy – and then you insult me.'

'I'm not insulting you, Mum, or if I have, it wasn't my intention. I'm very grateful that you've had Kyle for me and I won't ask again. I have a lot of rearranging to do in the next few days and that will include work, all the rest of it. It may mean we have to move.'

Her mother reeled back as though stung. 'Move? Where to?' To hear her talk it would be easy to imagine that she and Megan were joined at the hip. Chris and Megan had fallen into the habit of speaking of Margaret as though she was the devoted grandmother they both wished for, but in fact she would have been quite content if she never had Kyle to look after again. She liked tidy and he wasn't tidy. 'When would I see you and …' The pause was too long.

'Kyle? I'm not saying we're going to the moon, Mum, just somewhere less expensive.'

The look on her mother's face said it all. What could be less expensive than this poky little place?

'So, I tell you what, Mum,' Megan got up and went over to Kyle. 'Kyle and I are going out to see the ducks on the river. We could do with a blow of air, couldn't we, Kyle?' She had looked out of the window and seen the sun shining hot and yellow and was surprised – it had seemed to her that it must be raining.

The boy jumped around, scattering Lego bricks far and wide. 'Ducks! Ducks! We're going to see the ducks!'

'Go and get a juice, poppet and we'll be on our way.'

The child ran into the kitchen and soon there was the sound of doors opening and closing as he searched for his favourite drink. His voice echoed down the little hall. 'Mummy. Do we have any apple 'n' ba'currant?'

'Blackcurrant,' his grandmother muttered under her breath. 'Apple *and* b*l*ackcurrant.'

'Mum. He's a little boy. Leave him alone, just for a while. In fact,' Megan had to fight down her temper. 'Leave *me* alone. Just for once.'

Her mother smiled her little how-you've-hurt-me smile. Chris always said she smiled with her nostrils and Megan was flooded with a sense of loss as she remembered that. And how right he was. Margaret

Harris had developed gathering her things and making an exit into an art form and she did it now. She called 'Goodbye, Kyle,' from the doorway.

''Bye, G'amma,' he shouted back, voice echoing because his head was in a cupboard, seeking the elusive apple and ba'currant.

Megan watched her mother's lips move silently, correcting him and raised an eyebrow. Her mother got the message and clamped her mouth shut firmly. But she couldn't resist her parting shot.

'Are you going to leave those toys strewn all over the place?' she said, screwing up her nose as though the Lego smelt. 'This house is a … pigsty.' And she swept out.

Megan leaned against the door when she was gone and bowed her head. Well, if she could see her mother off the premises with no blood shed, she could do anything. Come on world – Megan Harris and Kyle Rowan are ready for you. Do your worst.

Tea was cleared away with almost supernatural speed. Chris had gone upstairs to unpack his bag and when he got back, everything had disappeared. It was like a scene from *Beauty and the Beast* although his mother bore next to no resemblance to Mrs Thingie, the teapot played by Jessica Fletcher. Chris was aware he was mixing his media, but he knew who he meant. Somehow, Mike didn't bring to mind any cartoon characters, so he let the analogy slide. He was aware that he was deliberately thinking about other things to stop Megan's voice ringing in his head. Every time he let his attention wander, he could hear her, calling him. He wandered into the sitting room to find his mother. He needed company, chat, meaningful conversation, *Antiques Road Trip* even; anything to keep that voice quiet.

His mother was sitting, knitting. He hadn't been far wrong in his prediction. It wasn't an antiques programme she had on, it was one where for some reason, a couple were looking at loads of homes they couldn't afford and subsequently didn't buy. He knew as an estate agent … as an *ex*- estate agent, he should perhaps be interested, but he could tell at a glance that to have a property like that at that price meant the programme had to be older than Kyle, so what was the point? But he had to silence the calling.

Sarah Green was never still. If she wasn't baking, she was knitting. If not knitting, she was sewing. But she put it aside when she saw her son's face and switched off the television. 'Sit down, darling,' she said, and patted the seat of the sofa next to her, pushing her wool and assorted blanket squares aside. 'We need to talk things over, don't we? No recriminations. No rehashing it all, just a bit of planning for the future.'

He plonked down on the cushion and the sofa sank in the middle. It was the only thing she had brought from her old house and it comforted him. 'I love you, Mum. Do I ever say that?'

She looked at him, sitting there, thirty-two, going on twelve. 'No need to say it, darling. I know you love me and I love you, too.'

'How many miles?' It had been a while, but the old mantra was never far away.

'To the moon and back.' Her eyes filled with tears and only she knew exactly what for. She mourned for a life she had lost, with her husband who was the love of her life, who she still cried for every day, alone in the shower, turning her face up to the hot water so the tears wouldn't dry on her cheeks and give her away. She mourned for the children who had grown up too fast, for the woman she had once been. Surely, she had used the odd bad word, once upon a time. Had had a bit too much to drink when occasion demanded it and even when it didn't. But now, here she was, the vicar's wife, knitting blanket squares in the vicarage. And she was also an ungrateful bitch, for not being as happy as a pig in shit. Sorry, she said to herself in her head, I just said 'Shit'.

'Let's try not to cry, Mum,' Chris managed to get out without his tears actually falling. 'I might not stop once I start.'

She sniffed and wiped her eyes on the back of her hand. 'Not crying. Just a bit watery.' Another quote from his childhood. Many more of these and they would be in pieces. 'So. How long do you think you might be here? You can stay as long as you want, of course. But I'm doing an online order shortly and I need to know what to get.'

'Mum! Online order? You?'

She swatted him with her hand. 'Cheeky. I'll have you know I am a bit of a dab hand. So … do you have any idea?'

He shook his head. 'Sorry, Mum. Can I just leave it open for now? Not too long, I hope. I need to talk to Dave Stanley. I have a feeling I can still pull something out of that particular fire, if I'm lucky.'

'And Megan …?'

'No.' He bowed his head. 'I think the fire has reached the roofspace, Mum. That house can't be saved.'

There was nothing more to be said. He leaned against the back of the settee and closed his eyes and after a moment or two, she reached for her needles. Knitting could keep a whole pack of dogs at bay.

In the Air

*

That Tuesday morning was not a good time to be in the offices of Stanley Associates. Jacintha sat bewildered and soggy with tears in the midst of a gaggle of twittering women. The men in the office herded in one corner, like wildebeest who smell cheetah on the wind. Cassie ignored it all. Although he had given her the brush-off, she had a very soft spot for Chris Rowan and suspected that knives had been, if not exactly placed in his back personally, definitely and resolutely twisted and rammed home by the self-serving little madam so as far as she was concerned, she had got all she deserved and not a moment too soon. She sat at her corner desk and got on with her invoicing, earphones in ears, eyes on the screen.

'... And it's not as if I didn't do *anything* he wanted,' Jacintha was sobbing, with artfully broken voice. She rolled her eyes up towards the door behind which Dave Stanley was lurking, keeping his head down. 'And I mean *anything.*' She dropped her voice on the last word and to the male contingent's annoyance, what followed was largely inaudible. It sounded good though; at least one of the twitter sisters said 'Pig!' several times.

The phones were beginning to ring and, one by one, the women drifted off to do what they were paid for. Soon, Jacintha was on her own, her face strangely unblotched but a soggy hankie in her hand still betokened her distress. One of the wildebeest wandered over and whispered something in her ear. She looked up at him appraisingly and after a second or two's thought, wrote her phone number on his hand. He didn't have much power and influence, it was true, but if half the rumours were accurate, he would be able to give her a much better time than old 'let's leave it a minute, see what happens' Stanley.

She bent her head to the letters on her desk and soon had them divided into two piles. One pile was to be distributed amongst her colleagues, the other pile, for Dave Stanley's personal attention, would be going with her to the Ladies' later, for some serious wiping. She had been planning to leave this dump anyway, so she might as well go out with a bang.

Her phone rang. 'Stanley Associates,' she said, mechanically, clicking her fingers at the girl at the nearest desk and waving the first pile of letters at her, her eyebrows up in mute appeal.

'Oh, Jacintha.' Chris had decided a phone call rather than a visit might work best. Then there would be no embarrassment if it didn't all pan out.

'Chris. Hello.' She didn't say more. She knew the dead reply made people feel awkward; they didn't know how to proceed.

'Ummm …'

Yup, it had worked again.

'Ummm … is Dave about?'

She looked about her ostentatiously, with the phone away from her ear. 'No.' She spoke into the mouthpiece from a distance, then closer. 'No, sorry. I don't know where he is.'

Cassie, the only person who might care what Jacintha might be doing, didn't hear or see a thing.

'Oh.' Chris felt bad. He was probably out, doing his viewings. 'Can I leave him a message?'

'You can leave him a message, yes.' There was no sin of commission there; she didn't say she would pass it on.

'You'll be seeing him later, I expect.'

Bastard! It was probably him who put the boot in with Dave, made him feel bad about their affair. 'Squalid little fling' he had called it at three that morning. After they had been in bed since ten, that was, she reminded herself; she felt more justified that way. 'No, I don't expect I shall.'

'Oh.' There was a pause. 'I'm sorry.'

Yes, that's it, my lad, she thought. Rub it in. You knew all along what he was planning. 'As a matter of fact,' she hissed into the receiver, 'you're not the only person leaving Stanley Associates. My resignation will be on his desk by coffee …'

Two of the wildebeest put their heads together and one of them guffawed. Jacintha didn't know for certain which euphemism the other had used for the part of her that was usually on Dave Stanley's desk, but she could guess.

'… and then I shall be on my way.'

'Jacintha,' Chris said, finally having regained the power of speech. 'I really am sorry. I … well, I don't say what you were doing was right, but there was no need for Dave to be …'

'Dave isn't being anything,' she said loftily. 'I got fed up with him and his limp dick and his excuses and reasons he couldn't leave his wife. I got tired of creeping around, only every eating at mine or in such crappy restaurants that only other people screwing around would want to go there.' She was on her feet now and screaming more at the closed door than at the phone. 'I don't know why his ugly, fat, horse-faced wife wants him anyway, but she's *fucking welcome to him*!' The last words were at a high-pitched wail and as she said the last, she threw the phone at the front door of the office. By much more luck than judgement, the potential landlord who had just pushed it open avoided serious injury. He stood there irresolute as the phone whizzed past his ear. It looked as though he would be continuing his search for a good agent, but on the other hand he didn't want to miss the fun. No harm in hanging around. One of the wildebeest hurried over and took him across to a desk in the corner, away from the chaos. But Jacintha had snatched up her bag and coat and was out of there, running wailing down the street.

Cassie looked up, aware for the first time of something amiss. 'What was that?' she asked, mildly.

As if it made perfect sense, the woman on the neighbouring desk filled her in. She was so used to writing copy based on the number of words, she had it in a nutshell. 'Dave has screwed Jacintha, in as many ways as the word covers. Jacintha just threw the phone out of the door and has now run home, one assumes, to mother.'

'Who was she on the phone to?'

The neighbouring woman shrugged but the junior wildebeest filled in the gaps. 'Chris Rowan.'

Cassie jumped up and ran into the street to retrieve the phone, which had skittered across the pavement and was leaning against the wheel of a parked car. 'Chris?' She was speaking before she had it to her ear. 'Chris? Are you there?'

But she was too late. Chris had gone.

Sarah Green had rung in to the café to tell them she had a family emergency and wouldn't be in. Her call was greeted with amazement and not a little resentment. Sally, who was briefly back from her childcare crisis but had an appointment for her nails later that day and wasn't planning to be there after two, turned to the other two helpers and raised her eyebrows.

'Well!' she said. 'I like that! As bold as brass, says she has a family emergency! Leaves it all to us!' Sally lived her life as a series of lurches from one drama to another, with brief pauses in between to dismiss the sufferings of others. Her colleagues that day were more generous.

'I understand her son isn't well,' one said. Her name was Sylvia although for reasons no one could remember, she was always called Poppy. Cruel observers whispered that it was because her eyes were virtually out on stalks, but in fact it was simply that it was the first word she had spoken. No one was left now to remember Poppy as a baby; she was seventy five, bent and weak as to wrists and eyesight, but customers all forgave her little errors in order delivery because of her sweet nature.

'Son!' Sally said, with a dismissive snort. 'He's not exactly a kid, though, is he? She should have more consideration to those of us with *real* children.'

The other two looked at each other with meaningful eyes. The third woman, Pauline, put in her oar. 'Your children are always your children, Sally. No matter what their ages. I would hope that mine would always come home to me and George if ever they needed us.'

'God!' Sally cast her eyes up. She was the only member of the café staff who actually got a wage packet. Everyone else was a volunteer and she somehow considered that made her exempt from toeing the Christian line and not taking the name of the Lord her God in vain. In fact, she had only said she believed in Him at all in order to get the kids into the church playgroup, keep the little bastards off her hands for an hour or so. 'Sod that. I can't wait for mine to be out of my hair.'

Pauline, who was unfortunate enough to live within football distance of Sally's house, thought that the time they spent *in* her hair was little enough, judging from the hours they spent playing in the street, but said nothing. Poppy had turned away and was wiping the coffee pot, over and over and over. They liked Sarah. Poppy was madly in love with the vicar, the nearly twenty year age gap notwithstanding. Each was quietly planning an early escape – Sally was hard to bear at any time. Without the filtering effect of Sarah, she was impossible.

'I don't see the vicar wearing it,' Sally added. 'He likes his peace and quiet. A man his age, never had kids, won't want her son cluttering up the place.'

This was news. Poppy had heard that Sarah's son was unwell. She hadn't heard he had moved into the vicarage. She wondered whether that was even allowed – didn't they have to ask the Church Commissioners or something? She had certainly heard Rev Mike say something along those lines when she had asked him how many Syrian refugees he was planning to take in. She would have to have a word, find out – those poor little babies on those dreadful leaky boats deserved a bed more than Sarah's son, she was sure about that. 'Are you sure he's in the vicarage?'

'Oh, yes,' Pauline chimed in. 'I saw him yesterday afternoon. He went home with Sarah; he was carrying an overnight bag.'

'Oh!' Poppy was relieved. 'An *overnight* bag. He's probably just come for a night or so.'

'Oh, no,' Sally said, triumphant. 'I heard his wife's kicked him out. Apparently, he was having it away with all manner of women. All over town, I heard.'

'Sally!' Pauline was outraged. 'How ever did you get hold of that? I've met him. A lovely young man. Works at that estate agent in the High Street.'

'My sister works in that GP Practice on Castle Street; you know, the one round the back of Argos.'

The others nodded.

'Well, she reckons that new manager there has been knocking him off for years. Nothing said as such, you know. Just hints. But there's no smoke without fire, I reckon.'

The older women took a step back, looking at Sally from under lowered lashes. Poppy had never married, although she had once come very close to a very intimate encounter with the cheese counter manager back in the day when she had worked at the Co-op. Pauline had had her moments, but generally she would admit to having been monogamously and monotonously married to George since Adam was in the militia. Lovely young man or not, he was clearly no better than he should be. And Sarah had had a day off because of him? It just wasn't right!

Poppy spoke for them all. 'I'll have a word with the vicar,' she said, firmly.

A bell pinged behind them and a cheery voice called out for the usual. The rush was on and that was that; Poppy would speak to the vicar and yet another brick tumbled into the void. The black dog rolled over to have its tummy tickled. It had never had any luck as yet, but it never gave up trying.

Chris Rowan had never been unemployed before and it was all new to him, the hours of time left unfilled, the bank account which looked impossibly small suddenly with no hope of replenishment. Dave Stanley, having not heard back from Chris to discuss his generous offer, had paid up the three months in lieu, he had added the tax rebate and had also – although he didn't have to – had topped it up with a couple of commissions; ironically, in the circumstances, that for the successful letting of the white elephant of Number Forty Three. But even so, he had less than two grand to his name – a huge amount had been swallowed up by the overdraft and so the bottom line was very small. He immediately transferred half of it to Megan's account; who knew when he could give her more? And that was it; almost before winking, he was down to a balance of three figures and that couldn't be good.

He had left his laptop back at the house and wasn't going back for it. Similarly, his clothes – some nice stuff too – that was staying there unless Megan had put it on eBay or taken it to the charity shop. His mother would keep his shirts circulating. He was already in his suit. And his couple of pairs of jeans would do for round the house.

He was hunched now over the vicarage computer. It was as old as the hills and you could almost hear the gears turning as he went online. Mike opened it up for him every morning, ostentatiously making him turn away as he entered the password. He asked him, extremely politely, to avoid downloading any large files. Their broadband package was very basic, he said, and so anything using a lot of data – he pronounced it 'dar-tar' and you could almost see the speech marks appear above his head – would be costly to the parish. This was usually accompanied by a smile and a ruffle of Chris' hair. The subliminal message was, you stay off the naughty websites, my boy. I know what you'll be doing as soon as my back is turned. You'll be surfing all the porn sites you can shake a stick at.

After the first couple of mornings he had feigned an urgent bathroom need to avoid the whole encounter. He then closeted himself away, registering on every site he could find to get a new job. Anything. Anywhere. As long as it was soon. It didn't take him long to discover that he was all but unemployable. His transferable skills were few. People management? Hmmm … not really. IT? Only just. Qualifications? Apart from an abortive stab at a drama degree when he was eighteen, he hadn't been in a classroom for fourteen years. Dave Stanley was very hot on courses and went on as many as he could find. If he forgot the content on the drive home, it didn't count. They usually came with a certificate churned out on the day and he could paper his office wall with them – in fact, he often had. Chris was kicking himself now as he saw all of the acronyms he had laughed into touch being listed on all the recruitment websites, all with an inviting little box next to them, just aching to be filled with a nice, fat tick.

CIPD. AAT. CIM. CAM. ADBLD. He wanted to add another; WTF. He could hear Dave Stanley's voice as clearly as if he was sitting in the little poky room with him; 'You'll be sorry, Chris. No one was ever hurt by getting a qualification.'

'Dave,' he said to the empty study, 'you're right. I give you this one.'

The door popped open and his mother's head appeared. 'Sorry, darling. Did you call?'

There was no way on God's green earth – sorry, Mike – that she could have heard him speak. She must have been outside the door, listening. A glowing ember of annoyance began to glow inside him, making his chest feel full and hot. 'No, Mum. I didn't call.' He could hear that his voice was full of stress and needless to say, she was on it like a Ninja.

She crossed the room and kissed the top of his head. 'Are you okay, darling?' she asked, queen of the stupid question as always.

'Well, no, Mum. I'm homeless, jobless, skint and my partner has chucked me out. So, no, I'm not all right. But I'm all right apart from that.' He screwed his head round to look into her face. 'Don't worry about me. This is just a blip. I'll soon be on my feet again, you see. Look – I've enrolled with all these agencies. Someone will be back to me soon, I'm sure.'

She leaned her cheek on his head and squeezed his shoulders. 'You're tense.'

Not a question this time, but nearly as stupid. He rolled his shoulders to show he was fine and eventually, when he simply sat with his hands over the keys without speaking, she left, with a final pat on his arm.

When she had closed the door behind her, he let his head loll back and let out his breath in one long sigh. She was his mother. He loved her; of course he did. But she could annoy for England. And now, he had completely lost the thread of what he was doing. Bugger it. He'd have a little wander on Facebook. See what was going on. He and Megan had never been Facebook friends – they had laughed at couples they knew who actually sat in the evening, tagging each other on Facebook whilst sitting in the same room. But now, he wished they were. He couldn't help putting her name in search and there it was. 'If you want to see what Megan Harris shares with friends, send a friends request now'.

He let go a hollow chuckle and looked at the door but this time there was no maternal concern. Either she had stepped down her surveillance or he had found the right level of sound that didn't carry through the wood. It's a bit late now to make a friend request, he thought. Too little and far too late. He scrolled down his own page. A few events. A few birthdays. He was tagged in Mark's stag photos of a year ago and his breath caught in his throat to see the image of himself. Most people would say he hadn't changed, but he could hardly believe the difference in his eyes. The eyes from a year ago looked out with such calm assurance. They said, to anyone who cared to look, 'Here I am, a man with a family, a better job than most of these jokers around me, a great future.' He picked up his phone and took a selfie, something he and Megan had always mocked. He uploaded it and paused over the comment box. What he saw made tears come into his eyes. He typed, 'Help me. I'm lost and frightened. Is there anybody out there?' Then, he pressed delete. Because there was nobody out there. No one to help him. And lost and frightened didn't really begin to cover it – not in a million years.

Forever Autumn

*

When Chris's phone rang he glanced at the number and almost declined the call. It was one of the office numbers, not Dave's or he wouldn't have hesitated; he was a little surprised to find how fast the small details of his working life were slipping away. Time was … and he was only talking a couple of weeks … time was, he would know everyone's number off the top of his head. He didn't want to speak to Cassie, that much he was sure of. But he thought that her number ended with a seven; this was a nine. He pressed 'answer'.

'Hello?'

'Chris? Hi, it's Gavin? Gavin, from the office?'

Oh, yes. Gavin. The moronic interrogative king. 'Hi, Gavin. How's tricks?'

'Oh, you know? All to buggery. Jacintha's left – threw her toys out of the pram good and proper. Dave doesn't come out of his office and his missus has taken over Jacintha's desk. She's bloody good, actually.' Gavin lowered his voice and it became a bit hollow-sounding; he was clearly shielding the mouthpiece with his hand. 'She gets on at me? She says I do that thing? That Australian, Californian thing? Anyway, I have to try not to do it, when she's around.' He gave a nervous laugh. 'It's hard not to do it once you're in the habit, but she doesn't take prisoners.'

Chris laughed. He knew Tamsin; one of the scariest women he had ever met, but also one of the nicest. She must be, to put up with Dave and his little wanderings, he thought. 'She's okay,' he said. 'Ask her if you can babysit one night – tell her you love kids. She'll be eating out of your hand in no time.'

'Really? Thanks, Chris. Anyway, I rang to say that it's my stag do this Friday. Wondered if you wanted to come.'

Stag do? How old was this kid? He looked about twelve. 'Umm … Gavin, that could be tricky. I mean, is Dave …?'

Gavin chortled and then his voice lowered again. 'Dave's grounded. For life, as we understand it.'

'It won't do him any harm,' Chris said. 'You know, Gavin, I'd love to come. Where are you starting off from?'

'We're not pub crawling. We've got the top room at the Greyhound. Do you know it? It's out on the Oxford Road?'

'That's a way out – are we car-pooling?' Chris hadn't gone out much since he had left his company car outside the office, keys in the ignition. He knew he could borrow his mother's but it wasn't quite the same – especially when it came to giving lifts to potential vomiters!

'Sorry, should have said. We've got two stretch limos to take us both ways – it's not every day you get married, after all.' There was an aghast silence. 'Er … sorry.'

'Don't apologise, Gavin,' Chris said flatly. 'These things happen. So … where do I pick up my carriage?'

'Pardon?'

Chris sighed. 'The limo. Where are we picking it up?'

'Oh, sorry. Carriage, yes. We'll get you. Where are you these days?'

'I'm at the Vicarage, St Blasius; it's on …'

'I know it. My mum goes there sometimes. Well, you know. Easter. Christmas. Harvest Festival. All the biggies. She doesn't like getting too involved – they're not a very friendly lot, but the vicar does a good service for the biggies.'

'Yes.' Chris knew. He had been dragged along on the previous Sunday and the congregation had not exactly welcomed him with open arms.

'We'll pick you up about eight, Friday. Okay?'

'Looking forward to it.' And Chris, as he put the phone down, found that he actually was.

The thing with summer nights and going out, Chris thought, was that you feel such a fool all dolled up to go out with the lads when the sun is still hot and high. It feels like going to a Birthday Tea when you're six. His mother had ransacked the charity bags in the church hall and had come up trumps; a pair of chinos, a linen shirt and a leather jacket. He could have gone back to the house – he couldn't call it 'home', not even in the privacy of his own head – to get more clothes, but he couldn't bear it. If she had cleared out the wardrobes, it would be unbearable. If everything was still there, waiting for him, it would be worse. So he hung the jacket out in the garden to rid it of its smell of charity shop despair and his mother laundered the shirt and chinos. She twirled him round as he came down the stairs and smiled approval. Yes, six years old and going out with friends – nothing changes. All it needed was for the stretch limos to be driven by Gavin's mum and dad and the picture would be perfect. And more than a little scary.

'You look lovely, darling,' his mother twittered. She patted his stomach. 'Better for those few extra pounds as well, I think.'

He looked down at her, smiling up at him. He could stove in her head, sometimes. He could hug her till she couldn't breathe on others. So he compromised with a peck on the cheek and before he had to ruin the moment with words, there was a toot on a rather classy sounding horn outside; his limo was here. He opened the door and was down the drive like a rat up a pipe. Saved by the toot.

The evening could have been worse. It could have been *better*, but it could certainly have been much worse. After the first few moments of frozen silence when he climbed into the limo, the conversation was fine. James's takeoff of Jacintha's exit made them all laugh until it hurt; there was something about the toss of his head to fling non-existent hair out of his eyes that made the whole thing perfect. James had embraced his baldness and shaved and polished his head to resemble something that Tim Wonacott would coo over on any antiques show you cared to name; it gave an added dimension to his parody that kept them going, on and off, until the drink made all outside help unnecessary.

Gavin reached leglessness first. It wasn't to be wondered at, James muttered into Chris's ear. Gavin had got his brainless little bit of tottie up the spout almost on their first date and instead of doing a runner like any sensible man would do, he was walking her up the aisle. James, twice divorced and loving it, couldn't see it lasting beyond the kid's first tooth, but you can't tell the youngsters, can you? Did Chris know Tamsin Stanley?

Chris nodded.

James nudged him in the ribs. 'Go way back, do you? You and Tamsin? She looks as though she was up for it, back in the day. I suppose …'

Chris put down his drink. 'No, Jim. You suppose wrong. Tamsin is too old for me, too married for me, too *not Megan* for me. I don't shag just anything with a pulse. In fact, these days, I have to burst your bubble and say I don't shag anything at all. I'm living in a vicarage with my mum, so go figure.' Somehow saying it all out loud made Chris need another drink and keep 'em coming. 'Sorry, mate,' he had noticed James looked a little crestfallen. 'It's just that my new reputation is very far from the truth.'

James clapped him on the shoulder and wandered away. As Chris got drunker that evening – and he did get *very* drunk indeed – the looks seemed to get more searching, more hostile and more annoying. The last thing he remembered before he was poured into a taxi, the stretch limo driver having refused him entry on the grounds of incipient sick, was that he tried to punch the groom-to-be. And after that, apart perhaps from an incident with the vicarage hanging baskets which was a bit of a blur, all was blackness. The dog didn't mind; he knew that he was harder to spot in the dark.

Sarah Green wasn't a strong woman, even her best friends would say that. She had kowtowed by and large to her first husband, even to the extent of colluding with him in ignoring the illness which killed him and so it wasn't really a surprise to anyone when she became the vicarage doormat. But, like many women, she discovered her inner tigress when one of her children was hurt and needed her. Claire was pretty much self-sufficient; Sarah had ticked that box years ago. Even when she was little she would put her own plasters on her grazed knees. Chris had always been much needier – even a close encounter with a wasp or bee would have him hiding behind the sofa; they didn't need to have actually stung him to make the yelling start. Actual bloodshed was enough to prostrate him for the day. Mike had never seen her in full mother mode, so it came as a bit of a shock when he tried to tackle her about the night before.

They were sitting at the kitchen table, the toast neatly stacked in the toast rack, the butter in curls, the marmalade glistening fatly from the cut glass dish. The cereal had been eaten in as much silence as is commensurate with Crunchy Nut Cornflakes and the first cup of coffee had been drunk. It was like a gavotte, not a step out of place, not a smile cracked. They were both waiting for the perfect moment and finally, it came.

'I notice the hanging baskets are not in place this morning.' Mike Green had rehearsed the start of this conversation for a while and had thought that this was the perfect opening.

His wife carried on buttering her first slice of toast, over and over, corner to corner as though her life depended on it. 'Really?' It wasn't what he had hoped for, but it was at least an opening for the next sentence.

'They're actually on my car. Upended on my car, to be exact.'

'I'll clean them off if you can give me a moment after breakfast.' She looked up at him and a more experienced husband would have known to say no more.

'It's not the mess I really mind,' he said, in his most sanctimonious tones. 'It's the fact that it was done at all. It's the lack of gratitude.'

'Gratitude.' It was a wonder the coffee didn't freeze over. 'Gratitude? You know who did it, then. Someone who should be grateful, I'm assuming.'

The vicar was a bit confused now. They had both been awoken by the noise the previous night or, to be more precise, the small hours of that selfsame morning. No words as such had been audible, but the gist was clear. And, just before the front door slammed as if to break off its hinges, there had been the unmistakeable sound of two large baskets of petunias hitting the bonnet of a 1999 Audi estate. 'Well … it was Chris, surely.'

'Surely?'

Even the fairly novice husband was beginning to grasp that all might not be well. 'It *may* have been vandals, of course …' He waited hopefully for a reply, but there was nothing. 'But I have to say, Sarah, that it seems beyond the bounds of coincidence that your son comes in blind drunk and the garden is ruined.' He picked up a triangle of toast and began to butter it. He then loaded it with marmalade and took a huge bite. 'Also,' he began, his mouth full but she had decided to speak.

'Do you know how repulsive I find that habit?' she said, in a mild, conversational tone.

His eyes bulged and he swallowed his toast. 'Repulsive? What?'

'You always talk with your mouth full. I assume you do it so that you leave no spaces for someone else to fill with words of their own. But as I seem to have silenced you temporarily, I will tell you now that yes, I expect it was Chris who tipped up your precious petunias. I hardly call that ruining the garden, however, which, when I looked last, runs to nearly an acre of lawns and flowerbeds, tended by me and a gardener. Tell me, Mike, where is the lawnmower?'

'Umm … it's in the … garage?' Gavin would have been proud.

'No. In fact, we don't *have* a lawnmower. Unless you count Mr Curtiss, the vicar's warden, who mows the grass every Thursday without fail after he has done the churchyard. So, don't whine to me about your bloody garden!'

'Sarah! Language!'

'Oh, please!' She was in her stride now and, although not a naturally foul-mouthed woman, could feel the words queuing up, just begging to be said. 'Don't be a sanctimonious arse, Michael. Chris has been through some of the worst weeks of his life. I haven't been much of a mother lately. I should have seen the signs. He was never happy, not even as a child, but I just didn't think. Claire more than made up for them both, she has done nothing but smile from the day she was born. I think I always considered them like day and night. But now, when he is struggling to rebuild something, all you can come out with is your sodding petunias.'

Words struggled for precedence in Mike Green's mouth but in the end nothing won and he sat there, mouth still half full of toast and marmalade, stunned.

'I married you against my own better judgement,' she continued. 'I have never been and never will be a religious woman. If you ask me, it is all a load of hypocritical, superstitious claptrap. However, I do, sometimes, quite like *you*. When you let your guard down you can be quite a nice man. But, honest to God, Mike, you really should learn to think before you speak. It doesn't matter how long we stay married; I will always be mother to my children before I am wife to you.'

'How long we stay married?' He looked stricken. He had assumed it was for life. If it wasn't, how would he ever hold his head up in the parish?

'Oh, don't worry,' she said, reaching over and patting his hand. 'I'm not going to leave you, not going to show you up. I'll do the café, I'll do the jumble sales. I'll be the vicar's wife, don't you fret. But the last days have opened my eyes, Mike. I had a child who needed me and I didn't notice. It's too late, I expect, but I am going to try and put that right.'

There was a crash overhead.

'Oh,' the vicar said, with a trace of venom in his voice. 'Number One Son is awake, from the sound of it.' The sound of scurrying footsteps and a hurriedly-slammed bathroom door completed the picture. The sneer on Mike Green's face nearly earned him a faceful of marmalade, but his wife had said her piece and she was back in vicar's wife mode again. 'Perhaps you should go up and see if he needs his arse wiping as well!'

The vicar hadn't used a dubious word since, as he recollected it, 1983 and the shock of what he had just said carried him out of the room and out of the house in a cloud of high dudgeon. The sound of his car reversing at speed out of the drive, accompanied by the crash of petunias hitting the drive and was followed by the blast of an angry horn.

Saturday morning at St Blasius' vicarage. Welcome to the weekend.

Chris didn't feel at all well. He did at least remember most of the night before. This was an improvement on some of his really wild nights – or, perhaps more correctly, his regretful mornings – from the days before he met Megan, but he still felt very, *very* ill. It was Saturday, it had that to say for it, not that that made that much difference to him these days. But he felt less of a pariah on a Saturday, because if someone met him in the street, they wouldn't immediately assume he was unemployed. He could also lie in bed a while longer and perhaps if he stayed there long enough, Mike would have gone out. Through a muzzy head, he thought he heard sounds of raised voices from the kitchen, which was immediately below his room. But he couldn't believe it – it must be just the ringing in his ears. What he *couldn't* mistake was the sound of a moderately clapped-out car reversing at some speed out of the drive. The blood drained from his face as he also recognised the sound of a couple of dozen petunias and their accompanying baskets and soil sliding off the bonnet. It may have been worse than he thought.

He dressed hurriedly, making sure to wear something different from his not-terribly-glad rags of the night before. Nothing screams 'Drunk!' than wearing the same clothes twice running. He went downstairs gingerly; there was nothing in the sound of reversing to tell him who was behind the wheel and he really wasn't up to Mike and his mock-gentle tones this morning. He stuck his head around the kitchen door and there was good news and there was bad news.

The good news was that it was his mother sitting there at the table, cradling a mug of coffee and looking thoughtful. The bad news was that he hadn't grown out of his unfortunate idiosyncrasy of being completely nauseated by the smell of toast when he was hung over. He legged it down the hall and made it by a whisker to the downstairs loo, where he was violently sick. It made him feel better, paradoxically and he made his way back into the kitchen, fairly sure that he would stay the course this time.

His mother looked up. 'Feeling okay?' she said, but her voice was devoid of even her fake bubble this morning.

He slid into Mike's abandoned seat. 'I'm as well as can be expected for someone who sank more alcohol last night than I usually drink in six months. Also, as well as can be expected for someone who – and I'm pretty sure this wasn't a dream, unfortunately – tipped a couple of hanging baskets over his stepfather's car.'

She smiled, but thinly, with no meaning in it. 'I'm glad you don't feel too bad,' she said. 'And no, it wasn't a dream.'

There was a silence, during which Chris wrung out a mug of coffee from the cafetiere. It was almost stone cold but at this point it didn't matter that much. It was wet. It was caffeine – that scored it two out of two.

'And, in case you were wondering,' she continued, as though there had been no pause, 'he was angry, yes.'

'Sorry.' There was probably more to say on the subject, but just at that moment, Chris was stuck for an answer.

'Hmm. Yes. Me too.' She got up and put the kettle on. This was going to be a three cafetiere morning, she could tell.

'No, Mum, really, I *am* sorry. I shouldn't have done that. But … well, it hadn't gone well, the stag do. And I just felt a bit …'

'Frustrated. Join the club.' She turned to face him. 'I know you and Claire don't like Mike.'

He made small noises of dissent, but nothing sounded very convincing, so he stopped.

'More especially, I think, you don't like what he's done to me. I know I'm not the woman I was, but I thought …' She bowed her head and buried her face in her hands. Then, she squared her shoulders and looked up, wiping her tears with angry fingers. 'I needed someone to lean on. He was there. That's all there is to it. And if I seem to you to be a sanctimonious old trout sometimes,' she looked at Chris and forced a smile, 'I suppose it's because sometimes, I *am* a sanctimonious old trout.'

He laughed and shook his head.

'But this morning, I decided to have a shot at being your mother for a bit. And so that's why the vicar has stormed out. I don't know when he'll be back but I do think it might be a good idea if the petunias had been swept up before then.'

'I'll get straight onto it,' Chris promised. It seemed the least he could do.

'But also, darling, I think it would be a good idea to look for somewhere else to live. Speaking for myself, you could live here forever if you wanted to, but … well, it *is* the vicarage, I suppose. And he *is* …'

'… the vicar. Yes, I had spotted that. I was going to go down to the benefits office on Monday anyway. I know I can't go on like this.'

'Are you *sure* that Dave wanted to sack you?'

'No, not at all. But he's moved Tamsin in and got rid of Jacintha. She was all bound up in it, I know. She wouldn't pee on me if I were on fire and I think I blew it when I let him know that his affair was common knowledge. There's no enemy like someone who knows you know where all the bodies are buried. And besides all that … I really can't gather up the strength to go through all that again. I'm not sleeping.'

'Is it the dream?' She had returned to the table with the fresh coffee and poured them each a mugful.

'Dream?'

'The one with the dog. You were always having it when you were a little boy.'

'Was I? It can't be exactly the same. In this dream, I'm showing someone a house.'

'When you were tiny, it was a dog in your bedroom. When you went to school, it was in the changing room. It just goes where you do. Your dad even suggested once that we actually get you a dog, but I thought it would scare you.'

'Dead right, if it was like this one. It's got jaws *this* big.' He stretched his arms out to his sides, to show the extent of the dogs bite.

'Well, it wasn't a good idea. And Claire was allergic to pets in most cases, anyway. That's why we never had any.'

Chris mulled it over for a moment. How could it be that he had been having the dream for so long with no memory of it? 'Anyway, yes, I do have the dream. But it isn't just that. I just can't get to sleep. My mind is always racing, but then, when I have to do something, I just can't get the enthusiasm.'

'Could you be depressed, darling?' she asked, gently. 'Dad used to …'

'No!' What was it with everyone? 'No, I'm not depressed. I'm just a bit miserable over this job and Megan and everything.'

'Look, darling, why don't I ring Megan and see if we can have Kyle tomorrow? I'm sure she wouldn't mind. The weather won't be nice for that much longer, autumn's almost here and we could take him to the park.'

'A bit of a cliché?'

'Pardon?'

'Dad taking the kid to the park? No. If I am to see Kyle, I want everything to be normal. I want to have my own place, with a room for him with some of his toys there. I want it to be an ad hoc arrangement, some days with me, some with Megan. I don't want it written in stone, every third Sunday afternoon until the crack of doom.'

His mother was stricken. Of course that's what he wanted. It was what they all wanted. But he was learning, on a sharp curve, that we can't always get what we want. 'Another time, then,' she said, burying her nose in the mug and steaming up her glasses. She looked up at him, going cross-eyed as she had when he was a child. She even got a small chuckle out of him.

'Can I just do one thing at a time? I might be able to manage that. Multi-tasking just isn't in my remit just now.'

'I understand, darling. And I don't want you to go straight away. It's just that I think it would be better for you if you were living somewhere else. You wouldn't have to be worrying all the time about whether you were being a nuisance. Not that you *are* ... oh, dear, I'm not making myself clear at all.'

He reached over and patted her hand. 'I understand. I'll do it on Monday. And meanwhile, to show willing, I'll make sure I haven't bunged up the computer. Can you get me in? Mike never let me have the password.'

'Oh, for heaven's sake! As if that matters. Yes, of course. Are you ready now?'

He drained his mug. 'Yes. I just need to clear out my browsing history – I know how annoying it is searching through someone else's crap when you're looking for something.'

'Why don't you pop outside and just sweep up those petunias?'

she suggested. I'll get you logged on and then we'll be back on track for the morning?'

He got up and went round to the back door, dropping a kiss on her head as he passed. 'Just fyi,' he said softly into her ear, 'Claire and I always knew that you were still our mum.' She squeezed his arm and leaned into him briefly. It wasn't perfect, but it would do.

Sarah Green was not really a computer person. She didn't do internet banking. She preferred to read her books on paper and watch her films on the television set, safely stowed behind faux Jacobean doors in the sitting room when not in use. She had heard of Skype but for all she knew, it could be one of those new breeds of dog, like a cockerpoo or a labradoodle. If she were to be asked to describe it, it would be somewhere between a Scottie and a Lhasa Apso. But she could log on and she could retrieve and send emails. And she was a dab hand at shopping online; she could whip around a virtual Tesco like a ninja. She could hear sounds of sweeping from the front of the house as she settled down at the computer. She pressed power and the computer leaped into life; it had only been sleeping. She tutted to herself. Chris didn't help himself, sometimes. He knew how annoyed Mike got when he didn't log off properly. The screen did its colour-changing thing as usual but didn't go to screen-saver; a picture of Mike and Sarah at their wedding reception, all smiles. Instead, a message told her that her browsing had been interrupted; did she want to resume? She clicked okay as a matter of course and in that micro-second between click and screen her world imploded.

Chris had swept up all of the petunias and the soil and had knocked out the moss which lined the hanging baskets. He looked at the remains and thought he could probably rescue a few plants, but would that then look worse than the missing baskets? He decided that no baskets at all would be the best plan; anyone seeing four rather crushed petunias with soil ground into their leaves might be rather puzzled. Not having hanging baskets, on the other hand, was more the norm than otherwise, especially with autumn just around the corner. He took a shovel from the garage and disposed of the evidence on the compost heap and stacked the baskets by the door of the shed. He realised that he hadn't been getting outside much the last few weeks. He had always been out and about in the course of his work, walking between houses whenever he could. But he had been hunched over the computer for too long, playing solitaire as often as not, but lacking the will to go for a walk for the sake of it. But he felt better already, his headache almost gone, the smell of fresh, clean air in his lungs and clinging to his clothes. Yes, from Monday he would make sure he walked at least five miles a day, until he got a job, that was, and he would soon be a new man.

There was something about the look of his mother's back as he went into the study that made Chris's heart hit the back of his mouth. There was no muscle tone in it, she was slumped, boneless, with her head dropped forward. 'Please, God,' he whispered as he tried to force his legs to work and run to her. 'Please, God, no … no!'

'Mum?' He tried to make his voice sound normal, but he knew it didn't. 'Mum? Are you okay?'

She didn't answer, but as he got closer and could see the screen, he could see why she was so quiet. Grimly, without even a glimmer of pretence of pleasure, two dead-eyed women writhed around each other on the screen. The lighting was bad, the direction worse and when any dialogue did briefly occur, it was banal in its gross obscenity. A horrible thought struck Chris.

'Mum. That's not what … I mean, I didn't …'

She shook her head and reached for his hand. 'No, darling,' she said, stroking her cheek with his fingers like a child seeking comfort. 'No, I know it isn't you. Look …' she pointed to the bottom of the screen. 'He didn't even bother to pretend.'

Chris leaned in to look at where she had pressed her trembling finger. 'Username and password,' it said. And the username was 'randyvic'.

'Mum.' He didn't know what to say. This was so far outside the usual parent and child issues that it almost met itself on the way back. 'I just don't know what to say …' He leaned over to switch the computer off, but she grabbed his wrist.

'No,' she said. 'Leave it on. In fact, let's turn the sound up.' She pressed the key over and over until the grunting, screaming and random obscenities filled the room. Chris suspected it could be heard outside in the road. He also suspected that that was her plan. 'Let's leave it,' she said, raising her voice over the din. 'Randyvic and I have a lot to say to each other when he gets back.' She stood and pulled him into the hall, where it was quieter. 'Is that a paid site, do you know?'

'Pardon me?' His eyebrows hit his hairline. 'Why do you think I would know something like that?'

'Don't all men do that?' she asked, checking her facts.

'No, they certainly don't! But the fact that there is a log in might point to it being subscription, yes.'

'Hmm. Something else for us to talk about. He blames my online shopping for the overdraft, but now, I wonder. Anyway, darling,' she seemed to have reached new reserves, 'could you pop out for the rest of today, do you think? I would rather be on my own when he gets back.'

Chris didn't need telling twice. He could start his new exercise regime right now. In fact, he would go to the park. He could feed the ducks.

How To Disappear Completely

*

The park was peaceful, although perhaps only Chris saw it that way. There were children everywhere, throwing hunks of bread to unheeding ducks. Once, he would have walked through the crowd not noticing what was happening, but now, he saw the skull beneath the skin. That mother, over there, with the three little kids; she was clearly on her own, no man in her life these days. But you could tell, just by looking at the children who all looked as unlike each other as it was possible to do and share a species, that she had had at least three and all in the space of about four years, making a rough guess as to age.

He watched as a man approached, being walked by a dog. It wasn't that the dog was particularly large or rambunctious. It wasn't pulling or jumping around, it was just a rather overweight Labrador, golden, to Chris's ineffable relief. He had enough of black dogs, what with the dream and all, so he avoided them like the plague. But he saw in the man's face his total disinterest in his task. He had been told to walk the dog. He was walking the dog. He could now go home and say the dog had been walked and there would be no need for further conversation. He wore a yellow sailing anorak which Chris knew without being told was one of a pair. The man's wife had one two sizes smaller, hanging on a hanger in the hall. But since she never walked the dog, it was considerably cleaner and didn't have a roll of poop-bags in the pocket. How lovely, Chris thought ironically, to have a pet.

And that guy over there. Allowing for the fact that he was three inches shorter and was carrying a couple of extra stone, he and his kid could be Chris and Kyle in a funny mirror, out for a walk in the park to feed the ducks on his one visitation a month. The father was on his phone, holding the boy by the hand. The child was leaning away, his mouth a dark hole of misery. In his other hand, he held a packet of sweets, full of banned e-numbers, and now his dad was reaping the whirlwind of a kid who didn't want to be there anyway but who was now rendered virtually psychotic by sugar and additives. In fact, everywhere he looked, people were generally unhappy and desperate. He could hardly believe he had never noticed it before.

Hang on, though. Surely, over there, that couple were happy? The girl was hanging on his arm and looking lovingly into his face. He had an arm around her shoulders and was swinging along as if he hadn't a care in the world. Chris felt a small pang; he and Megan had been like that, not so long ago. He was surprised he didn't feel more upset, but somehow he couldn't dredge up the enthusiasm to poke the painful part of his heart today. As he got nearer, he could hear what they were saying and the bluebirds circling around their heads suddenly turned into vampire bats.

'Look … um … Shaz, it was great, all right. I'm not saying it wasn't great. But … let's be honest, girl, we've got nothing in common.'

'But …' for all her pretty face, the girl had a voice like a circular saw. Chris could see that a lifetime of listening to that could easily get on your wick.

'What's your favourite film?'

'Yer what?'

'Book?'

The girl looked puzzled.

'So, you see what I mean. I'll buy you breakfast and then walk you home, shall I?'

'Get stuffed, you ungrateful pig,' she shrieked and pulled away from him. 'Got what you want and that's it, is it?' People were starting to turn and stare. 'Breakfast! You can shove it up your arse!' And with that, she stormed off, flinging her bag over her shoulder and stamping like a thwarted child.

Chris wanted to go up to the man; he was little more than a boy, really, a student he would guess, having a night of fun with a little bit of local tottie. Chris could tell him that that wasn't always where it ended, but how could you encapsulate a life in ruins in just one sentence? In the end, Chris walked away; if the lad was lucky, Shaz wasn't a psychopath. If he was unlucky, the damage was done by now.

Chris became aware that he was squeezing the bag of toast crusts in his pocket. Even the ducks wouldn't want them now and he walked towards a bin to get rid of it. Along the path, just coming through the gate, he saw a face he knew. It was Megan and, in front of her, pedalling his trike as though his life depended on it, was Kyle. Chris was sure that for a few seconds, his heart actually stopped beating and his feet froze to the floor. They were laughing and Megan had never looked so lovely. His feet unfroze and he took a step towards them but then thought better of it. What good would it do? He turned and walked away, towards the cafeteria. He could hide in plain sight there. And if by chance she saw him, somehow having a cup of coffee and a free read of the paper made him look a little less like a stalker. More like a normal person, if she could imagine that. But he didn't stop for a drink. Head down to hide his tears, he walked through to the other gate and disappeared in the Saturday crowd.

'Mummy,' Kyle said over his shoulder as he pedalled on ahead. 'Do you remember when we came here with Daddy once?'

'Not just once, sweetie. We came here a lot with Daddy.'

Kyle was puzzled. He had trouble with the concept of number and Megan made a mental note to look that up; she wasn't sure whether this was a milestone or not. 'Is Daddy here?'

'No.' Megan forced a smile. 'He isn't here today, sweetheart.'

'Why isn't he here?' Children's questions were usually direct and Kyle's more so than most.

'Umm … Daddy has to be somewhere else at the moment,' she said, trying hard to keep the tremble from her voice. She hadn't heard from Chris since the day he had walked out of the door. Some money had appeared in her account and then that was it. Nothing. She felt her lip begin to wobble. Didn't he care at all?

'I want Daddy to be here,' Kyle said, his voice rising and threatening a tantrum.

'Let's feed the ducks, shall we?' Megan was aware that she was using what she called her 'teacher voice' and hated herself for it.

'I don't *want* to feed the ducks. I want *Daddy!*'

'Okay, Kyle. That's enough. We're going home.' Even as she spoke, Megan knew that she was being short with Kyle more and more often. But she just didn't have the strength to deal with him. Not here, with all the perfect families looking on. Not now. Weekends were always the worst times. No lie in cuddles. No breakfast in bed, marmalade on the sheets and Weetabix everywhere. Just nothing; unless more of the same counted as something. Samantha was already on at her to go out, but to find herself a date and go out and make pointless small talk seemed to her to be on approximately the same scale as scaling the Matterhorn. So, she turned Kyle's bike around, clipped on the steering handle and pushed him, steely-faced and determined, out of the park and home.

Chris had made himself a promise to not spend money needlessly. His account was still reasonably healthy, but he had a long way to go on this small amount and he needed to think ahead. But even so, a coffee wouldn't hurt, not even an overpriced one with a fancy name in a cup the size of a bath. He settled down outside with the smokers and similar pariahs – inside was just too full of yummy mummies and their squalling progeny for his liking and anyway, autumn or no, it was a pleasant morning, sunny and warm. He sat there watching the world go by, the *Big Issue* seller crying her wares across the street. He had never actually bought a *Big Issue*. He knew it was all very laudable but he always felt that they surely had other options than standing outside in all weathers flogging a magazine nobody ever read. He watched her now, smiling, connecting, taking the right money and making the right change. This wasn't a handout; she was actually in business for herself, doing what she could to change her life. Like the lad after the one night stand, he wanted to go up to her and say something, just to show he was in the same boat. But he just sat there, watching the chocolate pattern soak slowly into the foam on his skinny nutmeg short flat latte or whatever it was. He usually just pointed and nodded in coffee shops these days.

'Chris?'

He looked up and almost groaned out loud. 'Cassie. Hello, how are you?' The social niceties just fell out of his mouth, without him having to think.

'May I?' She pointed to the chair on the opposite side of his table and he nodded. 'I've been thinking about you. How have you been?'

'I went to Gavin's stag do last night,' he said, deliberately avoiding a direct answer. 'So I am a little bit …' he waggled his hand to show how the land lay.

'Oh, I see,' she laughed. 'A bit hungover, I would imagine.'

'Just a bit. I …' he leaned forward, 'I tipped my stepfather's hanging baskets over his car when I got home.'

She dimpled her cheeks at him. 'You released your inner teenager, by the sound of it.'

'Something like that. He was rather underwhelmed, according to my mother.'

'But you get on okay, as a rule? You're happy enough?' She leaned forward and he realised that she was genuinely concerned for him, not just the nosy cow he had taken her for.

'Not happy, no, I wouldn't say that. It's got a bit … difficult …' And to his amazement, he found himself start pouring everything out, up to and including his mother's rather startling discovery that morning.

Halfway through, she stopped him. 'Sorry, Chris – I must have a coffee. This sounds like a bit of a humdinger.'

'You could call it that. Cassie, could you get me another coffee, too? I'll pay for it, of course – it's just that, if you're going …' He could have kicked himself. He had already become that person, the one who never bought a round.

'Don't be silly. My treat. What was that?' she peered into his empty cup. 'Hard to tell these days, isn't it?'

'I'll have whatever you're having,' he said. 'I can't honestly remember what that was.'

She disappeared and he leaned back in his chair and closed his eyes. The sun was warm on his face and he found that by concentrating he could filter out the sounds around him, one by one, until all he could hear was the *Big Issue* seller crying her wares. He concentrated harder and soon even she became quieter and more distant until she came and went, like the shouts of children dopplering in and out on a merry go round.

'Chris?'

The voice, much nearer, made him jump. He opened his eyes and saw Cassie's worried face across the table. He sat up straighter and rubbed his eyes.

'Sorry,' she said, pushing a cup towards him. 'Had you dropped off?'

'Sorry,' he said back. 'I haven't been sleeping very well.' He waited for the depression lecture, but it didn't come.

'I've left the agency,' she said, casually.

'Really?' Chris had often wondered why she worked there. She mostly did paperwork, rarely interacting with either tenants, landlords or colleagues. He had always come to the conclusion she needed the money.

'I don't really need the money,' she said. 'I only went out to work because … well, being on your own all day around the house, if you have a bit of a tendency to get into a low mood, it doesn't help. Too much time for introspection is bad for someone like us.'

He didn't take her up on her choice of word and she was grateful. He had either missed it or took it as it was intended. 'I thought when you said …'

'I know what you thought,' she said. 'I believe you thought that I would talk his hind leg off.'

He looked down, embarrassed.

'That's the thing with introspection, Chris, though I'm sure I don't have to tell you. One little phrase sticks in your head and won't leave. It's like a song that you can't get rid of, just going round and round. But no, it isn't a member of my family. It's me.'

'But you always seemed so happy. Well, I obviously don't know you well, but, you know … you were always the one going round collecting for birthdays and stuff.'

'Just because I have depression doesn't mean I can't be sociable,' she said with a smile. 'In fact, most of the time, I'm fine. But sometimes, just one thing will start me on the downward slope and that's it, then. It's hard to stop when you're on that slippery slide. And so that's why I spoke to you about it. You've been hit by the big life changers – a break up of your relationship and loss of your job and home. It's no wonder you feel you're out of control.'

'I'll be fine,' he said, taking a sip of coffee and nearly burning his tongue out. 'Ouch! How did you get them to make this so hot? It's usually almost stone cold when I get it.'

'Aah, my secret.' She smiled at him. 'All right, I'll share. I just get them to give it a shot of steam at the very end. Good, huh?'

'Now I'm used to it, yes,' he said. 'I'll remember that.' Even as he said it, he was reminded of his situation. Daily coffees were not going to loom large on his horizon, he didn't think. He did a quick sum in his head. To keep the maths simple, he assumed the smallest, cheapest drink would be around two quid. Times five. Times fifty-two. Ye Gods! Over five hundred quid a year. More than half of the total money in his account. He took another swig. Best make the most of this one.

'You were telling me about your mum. How is she going to deal with this? Your stepdad and the …' she looked around and dropped her voice. 'The pornography?'

He smiled to think she would talk about depression, about something he still called, deep in the silence of his head, being mental and yet wouldn't say pornography out loud. 'I don't know. I've been wondering should I tell Claire.'

She raised a querying eyebrow.

'My sister. She's never really cottoned to Mike – I suppose she would call it woman's intuition. She won't be surprised. Well,' he qualified it, 'she'll be surprised at what it is, but not surprised that he has proved to be less of a saint than he likes us all to think.'

'Hmm … I suppose lesbian porn isn't the worst thing he could be indulging in.' This time she didn't drop her voice and got some startled looks from the people on the next table. She smiled at the wife, who had frozen with a tarte au citron halfway to her mouth. 'Sorry,' she said. 'Speak as I find.' And then she turned back to Chris. 'It's a bit of a facer, though, isn't it? Do you dob him in, that's the question.'

'But … my mother knows.' Chris wondered if he hadn't made himself clear.

'*She* does, yes. But what about the bishop?' This time, the woman on the next table actually choked on a crumb of pastry. 'Sorry.' Cassie smiled again and waited for Chris's reply.

'But …' Chris wasn't good at decisions these days. But this was a decision too far. Yes, she was right, he should speak to the bishop. But in doing so, he would almost certainly make his mother homeless. And he knew himself how that made a person feel. 'No. I don't think I can do that. She's got enough on her plate.'

'Oh.' Cassie was surprised. She wasn't much of a churchgoer. 'Have we got a woman bishop here?'

Chris was puzzled, then the light dawned. 'No, no, not the *bishop*. My *mother* has enough on her plate.'

'Sorry. I thought you were worrying about the bishop for a minute there. I do see your point.' Cassie looked at her watch. 'I should go. I only popped out for a paper.'

Chris realised that he knew nothing about her, where she lived, who with; nothing. And he also realised he didn't want her to go. 'Can't you stay a while longer? I don't know why you left work or anything.'

She shrugged. 'It was time. Dave's wife is there now … oh,' she read his body language, 'I can see you know that. Well, she's an improvement on Jacintha, that's for sure. We can all stop looking for the knife in the back. But she runs a tight ship, I must say. And so I jumped before I was pushed.' She chuckled. 'I just hope Dave has the sense to do the same.'

Chris raised an eyebrow. 'Really? Like that, is it?'

'I think the way she sees it, she has been the housewife. It wouldn't hurt him to have a go at being a house husband. Watch this space.' She stood up and shouldered her bag. 'Bye, Chris. Don't be a stranger.' And she leaned down and gave him a peck on the cheek.

And she was gone. As he watched her walk away, he was surprised; walking a few steps behind her, its rear end wagging as it went, was the biggest black dog Chris had ever seen. He hadn't known she had a dog and had certainly not noticed it while they shared a coffee. Almost as if the creature read his thoughts it stopped and turned round, sitting down in the middle of the Saturday hurly-burly and staring at Chris with a penetrating stare. He tried to return it and looked away then forced himself to look again. But, like Cassie, the dog had gone.

Ain't No Man Righteous

*

Chris's stomach was rumbling as he turned into the drive of the vicarage but he didn't have high hopes of getting any lunch today. He had hung around in town as long as was feasible, but he was, after all, a grown up and so were his mother and stepfather; surely, talking things through had to be the best plan? All was silent when he pushed open the door. He remembered when he and Megan used to fight; before *the* fight, of course, which wasn't a fight at all, more of a mutual capitulation. Then, when all passion was spent, they would usually end up in bed and it was true; make-up sex was just about the best there is, beaten perhaps only by revenge sex, but his experience of that was minimal so he was perhaps not the one to judge. But his imagination baulked at his mother and the vicar upstairs working it all out that way; even so, he listened particularly hard at the foot of the stairs, to avoid embarrassment all round. Nothing. The house was quiet as the grave.

He went down the hall, aware that he was trying to walk extra quietly on the parquet floor. There was one loose block in front of the lounge door and he instinctively avoided it; it gave a click which in this boundless silence would have sounded like a pistol shot. He edged the door open into the kitchen and looked around. No one. The lounge, as he back tracked down the hall again and peeped in, was the same. The study was off to the left, in a little annexe; he guessed it had been originally intended as a utility room but had been remodelled for the vicar's use; there was a door out to the garden which he had always assumed was for the use of parishioners with something on their mind they wanted to share with Mike Green but now he wondered whether it had a more sinister purpose. Perhaps he had watched too many *Midsomer Murders* – only the old ones, before they got the new bloke in that no one he ever met could stand. In every episode, a sneaking figure would ooze round a half closed door. The next scene was always of a screaming cleaning lady who had come upon the body. Realistic, not. Anyway, no one in the study either, living or dead. Which, God forbid – he had stopped apologising in his head by this time – meant that they probably *were* upstairs, at it like superannuated weasels.

But, no – what was that in the garden, down behind the shrubbery? His heart stood still. He could see his mother, wielding a spade with unwonted fervour; she really seemed to be knocking seven bells out of something … or someone … on the ground. He wrestled for a moment with the door, but it was locked. By the time he was haring across the lawn towards her, Sarah Green was standing back looking down admiringly at her handiwork. He hardly dare look down but when he did he nearly cried with relief.

'A rhododendron,' he said, trying to keep his voice level.

'Yes,' she said, looking down at it fondly. 'Mike brought it back for me. I've always wanted one. It seems so … vicarage garden, somehow.'

Chris lowered his head and breathed slowly, in through his nose, out through his mouth, to a count of ten. When the red mist was starting to clear, he spoke, low and steady. 'So, that's it then, is it? You found some lesbian porn on the vicarage computer, but he bought you a …' he suddenly lost control and shouted in her face, 'he bought you a … a *fucking rhododendron*! And that makes it all right, does it? Naked women all forgotten, because of a *shrub*?'

'Don't swear, please, Christopher,' she said, as if he were twelve. 'The neighbours might hear.'

He took a step back, amazed at her hypocrisy. 'I'm sure if they don't mind living next to a porn-addicted vicar, they won't mind a bit of profanity now and again. If I can remind you, I walked off down the drive this morning to the background music of two women …'

'Chris! That really is enough!' She leaned her spade against a small apple tree which was fighting for breathing space in the already overcrowded garden, a garden that needed another shrub like a fish needs a bicycle. She lowered her voice and moved closer. 'Yes, you're quite right, what you're thinking.'

He looked mulish; she had always been able to do that, since he was a little boy.

'I am a hypocrite. But I am also a hypocrite who needs a roof over her head and a man to lean on.' She gave a laugh, but it was just a sound; there was no humour in it. 'I don't love Mike Green, as your sister has been heard to remark many times, perhaps the loudest at our wedding. I have never loved anyone except your father and that won't change until the day I die. But I have to live with someone, I just don't do lonely. Despise me all you like, but don't rock the boat. I've told Mike what I think of him which is best summed up by the phrase "not much". He knows what he did was wrong …' she stopped and wrinkled her nose and Chris saw through surprised eyes that his mother was still a pretty woman. He felt sorry for Mike, but, she was right, not much. He had bought the package and hadn't bothered to check the contents. 'Well, I may be overstating there. I don't think in fact that he *does* know what he did was wrong. He knows I don't like it. He knows not everyone does it. But he doesn't really see how hurtful it is to me. We … well, I don't have to trouble you with all that.'

Chris heaved a sigh of relief. Damn straight she didn't – he had enough to cope with as it was without hearing bedroom confessions from his own mother.

'So, anyway, long story short, we have agreed to a compromise.' She smiled at him. He knew what that meant of old. 'Which of course means that he does as I say. No porn sites. No porn magazines. No visiting … well, he says he hasn't done that since we got married, but even so, it needed saying. As long as he sticks to all that, I won't shop him to the bishop.' She started off across the lawn towards the house, with him in hot pursuit.

'But, Mum … that's just blackmail. Isn't it?' He looked at her, determined as ever, striding out across the grass. 'Can you live like that?'

She turned round and looked at him. The usual errant lock of hair flopped over her forehead and she pushed it back with a grimy hand. 'I don't know. When I do, I'll tell you. Deal?'

He walked up to her and put his arms around her. He could hardly speak for the love he suddenly felt for this woman, love he knew in his gut he would soon not be in a position to tell her about. 'It's a deal,' he murmured, and had to clear his throat to stop the tears.

She leaned against him briefly, then broke away. 'You'll have to speak to him, you know,' she said. 'And ... Chris ... I don't know how ...'

'You don't know how to say this,' he finished for her, 'but I'll have to go. Yes, I think I'd already decided that. I couldn't stay a night anyway under a roof with that total arsehole.' He held up a hand, stopping her protests. 'No, sorry, I can't pay lip service any longer. He is an arsehole, Mum, and you know it. Anyway,' he looked around the garden. It was a shame he had never really got round to doing his five miles a day. 'Anyway, no time like the present. I'll get my things.'

'Darling!' She grabbed his arm. 'I don't mean today ...'

'If not today, then when?' he said. 'Where is the ... where is Mike? I'd like to shake him warmly by the throat before I go.'

Alarm flared in her eyes.

'Joking. Just joking. I do want to give him fair warning of what will happen to him if he upsets you again, though. So, where is he?'

'He went upstairs. To pray, as I understood it.' She was straight faced and even her son couldn't tell what she was thinking.

'Well, call him down. I don't want to talk to him on the landing. I'll get my things after and then be on my way.'

'I've ... I've had a chat with Claire. She wants you to go and stay with her.'

'Really? She *wants* me to go and stay.'

'Oh, Chris. Will you two ever stop sniping at one another? You're like children, sometimes. No, I will admit she didn't say she wanted you to go and stay. But she did say you could, if you needed to.'

'Ah, now that's very different, isn't it? I'll see how I get on. I'll let you know. I'll wait in the study, shall I? For the arsehole?'

With a sigh, his mother went up the stairs, calling her husband as she reached the landing. Chris pushed the door of the study open but felt it was more than just a door into a rather bland and unprepossessing room. It was a door into the rest of his life and so far, he didn't much like the view. He pulled a chair across the room and sat in it with as much aplomb as he could muster. He didn't want to sit in the naughty chair and the vicar had his study arranged just so, with the spare chair across from his being a little lower and also in a bright spot from the lamp. The man had clearly watched an awful lot of *Apprentice* episodes. So, moving the chair across the room next to an occasional table to rest a casual arm on removed that advantage and levelled the playing field a little.

With a pounding of feet on the stairs, the vicar burst into the room, like a TV evangelist on some public broadcast station. He swung round behind the desk and leaned forward, hands clasped together and looked at Chris brightly for a moment. The computer was conspicuous by its absence.

'Well, Chris,' his stepfather said in jolly, kindergarten teacher tones, 'Shall we pray together?'

'No.' Before that morning, Chris would have dutifully bowed his head and thought of nothing for a moment or two, but that ship had sailed.

The look on Mike Green's face was enough to turn milk, but his voice was his usual faux-gentle sing-song. 'You don't mind if I do, I hope,' he said and bowed his head, muttering.

Chris could only think one thing – sanctimonious git. But he stayed silent. The moral high ground was his position of choice for what was to come.

Eventually, the vicar raised his head and smiled encouragingly, if the nervous baring of his teeth could possibly be called a smile. 'Now, Chris,' he said, lacing his fingers more tightly together so that the knuckles shone white. 'We have a lot to talk about.'

'Not really,' Chris said, slouching even more in his chair. He was trying not to behave like a truculent teenager, but this man just got him on the raw. 'Let's recap. Yes, I came home drunk. I had been out on a stag night, it is almost mandatory. Yes, I ruined your hanging baskets. But *you* have been accessing porn on the church computer. I think if you asked for a quick vote by your congregation on which sin was blackest, I don't imagine there would be many votes for my little lapses, do you?'

The man behind the desk said nothing, but a small muscle began to tic beside his eye.

'And also, to add to the detail in case anyone was in any doubt, I got drunk and committed petuniacide once. You, on the other hand, were on the porn sites … how often? Once a day? More than that? I can't think it would be less. And apparently, according to my mother, there are magazines and prostitutes in the mix as well. Lovely.'

'In my defence …'

'You *have* no defence.' Chris had never actually told anyone off before and he was loving it. He felt the power surge through his body. 'I'd love to hear it, though – just for the craic.'

'In my defence, I was alone for a long time before I met your mother. And added to which …'

'No!' Chris raised a hand. Not the parents' sex talk. He really didn't need that. 'If that's all you've got, I don't want to hear it. And also if I may pre-empt you; please don't give me the I-think-it's-time-you-moved-on speech. I've had it from my mother and I will be gone inside the hour. I won't say thank you for your hospitality, because the words would choke me. If there *is* a reason I will be sorry to go it is because I am leaving my mother on her own with you. But needs must when the devil drives and you can take that any way you like.' With that, he got up and walked out of the room, resisting by the merest whisker the urge to punch the man's lights out. Within the hour – very much inside the hour – he was walking down the drive, his bag over his shoulder, his black dog panting at his heels.

Why Megan found the weekends worse than the weekdays, she would never know. She had the odd day in work in the week, to break up the silent hours, but there was still small difference. A day was a day was a day. Get up. Feed Kyle. Deal with Kyle's increasingly frequent tantrums. Put Kyle to bed. Go to bed herself, often more than a little squiffy on cheap wine. And the wine had to be really cheap; she had some savings from the money her grannie had left her, she had the money Chris had transferred but it was all dwindling. She would have to do something, soon. But money worries could wait. Each morning, she had more of the same, with possibly a slight worsening each sunrise. But even so, weekends were worse. Families out and about everywhere she looked, friends too busy with their families to make any time for her, not that she would ask. She hadn't spoken to her mother in weeks; somehow the Monday Kyle-watch had just stopped happening and although it was driving her crazy to deal with his meltdown after every nursery session, it was preferable to having to look at those pursed and disapproving lips as they mouthed the words of criticism and spite that seemed to be the woman's only vocabulary. Her father, as usual, sat immobile and silent in front of daytime television and for all the good he was, he might as well have been stuffed. In fact, for all she knew, he had been, stuffed and mounted for posterity years ago, on the day he was made redundant from the insurance office he had worked in since he left school. At least he was harmless; people often said of him he never said an unpleasant word. Megan would go further – he actually never said a word at all.

Sam was her rock, as she had always been. She had even offered to babysit Kyle, although Megan knew that she would actually rather babysit a room full of angry scorpions. If she had anywhere to go, she would have accepted, just to see her face. But she didn't want to go anywhere and she was certainly not going to wander round town for a couple of hours, spending money she didn't have, just so that she could make Sam squirm. So Sam would come to her, with a cold bottle of white in a bag and they would drink it and talk endlessly about Chris and what he did until Megan could scream.

As the weeks had gone on, the whole situation had taken on the feel of something she had once seen or read; it certainly couldn't have happened to her, could it? She was too ordinary to have this kind of disaster visit her life. If she had ever thought about the future, it always featured a wedding – she in frothy white, Chris in morning dress, with an angelic Kyle, behaving perfectly, as ring-bearer. Perhaps even a sweet little girl, just toddling, their second and much discussed child, as bridesmaid. At no point did she see herself like this, a tear-stained, muddled wreck with a child who was fast becoming the kid no one invited to parties and just one friend in the whole world.

And weekends *were* the worst. They were the days when she would have had a lie-in and hear her boys creating havoc in the kitchen. They were the days she hankered after, yearned towards as though they were the Holy Grail. And yet she knew, if she was being honest, that she could actually count their occurrence on the fingers of one hand. She just didn't have that kind of family. Had never had that kind of family. She stood in the kitchen, no mess in sight, no smelly socks, no muddy shoes, no Chris. She closed her eyes and tried to see his face. She listened for his voice but realised, with a sinking heart, that his face was growing fuzzy around the edges and that all she could hear him say was 'I can't help it. I can't help it. I can't help it,' on and on, round and round in a loop. She couldn't bear it that they were the last words she would hear him say and picked up her phone to ring him, to tell him to come home, that they could work it out.

Then, by that strange alchemy of the mobile phone, it rang in her hand.

'Hello?' Her throat was tight with tension but she tried to sound normal.

'Megs? It's Sam. What are you up to this evening?'

She tried to think of a snappy answer, but there wasn't one to hand. 'Usual. Kyle. Telly.'

'Well, stuff that.' Sam clearly had something planned. 'I've found you a sitter, lovely woman, got loads of grandkids, she'll be good for Kyle, a new face.' The unspoken phrase 'and not your mother' rang in the air. 'I won't take no for an answer, Megs. Her name is Lily and she'll be with you at six. Time to get to know Kyle while you get your gladrags on. We're off out on the town. One of the girls here is getting married next week. We're having a bit of a do for her – not that she'll get much out of it, she's pregnant, silly bitch, but what can you do? They don't listen. So it won't be a late one. I've told Brian ...'

'Brian? I thought ...'

'I'll fill you in tonight. I've told him I won't be home. I thought I could crash at yours. Don't make the spare bed up, we can have a girlie night, share the old double, natter, see the dawn come up. Remember those times?'

Despite the fact that it seemed like something that had happened to her before the dawn of time, she did indeed remember those times, with an empty longing. She nodded, then remembered she was on the phone. 'Yes.' She couldn't trust herself to say more.

'Great. That's sorted then. Gladrags. Six. You're going out on the pull, my girl!' And that was it. Sam had gone, to do whatever her weekends were full of; Megan smiled softly to herself. She assumed that that was presumably Brian.

Chris's stomach was still rumbling when he got back into the city centre and he decided that he would treat himself – if that was the word – to a burger. It wouldn't make a hole in his bank balance and he was rather tired of his mother's gargantuan meals anyway. But he was really hungry for the first time for ages and it was in the mood for some grease in a bun. He sat as long as he could bear in the garish interior, his ears assailed by what sounded like a thousand screaming children. In the corner, a clown with his damp desperation making his makeup run, was entertaining a birthday party.

Chris realised, and not for the first time, that the burger on the poster outside and the burger in the off-beige polystyrene pack were not the same animal. In fact, the burger had more in common with the polystyrene than any animal product Chris had ever known. So he picked out the gherkin and ate the chips and left. The clown was looking really desperate now, two determined toddlers trying to climb down his capacious trousers and another trying to tug off his wig. Chris thought it was important for everyone's self-esteem that he wasn't there to see the inevitable meltdown into screaming, crying and chaos that seemed to be just around the corner. And that it would be the clown doing the screaming and crying was never in any doubt.

Chris had been in a dark tunnel now for months, perhaps even years and with the shedding of responsibilities, it had seemed lighter lately, but not really in a good way. It wasn't the light of a warm and cosseting sun that shone into his eyes. It wasn't even the clichéd lights of an on-coming train. It was just a cold and merciless light which showed all the flaws and pitfalls in his life and it wasn't very pleasant; it was like life in HD; all the blackheads, beads of sweat and face-lift scars shown clear as day and larger than life. He needed a nice Vaseline filter, some low lights, soft music and everything to be back the way it was. But time could do a lot of things, it seemed to him. It could crawl like treacle, it could fly, it could be wasted, it could wrinkle if the physicists were to be believed. It could do anything it wanted to; except go backwards.

'Chris?'

He looked up and focussed on the man in front of him. He toyed for a moment with punching him in the face, but decided against it. It was probably not his fault. Probably. 'Mark.' Had his voice always been that colourless?

'Woah, mate. You don't look too good. Um … can I get you anything to help? I'm on a late lunch, but …' he gestured behind him at his pharmacy.

Chris had to bite back a hysterical laugh. 'No, thanks. It seems I have a bit of an …' What to call it? '… an intolerance to your specials.'

Mark's eyes widened with concern. 'My God, Chris! What happened?' His face clouded over, suddenly. 'You … you didn't need A&E or anything, did you? Because I did say …'

'No, no, don't worry. I didn't go to anyone, or have a blood test or anything like that. It just made me conk out, that's all. Nothing major.'

'Conking out is pretty major,' Mark pointed out. 'I think I should give you a list of ingredients after all, so you, you know, can avoid them in future. Allergies are funny things, they can turn nasty when you least expect it. But you'll have to keep it to yourself, the list. It could get me into all sorts of trouble if it got out.'

Chris almost felt sorry for his friend who had, all unknowing, wrecked his entire life for him, with one tiny glassful of something dodgy. Lives were ended by less, he supposed; a car, a blunt object, a piece of lead, a blood clot, a rogue cell. But for now, Mark and his marvellous medicine had done for him. He forced a smile. 'Don't worry, I don't need the list. I won't take anything I don't recognise again. Believe me.'

Mark looked at him, closely as if he had never seen him properly before. 'No,' he said. 'Something happened. Look, if you're not doing anything tonight, why don't you pop round? I wasn't planning anything, just a few beers and a pizza. It would be good to catch up.' He saw the bag over his shoulder but hardly missed a beat. 'If you're footloose and fancy free, you can stay over. We could go out, you know, few drinks. A pretty girl.'

Chris smiled wanly. 'I don't think much of yours.' It had been their mantra, back in the day.

'Yeah, that's the spirit. We don't have to …' Here, Mark left a space. He needed to know a bit more about what was going on before he made any other gaffes. 'Just have a chat, you know. A bit of a laugh. It'll do you good.'

'Oh, I don't know about going out,' Chris said. 'I had a bit of a skin-full last night. Stag do, bloke from the office, you know the kind of thing. I don't know whether I really want another night out.'

'Okay then,' Mark said. 'Back to Plan B. I close up around six – I'll see you at seven, shall I? Door next to the shop, look,' he pointed. 'My flat is up above.'

'Handy,' Chris said, thinking how awful to live so close to where you work and then in the next breath, but how nice to have a job.

'Well, yes, and it saves having to buy anywhere else. It all comes with the shop. It was one of the reasons I bought it.'

Buggering hell! He *owned* a High Street shop. They were the same age to the week. Chris immediately felt significantly worse than he had before. 'Good plan.'

'Ah,' Mark gave him a friendly punch on the shoulder. 'There speaks an estate agent, eh? Anyway, must dash. I've had to close the pharmacy counter while I'm away and the dippy woman on the perfumes can't be left for long before the till goes haywire or some other disaster befalls. See you at seven,' and he trotted off, neat as a new pin and as annoying as a fly in your soup. Or ointment, perhaps, Chris thought to himself as he hefted his bag onto his shoulder again and set off on yet another perambulation of the High Street, head studiously avoided as he passed the agency. Never mind, annoying or not, he had a bed for the night.

The dog got to its feet with a sigh. It had been enjoying its bit of a lie down while they chatted. And it knew that whatever life might have in store, it was downward from now on. Downward all the way.

Through the Bottom of the Glass

*

Pizza and a few beers were as good a way as any Chris could think of for getting an old friendship back on track. He realised how hungry he was as soon as they lifted the lid of the box and there was something about pulling the slices apart then and there, no plates, no cutlery, certainly no sitting up at the table and setting Kyle a good example. Just two mates, tearing into a hot chilli beef Domino's; it surely didn't get much better than this. The little devil on his shoulder whispered in his ear that yes, it did; it was better at home with his family, even if Megan thought that meat on a pizza was an abomination, but he cocked a deaf one and carried on eating, stringy cheese clinging to his chin. The dog waited hopefully at his feet for scraps; not that it liked meat on pizza either.

'So,' Mark said, casually, when they had eaten the last tiny morsel and were lying back, one on each of the sofas in his surprisingly roomy lounge. 'What's with you wandering around town with all your worldly goods in a backpack?'

It was so matter of fact that Chris was surprised into speech. Almost without pause, he told Mark about what had happened since they had last seen each other, when he had taken that fatal migraine remedy in the shop just below them even as he spoke. Mark listened without comment, a skill he had had even at school and when Chris came to the end of his recitation, that he was now here, on the sofa and had no idea where he would be tomorrow, he still held his counsel for a moment. Chris waited, surreptitiously wiping the tears which had run unchecked down his cheeks and soaked into his collar.

Eventually, his friend spoke. 'I'm so sorry, mate. I mean sorry for you, I suppose I should say. How long has it been now?'

Chris could have told him to the day, to the hour, to the minute, but settled for a rather more casual answer. 'A couple of months, I guess. Since I ... well, you know.'

'Have you heard from her? The woman, what's her name? Louise?'

'No.' Chris realised with surprise that he hadn't thought of Louise for weeks. He had gone from hating her and wanting to squeeze the life out of her with his bare hands to forgetting as easily as that. These days he never thought of much that wasn't immediately in front of him. Cassie's warning of being over-introspective was wasted, he thought – he didn't think of much at all. Just the here and now. And the increasingly annoying sound-track running through his head; his life as film noir. 'No, I haven't. She'd have trouble finding me, anyway.'

'I guess that's true at least. She can't meddle in your life if she doesn't know where you're leading it.'

'Every cloud has a silver lining.' Chris smiled as he said it, but it was just a knee jerk reaction, just his facial muscles doing what came naturally. Smile. Conciliate. Get by.

'Why did she do all that, though?' Mark had always wanted to dot his tees and cross his eyes.

Chris put his head back on the cushions and closed his eyes. He was comfy, warm and safe here. Full of pizza and with a half-drunk beer within reach, why go there? But he owed it to Mark to tell him everything. And apart from that, it was doing him good. What was the word? Catharsis. It was feeling good in his soul to tell him everything. And the great thing about talking to a real mate was, there was no need to pull the punches. So he told him all about his one night stand. Or at least, he told him what Louise had told him about it; he had no clear memory of it himself.

Mark's eyes were wide when Chris had finished. 'Wow.' He

seemed lost for words for a moment. 'I had no idea. I suppose none of us has any idea about our mates … just, wow. And you remember all this, after so long?'

'No. I didn't remember anything about it until she told me, when … well, you know when.'

Mark frowned. 'This all sounds a bit dodgy to me, mate. I mean, if you really had that good a time … and believe me, that sounds like a *really* good time … surely, you'd remember it. I know I would!'

'I had been drinking. It was a works' do.'

'But even so … do you think someone could have slipped you something?'

Chris bit back a retort that would have included remarks such as 'you should know.' Instead, he said, 'You mean a date rape drug? No – women don't do that, do they?'

'I don't know what women do,' Mark said. 'I only know that you can pick up anything on the net, if you know where to look. And she does sound a bit … driven.' He decided not to use words such as 'bonkers', 'psychotic' 'certifiable'; his friend had enough on his plate without the unwelcome addition of a crazy stalker. Anyway, they only existed in fiction, surely.

'Well, it takes two,' Chris said, flatly. 'I could have said no.' He had no idea how much he sounded like his mother at that moment.

Mark decided suddenly that the mood had got dark enough and swung his legs round and stood up, stretching. 'What say we go out for a drink? It's not often I have company; I'd enjoy the change.'

Chris knew nothing of Mark's private life. The flat was neat, smartly furnished but there wasn't a feminine touch to be seen. The bathroom was devoid of even an extra toothbrush. It didn't have the look of somewhere where someone had cleared out, taking her half of everything. It just looked … if Chris had been pressed on the point, he would have said it looked like a Debenhams window; stylish enough, but a little bit soulless. But that was no guide – when they had gone out on the town together when they were younger, that same combination had been Mark's taste in women, too.

'Are we … picking anyone up?' That sounded bad. 'I mean … do you have anyone who …?'

Mark smiled at his confusion. 'No, I don't have a lady in my life currently. In fact, I rarely do, these days. The shop takes up most of my time. If I'm not actually there, I'm doing the books, inventory, that kind of thing. I am the only pharmacist, cost reasons, mainly. And I just have some part-timers for the other counters. But it pays the bills. Perhaps one day I'll be able to open another, put some staff in, semi-retire. And if I'm not too much of an old, worn-out git by then, who knows – I may find the woman of my dreams.'

'It sounds as if you have it all mapped out.' Chris couldn't help sounding a little bitter.

'Oh, mate,' Mark slapped his leg on his way to his bedroom, 'who knows what's around the next bend? I might meet her tonight. But I won't if we don't get a wiggle on. Come on. Make yourself lovely.' And he went out, to have a quick shower and a change.

Chris didn't have much to choose from in the way of gladrags. His mother had managed, in the middle of the morning's mayhem, to wash, dry and press his clothes from the night before. He wondered again as he often had, were these skills handed over with the baby? It seemed effortless, but he suspected it was what he always thought of as the swan effect – serene and elegant and calm on top, paddling madly below the waterline. He skipped a shower – somehow it seemed a cheek too far – and was waiting casually in the lounge when Mark emerged, on a waft of Calvin Klein.

'We set, then?' Mark shrugged on a leather jacket. With his hair gelled and the aftershave, he was a bit of a cliché but Chris knew that even in his charity shop clobber, he still stood out when he was with Mark. Like women always were reputed to choose friends fatter than themselves, so men always looked for a friend who, though not hideous enough to put off women, were none the less just that bit behind the door when the looks were given out.

Chris got up and tugged down the sleeves of his jacket, which were just that threat too short. 'Let's go,' he said. 'Anywhere in mind?'

Megan had not wanted to go out, but as the time approached she started to feel more in the mood. She was still in her Saturday slob clothes when Lily had arrived but Sam was right – she was a lovely woman and Kyle had taken to her straight away. She had turned Megan round firmly at the foot of the stairs and said, 'Shower. Change. Makeup. Go. Kyle and I have stuff to do.' And Megan had obediently gone to do as she was told. Every now and then, she heard Kyle's peals of laughter from downstairs and felt mildly jealous. The woman had a knack, there was no doubt about it. She showered, spending more than her usual mandatory two minutes about it, soaping and shampooing and revelling in the hot water running over her tired skin. Then she took her time choosing her clothes for the evening, something sparkly, not too short, not too tight, but something that looked as though she had tried at least. Then, the makeup; not the work-day slap, something more subtle, something to bring a bit of a gleam instead of her usual careworn self. She was ready just as she heard Sam's ring at the door.

Lily answered it, with Kyle in attendance. 'Look,' she heard her say, 'it's Auntie Sam come to take Mummy out.'

Megan held her breath. Kyle had serious separation issues these days. His meltdown in the park was mild compared to most of his tantrums. But no; this time he just bounced around, chanting, 'Come on, Lily. Come on, Lily. Let's play, Lily.' She wasn't that happy to hear him using her Christian name like that; she preferred him to be a bit more polite to adults. But, she shrugged, if it was working, don't knock it. She edged along the landing, still listening, but Sam came to the foot of the stairs and looked up, straight into her eyes.

'Hey, Kyle,' she called. 'Come and look at this. Come and look at your pretty mummy.'

Kyle put his head around the lounge door and squinted up the stairs. 'Pretty Mummy,' he agreed then was back to the game. Whatever that game was, she wanted names, she wanted details. She hadn't heard him laugh like that in ... well, possibly *ever*.

She came slowly down the stairs, teetering on unfamiliarly high heels. Sam was still waiting at the bottom, waiting to stave off any last minute maternal misgivings. She put her arm out, across the hall. 'No,' she said. 'No need to go in and tell Kyle not to worry. He doesn't know he should be worrying, why put the idea into his head?'

Megan tried to push past. 'When did you get to be a child psychologist?' she asked, testily.

'The day I was born, I suppose,' Sam said. 'Use your experiences, Megan, not the tosh you read in all those Mama magazines you devour.' She looked at her friend closely. 'I know you. You won't believe you're doing it right until some journalist or so-called expert has told you. That's your bloody mother, that is. She's left you with the confidence of an earthworm. Now, get your coat if you're wearing one and let's get out on that town. Those men aren't going to pick themselves up, you know.'

Megan looked at her, mulishly, then laughed and pecked her cheek. 'Mmm, you smell nice.'

'You too. Let's go and knock 'em dead, Megan Harris. Long time, no do. I wonder if we still remember how?' Then she answered herself. 'It's like riding a bike – once you fling your leg over, it all comes back to you!'

And, laughing, they went out into the dusk of the warm, autumn night.

Although the summer was well and truly gone, the nights were still warm enough to kid you that the winter was far away. The town centre was crowded with the usual Saturday night mixture of couples, groups and singletons but everyone had one thing in common; they were looking to have a good time. Bars and pubs in the traffic free areas were making the most of the unseasonably warm weather by putting some tables and chairs outside and these were filling up nicely. They were good advertising – everyone liked the idea of café society, even in this rather dull, middle of the road place; romantic, that was what it was and a few of the even more enterprising managers had put candles and roses out on the tables. Love was in the air.

Sam and Megan could see the gaggle of brainless tottie from quite a distance. The bride-to-be had, very predictably, L plates on and a sash. The others were wearing clothes that wouldn't disgrace a crowd of pole dancers from the lowest of the low club. The two friends glanced at each other and the thought was the same in both their heads; what in God's name are we doing here?

'I don't think we need stay long,' Sam said. 'They've got a table booked in that Chinese, look, the one just behind them. If we just stay for the mains, dip out before the lychees start flying, that'll do. Yes?'

Megan nodded. If that. 'I mustn't be late, anyway. Kyle …'

Sam put a finger to her lips. 'Ssshh about Kyle. No Kyle tonight. We're just two hot women on the town, okay?' She plunged into the crowd, putting an arm around the bride-to-be, the reason for her impending nuptials stretching the front of her skimpy dress. 'Hello, ladies,' she said, beaming around the group. Megan watched, smiling. Sam may be the boss but for tonight, she was just one of the girls. 'Are we all here?'

The bride nodded. She seemed a nice little thing, if on the dim side. Megan looked at her standing there, teetering on high heels, five month pregnancy straining at her dress and wanted to hug her. Tell her there was no need to do this. That she would be all right on her own. But everyone was different; perhaps she was embarking on a marriage made in heaven. It didn't do to judge.

So they all poured into the Chinese restaurant and the staff looked at them with the stiff smiles they kept for this kind of group. They had put four tables together but right at the back of the room. They knew these women would be raucous, messy and bad tippers. But business was business and you couldn't turn it down. They started bringing out the dishes and putting them on the little hotplates already in place down the centre of the table. Megan was between two girls who didn't work with Sam and the rest; they were friends of the bride from way back and were soon talking around Megan as though she wasn't there. After a while, she offered to swap with one of them and they grabbed the chance, so after that, she was alone to all intents and purposes, with an inedible spring roll and a pile of crispy chilli beef, which flew in the face of any trading standards rules in that it was chewy not crispy and possibly not even beef.

There were speeches, using more foul language in one five minute space than Megan had heard in the last six months. There was laughter, of the drunken, slightly hysterical variety. Megan was shocked to see that the bride-to-be was as drunk as the rest and this, as much as the horrible food, was enough to bring her to her feet, gesturing to Sam.

Sam leaned over to whisper into the ear of the woman sitting next to her and she came round to Megan's end of the table. 'Problem?' she said, brightly through gritted teeth.

'You have to ask?' Megan said, also through a fake smile. 'The bride is both pregnant and pissed, a combination I wouldn't think has been common since the Sixties. The food is vile. Let's go.'

Sam raised her voice. 'Oh, poor you,' she said. Then she turned to the table and made tummy rubbing motions, pointing to Megan. 'Not very well,' she mouthed and everyone smiled, nodded, put their thumbs up. To get rid of the boss and her miserable friend this early in the evening was an unlooked for bonus.

Once outside, both women exhaled. 'What a truly dreadful night,' Megan said. 'I couldn't believe it when I saw how drunk she was.'

'She has every reason to be,' Sam said, solemnly. 'She's marrying some brainless estate agent, begging your pardon. In fact, he's from Stanley's; do you know him? Jason. Gavin. Gareth. Something like that.'

Megan spluttered with laughter. 'There's a Gavin. A bit of a jack the lad as I remember.' She realised with a pang that she could say that without melting down. Perhaps she had turned a corner tonight.

'Well, he should have watched where he jacked his lad,' Sam said. It wasn't wit of the first order, but it would do for now. 'They'd only been going out about three weeks when she was pregnant and now they're getting married. I can't believe they're being so stupid. It can't end well.'

Megan forebore to answer that one. What was there to say, after all?

Sam swung on down the precinct, either unaware of what she had said, or very much aware; you could never tell with her how much havoc she intended and how much just followed her around. 'I thought we'd go to the Bell. There's no way that lot will end up in there; I don't think they know what Prosecco is!'

Megan smiled. 'Not such a good venue for us, then,' she said.

'There's more to life than cheap wine,' Sam pointed out. 'We're on the spirits tonight, my girl, and no messing.'

Megan groaned in anticipation of the hangover to come. 'You know gin goes straight to my head,' she said.

'Excellent. That's what we're after. Here we are.' Sam pushed open the doors and made a typically spectacular entrance. 'Grab a table and I'll get two doubles. Start as we mean to go on, eh?'

The pub wasn't as packed as the others they had passed. The manager had made a decision long ago. No bar snacks. No fancy, poncy wine list. Just beer and spirits. On a good night you might get ice and a slice, but only if he had remembered to get some in. But for anyone who just wanted a drink and some conversation, this was the place. There was a guitarist in the corner, strumming and muttering into a mic, but he was easy to ignore. His songs were all pretty miserable as well, covers of Radiohead and Leonard Cohen, so there was no risk of anyone dancing. In short, it was a perfect place for two women out to get drunk.

Sam was back at the table in double quick time and it was a good night – there was ice *and* a slice. They looked around the room and didn't see anyone worth talking to, so they settled in to bitch about the girls at the hen do – and there was plenty to bitch about; this evening could be a lot of fun after all.

'Where are we going?' Chris asked while Mark locked up his front door. He noticed that his host looked fondly into the window of his shop and wondered why pharmacies ever thought that things that scraped the dry skin off your feet and mosquito repellent ever made for an attractive point of sale display.

'I thought we'd go to the Bell.'

'Ah, no, Mark! It's such a crap pub. They don't even do bar snacks.'

'We have just demolished an enormous pizza with everything on it,' Mark pointed out. 'And just *because* it's a crap pub with no bar snacks, it means it doesn't get mobbed by bloody stags and hens.'

Chris thought it through. 'That's a point,' he said. 'And, it's in walking distance, so we can both have a drink.'

'Hell, yeah,' Mark said. 'If even half of us is sober by the end of tonight, I'll count it as a failure.'

Chris pulled his wallet out as casually as he could and looked inside. His eyes nearly popped out of his head. A hundred quid. Where the hell had that come from? He answered himself immediately. His mother. Sleight of hand was clearly another skill they handed over with the baby.

'Don't worry, mate,' Mark said, misinterpreting the bulging eyes. 'Tonight's on me.'

Chris was about to explain, but then changed his mind. Mark could afford it, after all, and if blame was to be placed anywhere, he would be at least a contender. 'Thanks,' he muttered. 'Things are a bit tight …'

Mark held his hand up. 'That's it!' he said. 'No more talk of who pays what. The only thing is, I may have to slip you a tenner if you're the last man walking. We don't want to miss any drinking time just because I can't get to the bar.'

'Deal,' said Chris, with a smile. His stomach gave a lurch, and not just in anticipation of another night on the booze. Somehow, he knew this night wasn't going to end well. He didn't believe in airy fairy crap like intuition, but sometimes, he was to find, it really is better to go with your gut.

Megan had only had one glass of wine with her meal but on the other hand she had only picked at the food so she was, to all intents and purposes drinking on an empty stomach. Nevertheless, on her second gin she was beginning to feel that she was approaching peak performance. Witty, amusing but not loud and given to random laughing and/or weeping. Perfect. If Mr Right didn't catch her now, he would be sorry. She was peering into her glass, watching the ice chase the slice as she stirred it with her swizzle stick, otherwise known as half a bamboo skewer, when Sam suddenly nudged her in the ribs.

'Here he is!' she hissed.

Megan's head snapped up. Chris? It had to be; who else would Sam call 'he'? 'Where?' All she could see were a couple of suits, walking in their direction.

'There,' Sam said. 'I admit that I've been a little less than honest with you, Megs.' As she spoke, she stood up and leaned against a suit, the rather less attractive one, to Megan's surprise, and gave him a long, lingering kiss. 'Megs,' she said, when she finally broke away, 'meet Brian. Brian, Megs.'

Megan took the hand he proffered and smiled. She looked at Sam with her 'just you wait' expression and then looked behind them both to the spare wheel brought along for Sam's desperate friend. Actually, he looked okay. He was wearing a suit, yes, which made him look both needy and nerdy. But there didn't seem to be any of the usual ref flags – shaving rash, pen in top pocket, bad veneers – so she pulled out the chair next to her and said, 'Hi. I'm Megan. And you …?'

He sat down in a waft of something expensive. Closer to there were still no warning signs; Megan could have kicked herself, but in fact that just made her even more suspicious. Left hand – no ring. Wait for the voice; the voice was going to like Daffy Duck, she just knew it. 'Hi Megan. I'm Will. Not called after the prince, in case you're wondering. Sadly, I predate him by a year or so.'

Megan looked closer. Hmm, yes, a bit more than a year or so, my lad, she thought. Possibly ten. But he clearly looked after himself and perhaps there was something to be said for someone who had been around the block a couple of times. 'Hi. I can't think of anyone famous called Megan – sorry.' She smiled. 'That's a great line, though; I'll have to try and think of some. For future use.' She knew she was prattling and looked into her glass for inspiration.

Sam had sat back down and pulled a chair round for Brian. She looked at Megan with a questioning look but got no evils back, so hoped they were good. Yes, Brian and Will weren't in youth's first flush, but look where a thirty-something got you; left holding the baby. These guys weren't bad to look at, but there was that added dusting of gratitude which meant they wouldn't stray too far or too fast. 'Brian and Will are in IT,' she told Megan.

She had had them down for bankers, so IT was a pleasant surprise. 'Really? I'm sorry to say that I can hardly manage my smartphone. Computers aren't really my thing. What is it you do, exactly?'

The two men looked at each other and laughed. 'We don't understand them much, either,' Brian said. 'We just got lucky when we were at university. My parents had some money they wanted to invest. We had some nerdy friends who needed jobs after they graduated …'

'Do you remember that one … what was his name? Those glasses and that hair … you know …'

'God, yes. Josh. He looked like nothing else on earth but could that boy program – I call him a boy because he got his place when he was fifteen. He'd graduated in eighteen months. He made the business for us, really.'

'And yet you don't remember his name?' Megan said, an edge to her voice.

'They burn out,' Will said, dismissively and she liked him a lot less, just like that, in the blink of an eye. He looked around the table. 'Drinks?'

While he was at the bar, helped by Brian who seemed to be attached to him by some invisible thread, Sam leaned over. 'What do you think?'

'He's an arsehole, Sam,' Megan said. 'What were you thinking?'

'No!' Sam was annoyed. 'Come on, Megan. You've only just met the guy. Give him a chance.'

'A chance of what?'

'Who knows? The night is young. I tell you something, though. If he knows half the tricks Brian has up his sleeve, you're in for a hell of a night.'

Megan looked and indeed was, outraged. 'I'm not taking him home tonight!' she hissed. 'What do you take me for?'

'A woman who hasn't had sex for months. A woman who needs to feel someone's arms around her. No one will judge. Go for it. He obviously likes you. So, give him a chance.'

Megan sat back and smiled up at Will just in time. He put a drink in front of her and pulled up his chair. 'So, Megan, Sam tells me you have a little boy. I've got two kids, not so little now, though.' He fished into his breast pocket and pulled out two photos. A girl sitting on a pony scowled out of one. A boy with a rather bad overbite wearing a very expensive-looking school blazer stared out of the other.

'Lovely.' She just wanted out. This guy had so much wrong with him and now, here was the baggage as well. She took a huge slug of her drink and felt her eyeballs shrivel. 'What the hell is that?' she gasped.

'Gin,' Brian laughed. 'With a hint of tonic.'

Megan's eyes were watering and to her embarrassment, one of her contact lenses decided to go walkabout. 'Ow!'

'What?' Sam's voice was full of concern.

'Oh, just this damned lens. I don't wear them enough, that's the thing … ow!'

Sam shuddered. 'I don't know how you can,' she said. 'I hate anyone fiddling with my eyes.'

'Look over here,' Will said, whipping a crisp, white hanky out of his pocket. 'I wear lenses, I don't mind hoiking it out for you. Look up.'

And that was how, walking in with Mark at that moment, Chris saw, in glorious technicolor, the love of his life, her chin held in a masterful hand, looking up with shining eyes into the face of Mr Perfect.

He hadn't needed an excuse to get hopelessly, roaringly drunk but it was good to have one. Mark could only look on in horror as his friend poured drink after drink down his throat. Having left the Bell in a slam of doors, they had started working their way back along the High Street, gate-crashing hen and stag parties without fear nor favour. Had he but known it, Chris was a major reason for many of the selfies taken that night being ditched rather than shared on Facebook. Who wants to post a selfie of themselves with a green-faced, belligerent drunk in the background? Finally, the worst happened. He found a woman even drunker than he was, sprawled on the pavement outside a gastro-pub, just managing to avoid rolling in her own sick. He pulled her to her feet and in doing so, she fell against him.

'You're a handsome one,' she slurred and collapsed against his chest.

'You're not so bad yourself,' he muttered.

She reached up and pulled his head down for a long kiss which both of them knew was a bad idea. But somehow, the bad idea turned into a good idea which turned into a desperate urge to give each other a good seeing to in the next dark alley they could find. She took his hand and set off at a drunken trot, ankle turning over on her fuck-me shoes every other step or so.

Mark was fairly hammered himself, but not so much that the beer-goggles won out over commonsense. 'Chris!' he called after his stumbling friend. 'Chris! You don't want to do that!'

A fist caught him in his back. 'Don't you talk about my friend like that,' an aggressively drunk voice said.

'What?' Mark turned round to face his attacker. A girl in a skimpy dress, her belly sticking out too far to be anything other than a pregnancy, stood there, an L plate pinned crookedly across her chest.

'Don't you call my friend "that",' she said. 'She may be drunk, but she deserves better.'

Mark's innate politeness kicked in. 'No, no I didn't call your *friend* that. I meant, he didn't want to do … well, what it seems he is already doing.' Mark sighed. He had heard some rumours, Chris had borne some of them out over pizza a lifetime ago, but this was beyond a joke. He couldn't see anything down the alleyway, but the drunken cries and shrieks of delight told him everything. 'I apologise for him, I really do. He's had a bad time of it, lately.'

'Well,' said a well-spoken voice behind him. 'He seems to be having a good time of it now. I suggest you look the other way, ladies,' and Brian, ever the gentleman, walked on the alleyway side of his little party as he shepherded them along to the cab rank.

In the back of the cab, Megan was quiet. Will had an arm around her shoulders and every now and then dropped a small kiss on the top of her head or nibbled her ear. He was murmuring things she probably should have been protesting against, but her mind was whirling. She was putting two and two together and making at least a dozen. The man at the end of the alley was Mark, one of Chris's best friends. The girl he was talking to was the hen she had started the evening with, the intended of one of Chris's ex-colleagues. The man in the alley, was clearly off his face on drink and god-knew what else when Mark was involved. So, who else could the man in the alley be, with the morals of an alley cat, appropriately enough, than Chris? The father of her child. Will murmured another question into her ear and she turned her head to look him straight in the eye.

'Yes,' she said, clearly and concisely, to everyone's surprise but especially her own. 'Yes, I would like you to come home with me and do all that. And a bit more, if it's on offer.' In the seat opposite, she caught Sam's expression. It was very mixed, to say the best of it.

'What?' she asked. 'Like you said, I'm a woman who hasn't had sex for months. It's time to put that right, isn't it, Will?'

He looked at her, delight all over his face. 'It certainly is,' he said. 'It certainly is.'

Stone Cold Sober

*

Sunday morning. Chris couldn't exactly call himself a Joni Mitchell fan, still less Neil Diamond, but nevertheless, the words to *Chelsea Morning* just wouldn't leave his head. There was no milk or toast or honey and if the sun had actually made rainbows on the wall he may have actually been sick. But the tune was there and the words, in no particular order. He would have to think about switching on the radio soon, before the damn thing drove him demented. Even something from One Direction or, God forbid, Justin Bieber would help to drive it out. He dozed again, an arm over his eyes. Mark's spare room curtains weren't doing much towards cutting out the light.

An hour or possibly a minute later, the door to his bedroom opened. No one spoke and Chris toyed with saying nothing in the hope that they would go away. The technique didn't seem to be getting him anywhere, though, so he opened one eye and squinted under his forearm. Mark was standing in the doorway, fully clothed, clearly showered and shaved. It was still Sunday, right?

'Morning.'

Why didn't he sound friendlier? People were such crap hosts these days. 'Morning.' Chris found he had to think very hard to get his lips in motion.

'Could you get up and get dressed, please?'

It was probably Mark's pharmacy training that made him sound like the nurse at a particularly draconian GP practice. 'Can I have another ten …?'

'No. I've made some coffee. I'm in the lounge.' And with that, the door closed and Mark was gone.

Chris rolled out of bed and onto the floor. His clothes, so lovingly pressed by his mother not twenty-four hours before, now lay in a foul-smelling heap on the floor. He could only find one shoe. Presumably the other would turn up eventually. He couldn't face his gladrags so he unearthed some of his other, more workaday clothes from his backpack. They were beginning to look the worse for wear, having been washed and reworn so often since he had left … he found he could hardly think the next bit without tearing up. He shook himself. He must learn to man up if he was going to make it in this life. He pulled on a sweater, thin at the elbow, and went out to see what the hell was biting Mark. He couldn't remember but chances were that his old mate was one of those who didn't cope with hangovers too well. He was surprised at himself, actually – bearing in mind how much he remembered drinking the night before, he didn't feel that bad.

A cafetiere of coffee stood on a place mat on the small dining table in the bay window. The High Street was quiet as yet, with a few strollers out in the early sun. At this time of year, it paid to make the most of every ray. If the forecasts were to be believed, the winter was not going to be easy. There was toast as well. Chris instinctively looked for the honey and the bowl of oranges, but Mark clearly didn't have *Chelsea Morning* in his head – there was some strawberry jam and some Clover. Take it or leave it. He looked up as Chris went in. 'Sit down, Chris,' he said, tightly. 'Let's have some breakfast while we talk.'

'Talk?' Chris glanced at the clock, predictably enough on the mantelpiece. Ten o'clock. Not bad, not bad. And it was Sunday, after all. 'What about?' He took a slice of toast, spread it thickly with the Clover and took a bite. Healthy or no, he really couldn't cotton to these spready things – butter was the only option, to his mind.

Mark snuffled. It could have been an ironic laugh. 'What about?' he said. 'What *about*? Let's start with the drinking …'

'We went out for a drink,' Chris pointed out, mildly. 'I would have been happy here with a pizza.'

'Fair enough,' Mark said. 'But when I suggested going out for a drink, I didn't expect you to get roaring, falling down, vomiting drunk.'

Chris looked a little shamefaced. 'I did have a bit too much, I suppose. Sorry.'

'A bit too much. Okay, I had a *bit* too much. But I could walk. I could speak. But, most of all, I didn't pick up a drunken slapper and have her up against a wall in an alley.'

Chris laughed, a short bark, cut off sharply. 'Nor did I!' he said. 'I don't do that kind of thing.'

'Apparently, you do. You weren't long, I'll give you that. In fact, as I recall, she had a few things to say about that as we made our way back here. I'm not really prepared to repeat any of it, but it was very graphic.'

'But …' Dim memories, flashes like a strobe light, began to surface. 'Was it … was it when we came out of that gastro-pub place?'

'No. it was when we were thrown out of that gastro-pub place. She was lying in the road.' Chris looked stricken. 'I can see it's coming back to you, now.'

The whole incident flooded over him like ice-water. She had been hard to handle, down in the dark of the alley. He had tried to prop her up, but she wasn't having any. They had ended up on a pile of bin bags, full of God knew what … he couldn't breathe. He couldn't breathe! He could hear Mark somewhere in the far distance but he wasn't making any sense. His blood was pounding in his ears and he knew he needed to breathe, but he couldn't. His chest was in a vice. He was dying, no doubt about it. He got up, knocking the table as he did so and he felt the hot coffee flood over his hand. The sun coming through the curtains was hurting his eyes. The black dog bounded around the room, tail wagging, eyes bright, mouth open and panting, spittle flying, ready for some fun. Chris flailed around, taking gasping breaths in, but unable to breathe out.

Mark came round the table and grasped him firmly by the

shoulders. He spoke clearly, looking straight into Chris's eyes. 'You're having a panic attack. You're almost through it. Listen to me. Breathe on the count of ten. Can you do that? Listen to my voice. Breathe with me as I count and when you can, join in. In your head and then out loud. All right? One ... two ...'

Chris relaxed into his friend's grip and listened to him counting. '... three ...'

'That's it. Count for me. Five ... six ...'

Slowly, Chris felt better. His breaths in were less trembling, more positive. Soon, he felt his knees begin to relax and he could sit down. He put his head down on his folded arms, still feeling sick and weak.

Mark lay a hand gently on his shoulder. Then, after a few moments' pressure, he patted him twice and left the room. 'Don't worry,' he called over his shoulder. 'I'm just making some fresh coffee. Actually, not coffee for you. Some camomile tea. Just keep your head down for a minute. I'll be right back.'

Chris was pleased to have the keep his head down instruction as he was far from sure he would be able to do anything else. Slowly, he got his breathing back under control and the trembling that seized him from his head to his heels every ten seconds or so finally stopped. When Mark came back in with a mug in one hand and a fresh cafetiere in the other, he was sitting up and feeling a little calmer. 'Sorry,' he muttered. 'I'm sorry.'

'What for?' Mark put a mug of pale liquid that smelled of lawn clippings down in front of him, then poured himself a cup of coffee. 'For having a panic attack – well, don't be so silly. No one has one of those on purpose. For getting falling down drunk and behaving like an animal, then I'm not sure that sorry will quite do the business.'

'Look ... Mark ...' Chris took a sip of his tea; actually, not that bad. Then, a thought occurred to him. 'What's in this?' It came out much more truculently than he meant, but he couldn't change that.

'Camomile,' Mark said. 'Don't worry, I haven't slipped you anything mind altering. In fact, I didn't slip you anything mind altering the last time, either. I just find that the placebo effect can do more when I tell someone they've taken something a bit dodgy.'

'So ... what did I take?' Chris was confused.

Mark shrugged. 'Just a few herbal bits, something to make it taste nasty. It's more than my livelihood is worth to do anything else. Sorry. If you had been blaming me for your … unfortunate lapse, shall we call it … then you'll have to step up to the plate. It was all you, mate. Sorry. And last night was *definitely* all you. She was almost unconscious. What were you thinking?'

Chris put his head in his hands and scrubbed at his scalp with his fingers. 'I don't know. I scarcely remember …' He looked up, haggard. 'Did anyone see me?'

Mark considered the situation. He had been pretty sure he had seen that friend of Megan's out of the corner of his eye. But he didn't expect Megan was with her; he had heard she was a bit reclusive these days and really, no wonder. But … what was her name? Jan? One syllable, anyway. But she would probably tell Megan; if she saw anything. Too many unknowns. 'Only me and her mate. The pregnant bride.'

Chris's stomach gave a jolt. Gavin's intended. But perhaps not; she couldn't be the only pregnant bride-to-be in town. 'Let's hope that's the end of it, then,' he said, hopefully.

'Yes, let's,' Mark said, then his training and his natural laser-like honesty rose up. 'But you might find it comes to bite you, mate. I mean, did you use any protection?'

'Of course I bloody didn't. I could hardly stand, let alone … oh,' as realisation dawned. 'Oh … I see.'

'Yes. Any or all of the following. An unwanted sprog for her, a nice STI for you.'

Chris took a gulp of his tea. He would have preferred something stronger, but for now, camomile tea it would have to be. 'How long …?'

'Pregnancy, who knows? If she's a bit more sensible than she came across yesterday, she'll be round the walk-in now for a morning after pill. If she isn't – any time in the next six weeks should be when the shit hits the fan. The other – all depends, but if I were you, I would be round the walk-in this morning, too.'

'Can't you give me something?'

Mark held his hands up. 'Sorry,' he said. 'I can help with

headaches and the odd allergy but prophylactic antibiotics are a bit out of my league.' He leaned forward across the table. 'But, look, Chris … last night notwithstanding, you need help. Your life has unravelled and you're behaving as if it's just a blip. Let's face it, you've always tended to suffer from depression …'

Chris's usual reaction reared up and his chest went tight. Then he remembered Cassie and it subsided. He could hear her voice. He could feel the gentle touch of her hand. 'I didn't know,' he said. 'I just thought …'

'Thought you were a miserable bugger?' Mark smiled at him. 'That's what we all thought when we were twelve, Chris. But you're old enough now to know it isn't normal to feel the way you do, surely.'

'We just never talked about it …'

'Well, no.' Mark cast his mind back to visits to the Rowans' house when they were all at school. Mrs Rowan, flying round like a bumble bee on speed, food every second, merry whitterings round the clock. Claire, morose and argumentative. He hadn't seen her for years, but he realised now she was clearly on some spectrum or another, just unacknowledged by the bumble bee and her husband, Mr Rowan. Quiet to the point of invisibility. Often in a shed in the garden, working on his projects, none of which ever seemed to emerge. Again, the bright light of hindsight and what Mark knew of his sad decline and unwillingness to accept his cancer made it clear that he was also a depression sufferer. What a family – but probably not much more dysfunctional than any other. Certainly no worse than his own, in the scheme of things. 'Chris …' Mark didn't want the next bit of the conversation to arrive, but the longer he put it off, the worse it would be.

'I know,' Chris said, looking up with a smile so infinitely sad that Mark's heart turned over. 'I can't stay. You have had a telegram from your aunt from Brazil …'

'… where the nuts come from …' Mark filled in, in a voice full of tears.

'… and, oh my goodness, she's arriving today.' He and Mark shared so much. He wondered whether anyone at all knew him so well.

'Not today,' Mark said. 'Let's leave it till tomorrow, shall we? But then ... it won't do you any good to hide here, Chris. You need to move on properly. Get your own place. A job. Get back on your feet.'

'It's for my own good?' This was a test question; he already knew the answer.

'Yes. That's it. It's for your own good.'

Bingo! The right or the wrong answer, depending on the point of view. Chris got up from the table. Suddenly, he ached in every joint and his head was hammering. His tongue grew fur and he was going hot and cold. Oh, hello, hangover, he thought. I wondered when you'd be putting in your six pennyworth. He managed a smile. 'No worries,' he said. 'I'll go now. Down to the walk-in and then ...'

'Then?' Mark was on his feet. 'Then, where?'

'Claire's?'

'Don't be daft. Stay here till tomorrow. Tomorrow's another day.' Mark had always been a bit of a shining light in drama class, but even he couldn't make much of a stab at Vivien Leigh that morning. But he was right, Chris thought. Tomorrow certainly was another day.

That Sunday morning, Megan had woken late; a luxury she hadn't really been able to enjoy for the past three years and more. She lay with her eyes closed, still smiling from the dream she had been having just before waking; she and Chris and Kyle were having a picnic, in a daisy-studded field, with the sun shining and larks singing overhead. Neither of them was complaining about what was in the sandwiches; they hadn't forgotten to bring the flask, everything was perfect. That was how she had known it was a dream. As she came slowly back to the here and now, she began to take in a few details and also to remember things from the night before. Some things were good; others, very bad indeed.

For instance, the warm body behind her in the bed. Commonsense told her it wasn't Chris; this wasn't a soap; she hadn't just been dreaming the nightmares of the last months. It definitely wasn't Sam; she knew from other clues that it *very* definitely wasn't Sam! Deep in her brain, she knew it was Will, a man she had met in a pub the night before, but she didn't want it to be. That wasn't because she disliked him; far from it. He was good looking, clearly not short of a bob or two and – as the memories lined up to be called properly to mind – he certainly knew what buttons to press when it came to sex. No, she didn't want to be the sort of person who took a stranger to bed on the first date; if being set up by your friend even counted as a date. And, more especially, she didn't want to be the sort of person who took said stranger home to where her three year old son, already damaged enough, was living.

As Kyle passed through her thoughts, so her breath constricted in her throat. Nine o'clock and no Kyle! She shot upright in bed, eyes wild, then lay back down again, another memory at the front of the queue vying for her attention. That's right – Lily had stayed over, on the little flop out bed in Kyle's room. She could hear them nattering away downstairs, if she listened really hard, over the mad beating of her heart. The woman was a saint and Megan smiled to herself, wondering how she could kidnap her and keep her for ever.

'Hello, smiler,' a voice said in her ear. 'How are you this morning?'

She turned to Will and smiled some more. He hadn't asked the test question, the one that would get him booted out before the kettle had even boiled. She gave him another second or two, because her life hadn't been this hassle free since before the dawn of time and she didn't want to believe it too soon. But no; there was no crass remark, just a long, slow kiss and a strong arm around her waist, pulling her closer. It occurred to her as she let herself melt into him that this could still be a dream. And if it is, her hindbrain said to her more sensible self, don't knock it; dreams like this, I could get to like.

Sam's awakening was a little more abrupt and the body in her bed rather more familiar, but she was also wondering if the last hours had been a dream. Looking at Will and Megan, she had wondered for a while whether she had lit a blue touch-paper that had better been left alone. But Brian had said he was a top bloke, not given to chasing women, not a serial heart-breaker, not a secret drinker, gambler or abuser. He had more money than he knew what to do with and … well, there was no 'and' so she had decided to let nature take its course. And it had certainly done that; in the cab, she sometimes hadn't known where to look. She had gone into the house with them, slipped Lily fifty quid and asked her to stay as long as necessary. Megan had a lot of ghosts to lay and if laying Will was part of the process, it was fifty quid well spent. She turned over and propped herself up on one elbow, looking at Brian with a dispassionate eye. His hair was going a little at the temples but by and large, he was quite a catch. Older, of course, but all the boxes Will could tick, Brian could tick as well. With knobs on. She poked him in the ribs.

He opened one eye. 'Mmphf?' he asked, cryptically.

'Brian. *Brian*! Wake up.'

'Don' wanna.'

'No, I don't expect you do.' She waited. 'Brian!'

He sighed and turned over, but his eyes were still shut. He reached across to stroke her stomach, but she slapped his hand away.

'Not till you've answered my question.'

'But … when I *have* …?'

She kissed his forehead. 'Depends on the answer.'

'Okay.' He opened his eyes. She smiled. She always forgot how blue they were in the morning sun coming through the blinds. She almost didn't bother with her question as they crinkled at the corners and his hand started creeping across the bed again.

'What's the catch?'

'Catch?'

'With Will.'

'There is no catch with Will. He is …' he couldn't help a little laugh, although he knew it was rude to laugh at your own jokes, '… *a* catch.'

'No wife?'

'Not any more. Safely married off to someone else.'

'Kids?'

'Vile children, though he tends to flash the pics. He sees them as little as possible.'

'No other worries?'

'No drink problem, doesn't chase women, nothing like that. Ooooh … hang on though …' Brian made a grab for her but missed. 'I believe he's a bit of a farter when he's had sprouts. Or so they say.'

'They? I thought you said he didn't chase women.' She looked at him sternly. 'This is my best friend we're talking about here.'

Brian gathered her to him. 'Well, there's a bit of a rumour going around that he sometimes likes to bat for the other side ...'

She struggled out of his arms and was standing by the bed almost in one movement. 'What? *What?* He's *gay?*'

'No, no, not at all. If anything, he's bi. But probably not even that. You know how people like to talk. And, honestly, Sam, why worry? He was all over Megan last night. He's obviously smitten. Don't rock the boat. Come back to bed.'

She climbed in, but slowly. 'Brian ... I should tell her ...'

'Why? And what would you say? Mr Right, Mr Gorgeous, Mr Moneybags who will take you and your frankly rather strange kid out of the shit your ex has landed you in, may or on the other hand may not be, a little bit bi, as in when he's had a few drinks and is out with like-minded friends? It's a bit of a mouthful, isn't it? And why meet trouble halfway? They might never see each other after today, so no harm, no foul. Hmm?'

She looked into his cornflower blue eyes and set her mouth. 'I don't know ...'

'Look,' he said, pulling her closer. 'Why don't you think it over in the next half an hour, if you don't have anything else in mind? Or, alternatively ...'

And this time, she didn't knock his hand away.

Monday, Monday

*

The remainder of Sunday had gone remarkably well, Chris thought. He wasn't feeling quite the ticket after his little morning meltdown and so, instead of going out for lunch which had been the tentative plan the day before, Mark had gone out and bought in all the ingredients for what turned out to be a darned fine Sunday lunch. It wasn't as though Chris hadn't been stuffed with food over the last weeks and on Sunday his mother went totally nuts, rather than the only slightly unhinged gargantuan weekday meals. But they usually shared them with at least one or two parishioners and this could put a bit of a downer on even the most melt-in-the-mouth Yorkshires on earth. So, if Mark's gravy was a little lumpy and the cauli a little too al for anyone's dente, who cared? They talked about anything and everything that had nothing to do with exes, children and drunken women and, somehow, by hook or by crook, they got themselves through to Monday morning.

To prevent unnecessarily prolonged and potentially heartrending goodbyes, Mark went down to the shop early. He had put Chris's clothes through the washer-drier and Chris gave them a cursory press. Although they were far from designer chic, at least he now looked and more importantly smelled clean. He had a shower, trying hard not to obsess about early signs of an unfortunate infection, and washed his hair. He felt ready for anything and even sat down at the table to write himself a list.

Mark came up the stairs at eleven for his coffee and found him still there, a blank piece of paper in front of him, a pen in his hand. He had written 'To do' and the top of the page and underlined it three times. He had drawn sun's rays around the holes on the left hand side. He had drawn a house, child-style, at the bottom, but no flowers adorned its garden, no smoke plumed jauntily from its chimney. Mark thought you could tell a lot from that house, but didn't say so.

'I didn't think I heard you leave,' he said, keeping his voice level. 'Let's just get your list sorted and then you can be on your way. I hope you don't mind; I made a few calls for you this morning. You've got appointments at the doctor, the job centre or whatever they call it these days and the housing office, all this afternoon. Look … I'll jot them all down.' He pulled the paper closer and wrote each appointment, neatly numbered. 'There. First one's at the GP at one. The surgery opens after lunch at one, so there'll not be a queue. I'll take an early lunch, shall I? We can stroll along together.'

Chris looked down at the paper and pushed it from side to side. 'I'm not sure if …'

'I am,' Mark said. 'I know you think I'm being a bit of a bastard and I suppose in some ways I am,' he said. 'But we go back a long, long way, Chris and I know that mollycoddling you is going to get us nowhere. Who ended up doing your Chemistry homework for years?'

'You,' Chris smiled. It was true; he had never done a stroke of work in Chemistry.

'And what did you get for your GCSE?'

'F.'

'So … I rest my case. It's time to do your own homework, Chris. Come downstairs at twelve, we'll grab something from Gregg's and I'll walk you to the docs. You know it makes sense.'

Knowing it and believing it were two separate things, but Chris nodded. 'See you at twelve,' he said. 'My treat.' If he couldn't manage a Gregg's, it was time to jump in the river.

'Thank you,' Mark said solemnly, and clattered down the stairs again, coffeeless as it happened, but at least he had got the worst bit over. If he got Chris to the doctor, it was a start; the rest, he would have to do for himself.

Twelve o'clock came all too soon. Daytime television only can go so far towards filling a person's mind and Chris was amazed again how banal the programming was. Mostly, it seemed to involve people not buying a house, or so it seemed to him. Either that, or they did buy a house and immediately regretted it. His inner estate agent rose up in despair – no wonder people almost spat on his kind in the street; they were held up as at best grasping, at worst grasping and also rather dim. He looked at his list. Job centre. He toyed with lying about his previous work experience, but felt on balance that would be counterproductive. He started to worry about what he was going to say. He knew that he wouldn't be telling anyone the complete truth and even as the thought went through his head, he knew that he was being stupid. Lying to the GP would only prolong the agony and certainly wouldn't get him better any time soon. Lying to the job centre he had a feeling probably came with an interview under caution or similar scary outcome. Lying to the housing office; all by himself in Mark's uber-tidy sitting room, watching day-time TV with the sound off, he laughed. How often had he had to deal with the housing office, from the other side of the fence? Should he ask for one of the names he knew, or would a stranger be better? He knew the answer straight away – a stranger, every time!

His attention was taken by a strange noise just the other side of the door onto the stairs. He wasn't sure whether the street door was left open for people such as the postman, so he went over and opened it. A black dog sat there, one paw up for a handshake. Somehow, it didn't look like the kind of dog that would be taught tricks – it had a hard gleam in its red-rimmed eye and there was the tip of a tooth overhanging its lip. Chris reached out to pat its head, to calm it as its hackles were rising and a growl was growing in its throat. He jumped as an ambulance went past outside, sirens blaring, blue light throwing eerie shadows on the ceiling and when he looked back, the dog had gone. Chris squeezed his eyes shut then opened them again. There was a plausible explanation. There was always a plausible explanation. He just couldn't quite put his finger on what it might be, not right now. In the distance, the church clock began to strike. Chris took a deep breath, shrugged into his coat and put his backpack over his shoulder. The next step on his path to … where? Not Oz, that was for sure. But, for good measure, he would make sure he took no notice of the man behind the curtain. Or his dog.

Opening his wallet in Gregg's to pay for a couple of baguettes, Chris felt a bit guilty. He could easily have taken Mark out for a pub lunch on the money his mother had slipped in there. But he knew that having the majority of a hundred quid still there tomorrow might be very important. His balance on his current account was frighteningly low and there were no savings any more. He pulled out his phone just to check with online banking; he tried not to do it too often, it was all too easy to get obsessed. The phone said there was no service, which was ridiculous. He always had all five bars here. He turned around, arm in the air.

'Not a selfie, surely,' Mark said as he fell into step.

'No. I'm just checking for signal. How's yours?'

Mark brought out his Blackberry and thumbed a key. 'Fine. Who're you with?'

'I don't remember, actually,' Chris said. 'This is a … oh, bugger.'

'What?'

'This is a company phone.'

'But it's been months. Surely, they would have cancelled it before today.'

'What's the date?'

'Umm … God, first of October.' He pinched Chris's coat sleeve and punched him lightly on the arm. 'Pinch, punch.'

'Well, how time flies. Here …' Chris handed his iPhone to Mark. 'Can you use one of these? I daresay there's someone in a shop along here somewhere who can unlock it for you.'

'But what's today's date got to do with it?'

'Contract. I remember we all got new phones last year on the first of October. Dave had wangled some amazing deal on the tariff by paying up front for all the phones for a year. He said it had cost him a packet, but saved him almost as much. The deal was, as I remember it, that there would be an automatic upgrade to the latest phones one a year. And so, today, he is going round the office handing out whatever is fancy and all singing, all dancing as if they were sweeties. And my phone is so much plastic.'

Mark looked stricken. His phone was his lifeline and without it for checking emails and all the rest, he would have been lost. But, now he came to think of it, Chris's hadn't so much as chirped since they had been together and he wondered if he would miss it that much. But, still … 'Look, Chris, why don't you keep it. Get one of those SIM-only deals. They're all over the place and really cheap.'

Chris shrugged and handed Mark his baguette. 'I can't really be arsed, Mark, to be honest. I mean, who phones me? Who wants to keep in touch?'

'Your mum. Claire. Me. Megan …'

Chris's laugh was bitter. 'Oh, yes. Megan. That would be the Megan smooching with Mr Perfect last night, would it? I remember that, all right, even if some of the other stuff is a bit of a blur. Let's compromise. I'll keep the phone and when and if I get myself a SIM, I'll let you have the number. Deal?'

'Well …'

'Deal?' Chris held the phone by his finger and thumb over a bin.

'Deal.' Mark unwrapped his baguette and took a bite. 'Here, I think this is yours. It's got hummus in it.'

'Sorry. I forgot you didn't like it. You don't know what you're missing.'

Mark ran a tongue around his teeth, trying to clear them of the gritty feeling. 'I think I do.' He peered suspiciously into the other sandwich. Cheese. Tomato. Not even any mayonnaise. When it came to his lunch, Mark was a bit of a stickler. Apart from anything else, he was hardly going to get more custom if he blasted them with garlic all afternoon.

They walked along in silence for a while, their lunches taking all their attention. They still ate at the same speed, walked at the same speed, just like they had as children. Some things never change.

They had finished eating before they reached the surgery and they had some time to spare. Mark pulled Chris over to a concrete bench which encircled a bed of flowers, reduced now to a few rather sorry-looking pansies. 'Look, Chris. I've been thinking … I was a bit harsh, kicking you out. You can stay if you want.'

Chris nudged him companionably in the ribs. 'Don't be daft. I can't stay with you forever and I don't want to jinx it. We've been friends for too long to get to hate each other. Guests and fish stink after three days and I stank long before that. So, let me go, Mark.' He sounded unutterably sad but there was no response possible. 'I know you love me, mate. It's not something that we say to people often enough. But you have to let me go. I can't get on with the rest of my life if I just hang around being a taker.'

'No!' Mark almost shouted, and a woman pushing a shopper past their knees flinched and scurried away. 'You're *not* a taker, Chris. Don't say that about yourself.'

'Well, it strikes me that I don't give much to anyone, except heartache and pain.'

'Foreigner,' Mark said, in a kneejerk reaction.

'What?' Oh, yes. Sorry. I didn't mean to quote. Damn. I'm going to have that bloody song in my head all day, now.'

'Me too. Thanks for that.'

'But, seriously, it's time for a new beginning. But I promise I'll let you know when I'm back on my feet.'

'Make sure you do.' Mark looked at his watch. 'Ten to. I suppose …'

'Yep. No time like the present.' They stood up and hugged each other, not awkwardly but with real emotion behind it. Neither of them wanted to let go and Chris felt a surge of love, just as he had when he had parted from his mother. Just what was still missing from his parting from Megan. And he had never even said goodbye to Kyle. They were holes in his heart that he would never be able to seal.

Finally, Mark broke away and patted Chris on the shoulder. Not until he was lost in the shopping crowd did he put his hand up and wipe away his tears.

The doctor's receptionist looked up and tilted her chin, nostrils flaring. Chris took against her on sight; so, all the stories about her kind were true. He hadn't been to the doctor's in ages although it sometimes seemed Megan practically lived there, what with her own ailments and Kyle's. The woman spoke, but it was as though each word cost money. 'Name?'

'Rowan.'

'Last name?'

'Yes.'

The woman sighed. 'I thought Rowan was your forename.' She tapped impatiently at her screen. 'I'll begin again. *Fore*name?'

'Chris. Er … Christopher. Christopher Matthew.'

'Sorry, Mr Matthew, we don't seem …'

'No. My middle name is Matthew. My surname is Rowan. Christopher Matthew Rowan.'

She clenched her lips together; in no universe known or yet to be discovered would it count as a smile. 'Thank you. Yes, I have you. Could you confirm your date of birth, please?'

At least that was simple; a number, a month, another number. What could go wrong?

'Thank you. And your address?'

Not so simple. 'I … well, I don't actually have one at the moment.'

'No fixed abode?' she said, as though each word was a vile obscenity.

'Well, I'm not sure …'

She whipped her glasses off and tapped them on the counter. 'I have to put something,' she said and swivelled the screen around to face him. 'See. Here. It is a required field.'

'I suppose you could leave it as it is,' he said. His heart clenched at the sight of his old address, his happy address, there in white on grey. He looked at the line below. It said 'Linked' and alongside it were the names of Megan and Kyle.

The glasses were back on. 'I certainly can *not*, Mr Rowan. Not now that I know it to be false. The records must be accurate.' She peered at him over her screen, now facing her again. 'We do get *audited*, Mr Rowan. How would you feel if an inaccuracy in your record got us into *trouble*?'

Clearly, the answer 'I couldn't give a toss' was not what she was expecting. He smiled and said, 'Is a care of acceptable?'

'Yes.'

'Then put, "care of Mrs S Green, St Blasius' Vicarage."'

'Oh, the vicar's wife. Is she a relative?'

'My mother.'

The receptionist's face froze. So, this was the son, was it? She had heard all about him from her sister. No better than he should be, by all accounts. She looked at the clock. Shame, but she didn't have time to bring the doctor up to speed on it all. Never mind; he was probably just here to get drugs. She had heard he was a hopeless addict, as well as mad on sex. It went together. She didn't even think of rock and roll. 'I see that a … friend … made your appointment.'

'That's right.' He didn't see why he should give this frosty cow any more information than necessary. She had clearly already made her decisions about him, so why disabuse her.

She looked him up and down and her nostrils flared again. 'Wait over there and the doctor will call you through.' She looked as though she would have preferred him to wait out in the road, in the traffic if possible, but it was against the rules.

Chris decided to stay polite. 'Thank you.' He wandered off into the corner and looked around for a dog-eared magazine three years out of date. Surely, that was another thing – along with a miserable receptionist – that told you that you were waiting at the doctor's. But there was nothing. Not even a coffee table. There were posters on the wall, but all so depressing he decided to look elsewhere. And when he did, he almost jumped out of his skin. Sitting across diagonally from him was an old lady, bent almost double, with the most enormous shopping bag he had ever seen on her lap. She and the bag were a uniform shade of grey and that was why he hadn't noticed her. But her eyes were bright and she was smiling, so he smiled back.

'That's better, duck,' she said. 'Cheer up, it might never happen. Worse things happen at sea.'

'Sorry,' Chris heard himself say. 'I'm not really feeling quite the ticket today.'

The old woman laughed phlegmily and coughed as though she

would break in two. 'Ooh,' she said. 'My chest is something awful. I have the flu jab and the pneumonia jab and any jab they have going, but you can't do nothing about old age, can you?' She knocked on her chest as though it were a door she could open and make everything well inside. 'It's the fags, that's what's done it. Forty a day since I was twelve.'

'You were on forty cigarettes a day when you were twelve?' Chris couldn't help but ask. She was old, but surely, not *that* old. She'd be telling him she worked as a chimney boy next.

'In my day,' she said, 'you didn't stay at school till you was eighteen, oh, dearie me, no. Twelve, that's when I left school. Had to help in the fields.'

Not up a chimney, then.

'Travelling people, we was. Hopping.'

Chris was puzzled. She looked in pretty ropey shape, but she clearly had two legs.

'Hopping down in Kent.' She peered at him. 'Picking hops. For beer.'

'Oh, I see. Sorry, I was a bit confused for a moment, there.'

Suddenly, the old woman lost her twinkly charm. 'Trouble with you youngsters, with your fancy ways and your phones and your computers.' Her voice rose to a wail. 'I haven't got a computer,' she cried. 'I don't understand computers. I don't understand phones. I like a bit of fish.' Her voice had dropped to a conspiratorial whisper. 'The Queen Mother used to like a bit of fish. I haven't got a computer.' And there she was, back with the wail. Chris pressed himself back against the wall, eyes wide. The old bat was clearly as doolally as all get out.

The receptionist stormed round from behind her counter. 'Mr *Rowan*!' she said. 'You're upsetting Mrs Murchison.' She bent down and patted the woman's shoulder. 'Don't worry, Mrs Murchison,' she soothed. 'The nurse will be with you in a moment.'

The woman looked up at her, with trusting eyes. 'I haven't got a computer,' she muttered.

At that moment, to Chris's relief, a door opened and a woman popped her head out. 'Mr Rowan?' she asked, pleasantly. 'Would you like to come this way?'

The consulting room was a pleasant surprise. It wasn't, like the reception area, painted a glacial white. The walls were a pale primrose and the posters on the wall, though perhaps a little on the graphic side, were not as noticeable. There were pictures on a shelf above the computer screen, of three smiling children, all leaning on a black Labrador, which was sprawling in front of them; and if a dog could smile, surely this was doing just that. The doctor herself was in her early forties, he guessed, with untidy fair hair escaping from its pins. A cup of coffee steamed faintly on the desk. She noticed his glance.

'Sorry about that,' she said, moving it to the other side of the screen. 'I had rather a hectic lunchtime; one of my patients had a fall and I had to dash out.' She smiled at him. 'But what can I do for you, Mr Rowan. We haven't seen you for a while. In fact, *I* haven't seen you at all. I inherited you, if that's the word I want, from my predecessor.' She sat back, smiling. It was clearly his turn now.

'I haven't been very well.' It was as good an opening as he could come up with.

'Now, strangely enough, that is something you share with most of my patients,' she said, still smiling. 'Can you be a little more specific?'

He sat there. He knew he only had ten minutes, if that. How could he tell her that his life was in ribbons, that he had started seeing things, that the lights in the tunnel were worse than an oncoming train, in that they seemed to be going out one by one and leaving him in an impenetrable dark. 'I have headaches,' he said. It wasn't really accurate, but it was a start.

She looked at his record on the screen in front of her. 'I see you have a prescription for naproxen, but you haven't had a refill in … gosh, years. So,' she looked at him, 'have they started increasing in frequency? Severity? Perhaps it's time for an MRI; I see you turned one down last time. Oh.' She looked at the screen and then at him, with no further comment.

'Oh? What does "Oh" mean?' He was beginning to feel the tightness in his chest.

She turned the screen further away from him. 'Mr Rowan,' she said. 'I will give you something for your migraines, of course I will. An MRI wouldn't hurt, either. But I so have a note here that says your …

wife, is it? Partner? Anyway, she has expressed concern about you over the past year or so. When she has been here for herself or,' and she leaned back to check, 'Kyle. Something about nightmares? Mood swings? Does that sound about right?'

His mouth had gone dry. He didn't know whether to be furious that Megan had been talking about him behind his back or to break down in tears of loss and pain that he had had someone who loved him that much and had thrown her away.

The doctor reached over and took one of his hands in both of hers. 'I can see you are in a very bad place, Chris,' she said, gently. 'Now, I see you have moved out of your previous address, so I assume that you have perhaps experienced a loss.'

'Nobody's died,' he said, his voice coming thick with tears.

'A loss isn't just a death,' she said, softly. 'A loss can be anything from a change of home to a loss of a job.' She read his face. 'Or even all of those. Tell me, have you had any panic attacks?'

He nodded. 'Yesterday,' he muttered. 'And I think sometimes before that. Little ones.'

'I see.' She still held his hand and he didn't want her to stop. Her palms were warm and dry and the pressure of her fingers soothed him. 'I think we need to try and deal with those, first. Then the depression …'

He pulled his hand away and began to say that he didn't have depression. Then, he remembered Cassie. He tried to put his hand back between hers, but she was tapping on the keyboard now, the moment lost. 'I … yes, I do sometimes get a bit of depression.'

'Hmm. Well, as I say, let's deal with the panic attacks for now. You can come back in, shall we say a month? Yes, in a month and by then I will have been able to make you an appointment with a therapist.' She saw his expression. 'Now, don't go all macho on me, Chris. You've come in here today and that shows you know that you need help.'

'My friend made the appointment,' he said, sounding sulky even to his own ears.

'Then, he's a very good friend,' she said. 'I've sent a digital scrip to the chemist in the High Street. You can pick it up in half an hour. It's something to help for now. Is there anything else?'

The drunken woman on Saturday night rose up accusingly and sneered at Chris. 'There … there was a woman. On Saturday …'

'Unprotected sex?' The doctor was matter of fact. 'Never very wise, Chris. But I understand. Sometimes we all want to be hugged, don't we? Well,' her fingers walked through a display of leaflets on her low shelf, 'pop yourself round to this clinic and they'll be able to give you a once over. Now, don't worry; they don't judge.' He reached out for the leaflet but she hung on to her end. 'Now, Chris, don't just bin this. Go round to the clinic now. Today. This isn't something that should wait. Do you hear me?'

'Yes. Thank you.'

'Right, so, your tasks for this afternoon. Pick up your scrip and then go to the clinic. Taking every day one at a time helps, believe me. Where are you staying at the moment?' She glanced at the screen again. 'Oh, with your mother and Rev Mike. That's nice. Well, I'll see you in a month, Chris. Things will be looking brighter then.' And she turned back to the screen, tapping keys once more.

Chris found himself back out in the reception area, like Adam cast out of Eden. Happily, Mrs Murchison, as far from an angel with a flaming sword as it was possible to imagine, had gone, leaving only a faint, grey whiff behind.

Outside the surgery, Chris hesitated. The leaflet was still in his hand and he looked briefly through it. The clinic was at the hospital, in the corridor to the left of the A&E entrance, just before you got to the Fracture Clinic. It assured the potentially pestilential that no one would judge, that they would just give sound advice for future sexual health and also make sure that any current infection would be dealt with. Speed was of the essence and the morning-after pill would also be available to suitable recipients, on request. That clinched it. There was no way he was going there when there was even the slightest risk of bumping into his … whatever you could call the woman from Saturday night. He dropped the leaflet in the bin. Now, just one more choice to make. To go to Mark's pharmacy and pick up his happy pills, or not. No choice, actually; he needed to move on and move on he would. He'd go to another doctor if he had another panic attack. Until then, the tablets could wait.

Although he was actually no further forward, he felt as if he had taken huge strides down the road to wellness. He had *done* something. Even though Mark had made him go and then the doctor had made all his plans for him, it still felt empowering that he had walked up to the counter and made himself known, even though that had taken a while. Now, another counter beckoned. Two more counters. He pulled the paper from his pocket, with Mark's neat writing on it. Right. Half an hour to get to the benefits office. And then after that, another hour till housing. With any luck, he would have a job and a roof over his head by nightfall. Bosh! He hummed as he walked along. One thing you could rely on, he told himself. You always got a good hummable tune out of Foreigner.

The dog watched him go, its wagging tail slowing to a halt. Then, it lay down to wait.

He'd be back.

God's Away on Business

*

The benefits office, job centre, whatever it was calling itself these days, was squeezed into a space between a boarded up shoe-shop and an Oxfam charity shop, which somehow put a bit of a crimp in Chris's good mood. On the concrete benches outside, a number of people sat hunched over roll-ups and just one or two had an empty Starbucks cup at their feet with a few hopeful pennies in the bottom, to encourage the others. Chris tried not to judge them, but really! They looked unemployable and so they *were* unemployable. He wasn't a political man, but the government should be addressing this kind of thing, they really should. He pushed at the double glass door and went in.

The first thing he noticed was, yet again, a boot-faced woman behind a reception desk. Was that going to be the recurring theme today? He tried not to breathe too deeply; he wasn't sure what the smell was in there. Surely, despair didn't have an actual smell, did it?

He walked up to the desk and waited to be noticed. But it appeared that the woman's expression was just a default; when she looked up at him and smiled, it was as though the sun had come out. She was younger than she had first looked and her eyes smiled along with her mouth. Chris wished she would go and give lessons to the rancid trout at the doctor's and make everyone's lives that bit more bearable.

'Chris Rowan,' he said. 'I have an appointment.'

She glanced at her screen. 'Ah, yes; you're a tiny bit early and I'm afraid we're running a tiny bit late.' Even that statement made her smile. 'Here,' she rummaged in a drawer, 'here's a token for the coffee machine. Why don't you get yourself a hot drink and grab a magazine while you wait. Mr Jefferson won't be long.'

'It's okay,' he said. 'I don't need the token. I've got plenty of change.'

Again, the smile. 'It only takes tokens,' she said. 'It prevents … you know …' and she mimed an angry shaking. 'It's best if there's no money in it.'

'Oh. I see.' Feeling a little silly, he took the token and got a coffee, in perhaps the flimsiest paper cup in the western world. Juggling the red hot liquid made it impossible to read as well, so Chris filled his time between careful sips by looking round at the others waiting patiently – or otherwise – to be seen. The receptionist called out names from time to time but didn't give any hint as to who they were going to see. The poor benighted soul in office number one seemed to get the lion's share of the work, but that may have been because he or she kept things short and sweet. On average, anyone who went into office number one was in and out within five minutes. Office number two averaged ten and whoever lurked in office number three had only taken one person since Chris arrived and he hadn't come out yet.

Chris was still mulling over which office would be best – short and sweet or a thorough grilling – when the receptionist called his name.

'Mr Rowan,' she trilled. 'Office number three, please.'

'Thank you,' he said and walked towards the door.

'Do you have all your paperwork?' she asked.

'Paperwork?'

'Our letters, benefit details, NI number. That kind of thing.'

'No. I don't have anything. I know my NIN, but that's all.'

Her smile froze. 'I see. I'm sure Mr Jefferson will be able to help you, nevertheless.' As he walked away, he saw out of the corner of his eye, that she turned to a colleague behind her, mouthing 'No paperwork' and pulling a face. This wasn't going to be pretty.

Once inside the office, things began to head downhill at a rate of knots. Mr Jefferson looked as if he had been dug up after a long and uncomfortable burial. Back when TV watching was in his own hands and not those of his mother and the vicar, Chris had been a staunch *Sleepy Hollow* fan. Megan had enjoyed it too, but mostly for the hero, who made her go all gooey. Chris enjoyed it for the sly humour and the special effects, which were pretty good. Mr Jefferson looked just like the horseman's severed head, underground for two hundred years and counting. The man finished writing and then put the pages in a file. Only then did he look up.

'Mr Rowan.' It wasn't a question, or a greeting. Just a remark.

'Yes.' Chris pulled out a chair and sat down, his bag at his feet.

The man at the far side of the desk held out his hand. 'Paperwork,' he said, moving his fingers impatiently.

'Umm ... I don't have any.' Chris saw the skull's mouth tighten. 'I do know my NIN though.' He recited it, proudly. He was the only person he knew who could do that.

'No paperwork *at all?*' The head was outraged. 'Well, I suppose we *can* start from scratch. Hmm ... I need to find the right forms. I don't usually need them ... if you will hold on a moment.' He swivelled his chair around and searched through a filing cabinet behind him. 'Yes, here we are. I prefer to work on paper first, then transfer it to the system.' He said the word as though it had holy significance. 'The system is very unforgiving of errors, Mr ... umm ...' he consulted his screen, 'Rowan. Best to make them on paper, I always say. Less trouble down the road that way.'

'Yes.' Chris felt it might be his turn to speak but had nothing to say.

Jefferson pulled the sheets across and uncapped his pen. He shot his sleeves, adjusted his glasses and was finally ready to begin. 'Let's start with full name and date of birth, shall we?'

Chris trotted them out.

'Address.'

'I don't actually ... well, I was living with ...'

The man held up a testy hand. 'Please, Mr Rowan. Just information at this stage, please. Excuses we will explore later. So, you are no fixed address?'

'Yes.' It sounded bald and brutal but was also true.

'But you have an address to which we can send correspondence. Somewhere where you visit from time to time?'

Chris thought of Mike Green's face contorted with fury. He thought of his mother's tears. 'I ... I'm not sure.'

'Well, we can hold post for you.' He made a note. 'Right, now, on to your previous employment. What was your job? I assume you are unwaged?'

'Yes. I thought that I would be ... well, talking about a new job today.'

'First things first. That is another department and I will give you details of that shortly. For the moment, we need to see what benefits you may be entitled to.' He looked over his glasses at Chris and bared his teeth in a ghastly smile. 'We are not heartless here, Mr Rowan. But we need to do things in the right order.'

'The system,' Chris said.

'Precisely. Now. Previous employment?'

'Stanley's Estates.'

'Ah, yes. In the High Street.'

'Yes.'

'And you had been with them for ...?' The pen hovered.

Chris cast his mind back. 'Four ... no, nearly five years.'

'I see. And did you hold any seniority?'

'I was ... well, it didn't have a title as such. I was the second in command, I suppose, to Mr Stanley. When he was on holiday and such, I was in charge then.'

'Right.' Another note. 'So, you lost that position because ...?'

Chris looked down at his hands, which he realised were clasped tightly together in his lap.

'Mr Rowan?'

'I ... Mr Stanley and I ...'

'An altercation.'

'He said he had had complaints ... he brought in my personal life, but he had that all wrong. I ... I walked out.'

'He sacked you?'

'Well, yes, but ... I'm not sure he meant it. I meant to go in, talk it over, but … I rang up, but he wasn't available.'

Jefferson put down his pen and took off his glasses. He took a little cloth out of a drawer and polished the lenses furiously before putting them back on. 'I need to get this right, Mr Rowan, before I enter it on the system. You were sacked, you think, because of an inaccurate personal slur and you rang back once but didn't speak to Mr Stanley. Is that it, in a nutshell?'

Chris nodded. Put like that it sounded stupid, but it *wasn't* stupid. His chest started to tighten and he concentrated on his breathing. Jefferson was beginning to recede down the tunnel.

'Did you seek legal advice?'

Chris shook his head. 'No,' he said. 'I … it seemed like a lot of trouble.'

'I see.' This time the note was long. 'Would I be right in saying, Mr Rowan, that in essence you made yourself unemployed? That steps that a reasonable person would have taken, the man, as it were, on the Clapham omnibus, to use an old analogy, would have taken, were not taken by you?'

'Well, I didn't *make* myself unemployed, no. But I suppose that, yes, I might have tried harder to fight my corner. It all seemed …'

'Like a lot of trouble. Yes. I understand. Tell me, Mr Rowan, and forgive me if this question seems a little personal, but do you take drugs of any kind?'

'No! No, I don't!'

'Please don't take offence,' Jefferson said, 'but your rather lacklustre demeanour made me wonder. Are you, then, suffering from any mental condition for which you receive medical assistance?'

The trouble with this guy, Chris decided, was that he never used one word when a dozen stupid ones would do. His hands weren't clasped any more; each one was a fist. 'No. I'm not mental!'

'I don't believe I said that.' To give Mr Jefferson credit, approaching the end of a very long day, his tone was still even. Mrs Jefferson often boasted to her friends that her husband hadn't got a temper, and this certainly had to be true. It was the only way he kept the job for so long without going stark, raving bonkers. 'If you had a diagnosis of such a condition, it would help your case immeasurably.' He didn't have a temper, but on the other hand, he couldn't tell with any accuracy whether someone else across the desk was about to lose theirs, a serious flaw which had caused quite a lot of broken furniture in office number three.

When no answer was forthcoming, Mr Jefferson carried on delivering the bad news. 'As you did, in the letter of the law, make yourself unemployed, there is no benefit I can pay you now. Taking your last day of work … did you receive money in lieu of notice?'

Chris's nod was almost imperceptible.

'Then I am afraid it will be some months before I can arrange any benefits. Are you in need now? What, for instance, did you do with your payment in lieu?'

'I paid it over to my partner. My … ex.'

'I see. And are there children of the union?'

God! Why couldn't he speak like a normal person? 'I have a son, Kyle.'

'Aged?'

'Three.'

'I see. Have you undertaken to make provision for Kyle? And has his mother, to your knowledge, registered to receive any benefits for the child?'

'I don't know. I don't *know*! I haven't spoken to her since she kicked me out. Go on!' Chris was on his feet now. 'Go on! Write that down as well.'

'I already have a note that you are of no fixed address, Mr Rowan,' the skull replied, mildly. 'I really think that I must ask you to sit down. Otherwise I won't be able to help you further.'

'Help me further? Help me *further*? You haven't exactly helped me at all, have you? Let alone further!'

'I do have a discretionary contingency payment which I can discuss with you, but only if you sit down.'

Reluctantly, Chris sat on the edge of the chair, but he could hardly see the man opposite now, for the swirling black and red mist. The black dog, which seemed to have slunk in unannounced, sat by his side and pressed itself against his leg.

'Do you have a bank account, Mr Rowan?'

'Yes. Yes, I do.'

'And are there funds available?'

'I'm still just about in credit, yes.'

'I see.' Jot. Jot, Jot. 'And do you have any cash on you?' He looked up and for a moment, a human being looked out. This was the bit he hated. The snooping, the picking apart someone's life.

'My mother gave me some ... most of it's still left. About seventy-five pounds, I think. It won't go very far.'

'Mr Rowan.' The pen was recapped and put down for the first time. 'I think you will have to make a change in your perceptions before much longer. Seventy-five pounds to someone with a roof over their head, with a salary coming in sounds like nothing. What do they call it? Pocket lint. But for someone with nothing, and I mean *nothing*, Mr Rowan, seventy-five pounds is a fortune. I can't help you today. You don't qualify for an immediate benefit, nor a contingency loan. Compared to most of the people I see from day to day, you are as rich as Croesus. I would urge you, Mr Rowan, to try and rebuild some of the bridges you seem to have burned with such abandon. I will put your details on file in case I need to see you again, but, believe me when I say, I hope you never feel the need to come here again.' He stood up and extended his hand, but this time to shake Chris's, not to gather in non-existent paperwork. 'Goodbye, Mr Rowan.'

Chris got up, confused. 'So ... that's it?'

'I'm afraid so. If you speak to Angela on the desk, she will give you some literature on how to progress to seeking employment. Good*bye*, Mr Rowan.' And before the door had closed behind Chris, Angela on the desk was calling the next person in.

Chris wanted to sit down until his legs stopped trembling and his breathing settled down but clearly the benches immediately outside were out of the question. The comment about the seventy-five pounds had hit home and he felt as though he had a neon sign on his head that said 'Mug Me'. He didn't see individuals any more, just a roiling mob of people. He felt as though he was on a caffeine rush, but filtered through a blanket. He just had to go somewhere quiet, somewhere where he could shut his own door. He pulled the piece of paper out of his pocket and there was his salvation. Housing offices in another half an hour. If he walked slowly, he could get himself back on an even keel.

The housing offices were part of the council building and so not as intimidating as the benefits place. There was no double glass door to negotiate, no crowd of people who all turned to look at him. Even the receptionist was absent; there was no desk, no boot-faced woman, not even Angela. Just a window and a bell. Not very high on the friendliness stakes, possibly, but rather less public and much less scary. He rang the bell and waited, as instructed. He settled himself in the classic queue position of all the weight on one leg, hip out, hands in pockets, but there was no need. The window slid back and, rather disconcertingly, a voice spoke from below the sill. He looked in and saw that the woman who had answered him was sitting at her desk.

'Sorry,' he said. 'I …' Her face was not very welcoming. He realised that she heard it dozens of times a day. It wasn't her fault, after all, if the office designer was clearly nuts. It was just crying out for an injury claim for repetitive strain. 'I have an appointment,' he said.

'Name?'

He really ought to get a badge. 'Christopher Matthew Rowan,' he said, speaking clearly.

She glanced at her screen. 'Mr Rowan. Yes, I have you here. Thank you for being early. We have had a cancellation, actually; would you like to go straight through?' She gestured with a nod of her head to the door in the wall to his right and he knocked and went in.

The woman behind the desk was leaning back in her chair, a phone in one hand and a mouthful of biscuit. She bounced upright in a spray of crumbs. 'Oh, sorry,' she said, laughing and brushing bits of biscuit off her front and off the papers on the desk. 'Just having a bit of down time because of a cancelled appointment. Are you … no, you're clearly not Mrs anyone, are you? Am I still allowed to make that kind of assumption, I wonder, in these politically correct days? No, but you must be Mr Rowan.'

Chris warmed to the woman. She had a pleasant face, nothing special, nothing you would recognize again unless she was a friend or relative. But she was, for that same reason, non-threatening. She was probably ten years his senior but didn't have the family photos all around to rub in the fact that she had it all and you had nothing. She held out her hand and he took it, gratefully. It was warm and still a little bit crumby. She felt the crumbs dig into her palm and apologised again, laughing.

'Sorry. Hobnobs are a bit of a failing of mine. Like one?' She proffered the packet.

'Thank you.' He realised that he was hungry. His ham and hummus baguette seemed a very long time ago and the scalding coffee was a memory he would rather forget.

She turned to the shelf behind her desk. 'Tea? Coffee?' she asked. 'I hit the wall around this time of day and need a bit of a pick-me-up.'

'I'd love one, thank you.' The coffee arrived, over-heated and acrid but with real milk, real sugar and in a mug which said 'World's Best Golfer'. He held it up. 'Golfer? I've never really taken to it, myself.' Dave Stanley had dragged him round a course once or twice but it had been something of a fiasco.

'Me? Heavens no! That mug's been here since Adam was in the militia. It kind of went with the job, if you see what I mean. Along with a four year backlog of files, but we'll draw a veil over that. Now, then, let's see ... Do you have a file?' She looked around her at the teetering piles. 'I really hope not, because the chances of finding it are slim.' She smiled at him again. 'Sorry.'

'No. I don't have a file. I ... it's a long story.'

She spread her hands. 'I have some time. Why not tell me?'

And he found himself doing just that. He sanitised it a bit; he didn't want this nice woman to think he was as promiscuous and drunken as the last few months made him sound. He wasn't that person. But he needed to lay it on the line. He needed somewhere to stay and that was it.

She made suitable noises throughout his recital and at the end, leaned back in her chair again, making the springs protest. 'Mr Rowan ... may I call you Chris?'

He nodded.

'I think that is one of the most dreadful things I have heard in this office, and I've heard a few. May I ask ... have you been to your GP?

It sounds to me as if you may have a bit of a problem with depression. Hmm?' She raised an eyebrow.

'I saw her today ...'

'Good. Now, the news on the housing front isn't great. You don't really score enough on my scale to get you anywhere any time soon, I'm afraid. And I have to warn you, if and when somewhere does come up, I doubt it would be what you're used to. It would be a one bedroom flat, at best.'

'I don't expect anything much ...' although as he spoke, Chris realised he had been imagining a cottage with roses round the door. 'I was a letting agent, don't forget. I know what's out there.'

'Yes. You know what some of your tenants were running from, but I doubt you ever went there. However, let's not be downhearted. I imagine you've been to the job centre? Applied to agencies online, all that kind of thing?'

'I haven't been to the job centre, no, but I am with all the agencies ...' It suddenly struck him like a hammer that he didn't have a computer any more; he could have had a dozen offers that very day and he wouldn't know. He had also given out his mobile number as first contact. He jumped out of his seat in panic and shock.

'Chris?' She half got up, in sympathy. 'Are you all right?'

He turned a haggard face to her. 'I ... I just realised. I don't have access to a computer. My phone ... I ... I ...'

'Sshh. Sit down. Let me get you a glass of water. Stay there.'

She went through a door at the back of the office and he heard her ask someone for the water. He heard his name. Then he heard her drop her voice and say something he couldn't catch. But he could guess. Is that Chris Rowan in there? Chris Rowan from Stanley's? How are the mighty fallen. He slumped with his head in his hands and felt the black mist swirling. It must have come into the room with the dog.

He felt a cool glass being pressed into his hand and a warm hand on his back. Slowly, he felt better and sat up.

'Sorry.'

'No need to apologise. It's a frightening world, sometimes. Now, just so you know for the future, there are computers at the job centre and in the library which are free to use. Just a word to the wise, they will probably condescend to you and assume you don't know how to switch one on. Be patient with them; they mean well and they deal with computer duffers all day long. But you can log on and check your job offers from there as often as you want. But for now, as I said, the news isn't great. I'll just check what we have as emergency rooms.' She tapped the keyboard and tutted as the mouse refused to do its stuff. 'I do apologise,' she said. 'These computers are out of the ark. Umm ...' she peered closer. 'I have a room in ... no, no, that's not really ... umm ... personal question, Chris, but we have to ask this. Do you have *any* money?'

'Some. I have some cash and a few hundred in the bank.'

'In that case, I can help you in the short term. I have a list of bed and breakfast places that will take people on our recommendation for a nominal sum. They just don't want to lie empty, is the thing, really. Breakfast is extra, but you don't have to have it. They vary in how much value they are, in fact, so ... hello. This is a nice one. Niceish. Owned and run by a couple, very pleasant. The snag is some of their rooms are twin. You may have to share. How do you feel about that?'

Until he had moved in with Megan, Chris had never shared any sleeping space with anyone for more than a night and certainly never a stranger. 'I'm not keen,' he said. 'If there is anything else ...'

'The snag is that it isn't after half term yet.'

'Sorry?'

'Amazingly, there is a tourist season, even here. We're a cheaper option than Oxford, apparently.' She shrugged her shoulders. 'Who knew? But it does mean that some of our rooms aren't available until after the October half term. That's only about three weeks away. Look – I don't usually recommend this but ... can you sofa surf until then? This isn't official policy, so don't hare off round to the local paper telling them I said so. But in your situation, deliberately homeless, deliberately jobless – my hands are tied. I will put you on the list. I *have* put you on the list; but unless you can suddenly conjure up a few dependants and a darned good reason for not having a job, I don't see my being able to help you within the next six months, to be optimistic about it. Chris.' She reached forward and took his hand, the second time it had happened to him today and this time he clung on. 'I am so, so sorry I can't help you. But something will turn up, you'll see.'

'Sofa surfing it is, then,' he said, getting up, still reluctant to let go. 'I'll keep checking my emails. Thanks for the tip on where to go online.'

'Good luck, Chris,' she said, and clearly meant it. 'Can you flip down the name tag on the door as you go out? You're my last for today.' She waved at the piles of manilla. 'I think I'll fill in the last hour or so with a spot of filing.' She took the top file off a pile and blew on it; the air filled with dust and fluff. 'Or dusting. Possibly both.' She looked up at him with a sweet smile. 'Goodbye.'

He went out gently, so as to not make any more dust fly in the golden afternoon light just filtering through the filthy council windowpane. She heard him obediently flip down the name tag. Only then did she put her head in her hands. 'God,' she muttered to herself through her fingers. 'God, I hate my job.'

I Can Let Go Now

*

Outside once more, still jobless, still roofless but now more dejected than ever, Chris walked on into the gathering dusk. The backpack bounced on his kidneys with every step and he toyed more than once with binning it. But as it contained all he owned, he thought twice. Actually, he thought, it wasn't all he owned. He owned half a house or, perhaps more accurately, half of the equity in a house. He owned a lot more clothes; not exactly designer, but they were his and they were still hanging in a wardrobe, just a few miles away. Unless they were in a charity shop somewhere, dumped in black bags by Megan or, more likely, her mother or Sam. He had a son, too; not exactly a possession, of course, but nevertheless something to call his own. However, to all intents and purposes, all he really owned was bumping now with every step, onto his kidney. Bump. Bump. Bump.

He looked at his options as he walked, the thoughts somehow getting into time with his steps. Soon, they were just one word. Claire.

Megan picked up the phone as soon as the first ring sounded. She had rejected all calls from Sam on Sunday. Lily and Will had ended up staying for lunch and as she looked around her table, Megan couldn't help smiling. To anyone passing by and glancing in, they would have looked like a normal family. Husband, wife, pretty kid, mother – or mother-in-law, depending in the angle of view. They didn't look anything like their actual selves: the woman who slept with a bloke on a first date, and a blind one at that; the bloke who actually agreed to sleep with the aforementioned woman; the babysitter who had a magic touch with kids but nevertheless not much of a home to go to if she could extend her stay by 18 hours and more and the child, the only one of the party who actually was what he was. She tried to imagine Chris sitting in Will's place, carving the chicken, teasing Kyle with the hated sprouts but try as she might, she couldn't. It was probably her fault, she told herself. No one knew how to be someone's significant other just naturally; there had to be a bit of training, perish the thought. Unless you were a mind reader, and who could honestly say they were one of those? Will had had at least one trainer, she knew, so perhaps that explained why he was so good at being the man of the house. Lily … well, she was just that rare person, an adult who actually liked children. So that left her – she was the joker in this pack, for sure.

But now, Monday afternoon, taking Kyle back from nursery, tired, cranky, missing Lily, she began to think that perhaps the whole weekend had been some kind of dream. You heard of these things – people who had functioned perfectly normally for weeks on end, without anyone being aware that what they saw and what the somnambulist saw were completely at odds. But that would be pushing it. No, it had happened and although she knew it wasn't going to change her life, she was glad it had; she had had a small taste of normality and nurturing after what was now beginning to feel like a lifetime of … what? There wasn't a name for it, unless it was 'Less'. That was it; her life had always been less than it could be.

And now the phone was ringing. It was Sam; it had to be. Her mother never used the mobile, because she couldn't remember the number, she said. Megan didn't care about the reason; it was good to know that there was at least one place she could keep mother-free with no discernible effort.

'Sam. Sorry, I've rejected your calls. I didn't want to …'

'Megan. It's Will.'

'Oh, I'm sorry … I thought …'

He chuckled. 'I thought I'd jump in quickly before you said something that perhaps I didn't want to hear. Such as "I didn't want to ever see Will again" or "I didn't want to tell you what a total dick Will is". See, even if I am a dick, I'm a thoughtful dick.'

She laughed down the phone. 'Fool,' she said. 'Of course that wasn't what I was going to say. In fact,' she took a deep breath. This wasn't like her. She didn't say sloppy things, not ever. 'I was going to say, I didn't want to interrupt my day with Will.'''

There was a silence at the other end, long enough for her to know she had blown it. She put her head down on the work surface in the kitchen and bumped it gently up and down. 'Wow,' he said, finally. 'I wasn't expecting that. Thank you. I … I know this sounds ridiculous, we've only just met, but … I've really missed you today.' His little laugh sounded like a teenager. 'I feel such a fool. Look, I'm sorry. That's too much pressure. You've got enough on your plate …'

'No, really. Will, hush, just hush. I've missed you too. I can't explain it, it's just that … I seem to have spent my life apologising to people for their own behaviour and … well, I don't need to do that with you.'

'Because I'm perfect, clearly.'

'No,' she said, laughing. 'Because you don't have to be bolstered up all the time. And now who's doing the pressure?'

'I need to come round. There's something I have to tell you.'

And bosh! There it was, Megan thought. Just when you thought it was safe to relax, the sucker punch. 'Oh.'

'Don't say "Oh" like that. It's nothing bad. Well, I don't think it's bad. But I need to be the one to tell you. Okay?'

'Okay. Nothing bad.' She sounded like a little girl, she realised, but she couldn't help it. She hadn't liked this guy at first, he wasn't her type, no matter how you looked at it, but she really needed to be looked after right now. And she thought that, for a while, he might.

'Nothing bad, I promise. I've been a bit cheeky and got Lily to come round tonight. We don't have to go out if you don't want to, but it will save you having to worry about Kyle. If you want to go out, fine. Come round to mine, fine. It's your call.'

This was crazy. She just couldn't make decisions any more. 'Yours?' It was half question, half statement.

'Mine it is. I'll pick you up at seven. We'll order takeaway, so don't eat. See you.' And that was it, phone down. Businessmen didn't hang about, she thought. Sometimes when she had been on the phone to Chris, it had taken them ten minutes to decide who would hang up. She gave herself a mental slap – stop comparing this guy with Chris. It was like comparing chalk with cheese.

The phone rang again. Sam. She thought for a moment, then rejected the call. Tomorrow; tomorrow she would talk to Sam, but before that, she needed to know what Will had to say.

Claire opened the door to Chris with the same enthusiasm as he imagined medieval peasants did to the plague doctor. 'Chris.' It was neither statement, nor question, nor welcome.

'Claire.' Right back atchya. 'I guess Mum has rung ...'

'Oh, yes. She has. I gather the vicar got sussed at last.' Claire always called him 'the vicar' as if to use his name would choke her. She looked at her brother, standing on the doorstep. When they were kids, they had got on; they got on now, as long as they didn't see too much of each other. She missed him sometimes, just as he missed her. But the memory always turned out to be better than reality after an hour or two. But for this evening, dissing Mike Green up hill and down dale would keep them off the usual argument subjects like ... everything. She smiled and reminded him of Cassie. 'Come on in. Tell me all about it. But, Chris, we have to have this clear. One night. No getting pissed.'

'One night. Sober as a judge.' Chris stepped inside and reached for a hug. She squeezed him once, then let go.

'You smell a bit ...'

He sniffed his sleeve. 'Smell? Do I? What of?' Surely, not desperation already, like the guys on the benches outside the Social?

'It's just ... old clothes, I think. I'm guessing ... Mum rifled the jumble sale pile, yes?'

'Well, yes ... but a while ago. These have been cleaned, washed, everything.'

'Yeah, but it lingers, doesn't it?' She looked down at their feet. 'That bag. Is that all you've got?' She could always cut straight to the chase, straight to his heart.

'I … I didn't bring stuff with me,' he said, hearing the whine enter his voice. 'I just …'

'Walked out. Yes, I know.'

'How do you know?' Belligerent, now. They seemed to be packing at least a week of arguments into five minutes.

'Well, I rang Megan, of course. Kyle is my nephew, after all. Nothing is going to change that. She wasn't very forthcoming. Let's face it, Chris, she and I never exactly saw eye to eye. But she did mention that you hadn't taken much.'

'Umm … did she say what she had done with my stuff?'

'It wasn't that kind of conversation. Anyway,' she sniffed again. 'Sorry, Chris. You really do pong.' She glanced up at the clock on the wall and reached for her car keys. 'Look. Let's go out to Tesco. We can get something for supper that isn't takeaway; do you fancy steak? I haven't had red meat for ages but once in a while can't kill us, can it? And while I do the food shop, you can choose some new clothes. If you pick with care, you won't look *too* Florence and Fred. Or we could do Asda, for some nice George. Or Sainsbury's …'

'Claire. Stop. I've got hardly any money. I was told today … well, I'm not going to tell you everything I was told today, but let's just say I'm not getting any help any time soon. So, clothes are way down my priority list.'

'What did I buy you for your last birthday?'

He was startled. 'Nothing. We never buy for each other at birthdays. Never have, as far as I can recall.'

'Well, there you are, then. We've got a few decades of presents to catch up on. So a few pairs of jeans and some jumpers won't hurt. Put your bag in the corner, there, and let's get going. The Tesco is 24 hour – let's go there. They've got a better choice for men as well – Gok Wan isn't really in touch with his masculine side.'

'You know you're speaking a foreign language, don't you?' he said, giving her a brief hug. He knew when his sister wasn't going to take no for an answer.

She looked up at him and smiled Cassie's smile again, with a hint of Kyle around the eyes. 'I asked for a sister,' she said, 'and I just got you. I complained, but apparently, you can't send babies back.' She crossed her eyes. 'I understood why not when we had sex education lessons.'

They went out, laughing, to the car. But just for one night, Chris thought. Let's not spoil it. The Chinese might say that guests and fish both stink after three days, but in Claire's book, guests just stank. Full stop.

Megan was excited in a way she hadn't been for years. Part of the reason for the butterflies in her stomach was anticipation. But a far greater part was fear. She felt like she had as a child when she couldn't have a favourite toy. Her mother's idea of parenting had been reward and punishment, with the latter being her own personal favourite. Megan had learned not to show she liked something because that was the best and quickest way of having it taken away. And that was what she was feeling now.

Kyle had greeted Lily with more enthusiasm than Megan had seen him show in months. They had gone off into the autumn garden on business of their own and she had got ready with far more care than she had the previous Saturday night. Then she had something to prove. Now, she just wanted to look her best. She had never felt this before, this sudden onset of what some might call stupidity. She had known Chris for ages before they even spoke. Moving in together, having Kyle, had all been done because it was expected. And the fact that most of her friends and none of her family had liked Chris was almost an added bonus; if no one thought he was all that special, no one would try and take him away from her. Her heart jumped at the thought of him; she still loved him so much, but knew for her own sake she had to try and stop. Because here was the rest of her life. And if she wasn't very much mistaken, it was pulling up outside now and pipping the horn.

Kyle rushed over and gave her a hug as she popped her head around the back door but there were no tears, no tantrums. She wondered whether she would ever be able to make him smile like that; somehow, Lily had found a way into his little world and he was happy to have her there. Never mind; time to worry about that another day. For now, she just needed to make her heart beat quietly enough to allow normal conversation.

She shut the door and walked the few steps to the kerb. The car was, of course, long and sleek. It didn't have a child seat in the back. It didn't smell just ever so slightly of old sandwich wrappers and small boy. She reached for her seat belt and bought herself a few seconds of not having to make eye contact with Will, not having to decide whether to kiss him or not. He smiled at her and put the car in gear. She felt that he knew all the tricks, that she couldn't make him feel awkward, no matter what she did and although she didn't like smooth men as a rule, it was certainly nice not to have to second guess him all the time. The car was as smooth as its owner. There seemed to be no sound inside the leather-scented cocoon. She turned to him eventually and returned his smile.

'You must think I'm weird.'

'Not really.' He smiled again. 'Well, possibly a little. But in a good way.'

'There's a good way of being weird?'

'You don't seem to be a homicidal maniac. You had plenty of chance to hatchet me to death over the weekend and you didn't, so that's a bit of a plus in my book. My mind was often,' he lowered his eyelids and smiled a slow smile, 'elsewhere.' He slowed down, looking carefully for a parking space. 'Hold on a minute. This is where I show my inner psychopath. Finding a permit space here is like finding the Holy Grail.'

'There's one!' She pointed excitedly.

'Good girl!' He slid the car effortlessly into the space. 'And just outside, too.'

Megan had never been that keen on being called good girl. It was demeaning and condescending ... wasn't it? But there was nothing like that about Will. He handed her out of the car, he pushed open the double glass doors of his block, he ushered her into the lift. None of this seemed demeaning to her. In fact, it made her want to purr like a cat that had finally found the cream. And she would have purred, except that there was still the nagging voice in her head, the voice that sounded sometimes like Sam and sometimes like her mother, that said that surely, surely this was all too good to be true. Why should this all be happening to a loser like you?

The flat he ushered her into was like something out of a magazine. She and Chris had often laughed at the places they saw on TV – not a newspaper out of place, not even a single wilting leaf on a plant. No dog or cat hair, no coffee cup with the dregs gone hard and just that bit furry. Megan's place was looking the best it ever had, her evenings lately being full of nothing but time, but it would never be as clean as this. She looked at Will and laughed.

'God, this is tidy!' she said. 'I don't know where to sit in case I squash a cushion.'

He shrugged. 'It's only tidy because I'm hardly ever here,' he said. 'I often sleep at the office. We've got a little bedsit thingie there. Brian doesn't use it because …'

'He's got Sam.'

'Well, yes, I suppose that's right.'

Megan looked dubious. 'You mean Brian's playing away?'

Will laughed. 'It's what Brian does. You don't get to his age with no wife, even an ex one, without being a bit … unreliable. I'm sure Sam knows what she's getting in to. She's not exactly monogamous, if what I hear is true.'

Megan took a step back and set her mouth. 'That's my best friend we're talking about,' she said, coldly.

'I'm sorry,' he said. 'Speaking out of turn. Let me take your coat then you can squash the cushion of your choice while I get the takeaway menu.'

She shrugged out of her coat and chose a chair that was so huge she felt like Kyle must do every day of his life; as if she was in a land of giants.

He walked across the room from the hall with a tablet in his hand. 'Budge up,' he said, squeezing in beside her. 'That chair is a bit big for one though,' and he eased a thigh for a moment, trying to get comfortable, 'just a threat too small for two, I admit.' He held up the tablet. 'Chinese? Italian? Indian? Mongolian? A combination of all four?' He looked at her. 'Megan. Say something.'

'I'm not hungry,' she said.

'You're not hungry and …?'

'There's no and,' she said. 'We'll eat later.'

'Did I upset you, talking about Brian?'

'No. Well, yes. But I know you brought me here to tell me something and suddenly, I need to know what it is. Then we'll eat. If … if I still want to stay.'

'You can go when you want,' he said, 'but I don't think what I'm going to tell you is going to put you off your food, you know. But if you'd rather wait …'

She nodded. It was hard to speak with her heart in her mouth.

'Okay,' he said, and pulled her closer so she was half on his lap. She rested her head on his shoulder and closed her eyes. It was easier that way. 'I wasn't sure how much if at anything Brian and Sam had told you about me.'

'I hadn't even heard of you until I met you on Saturday. I hadn't heard about Brian, either, to be honest. It's not like Sam to keep things back, but she had.'

'Right. Well, in that case, this is going to be easier. Brian is prone to telling everyone I'm gay …'

She twisted her neck round to look up into his face. 'Pardon?'

'Well, it's not unknown, is it, for fathers of ten to suddenly come out. But in my case, it isn't true. I had a … I don't know the word. A troll. A stalker. A cross between the two. I think I know who it was, but we'll get to that later. For about the last three years, there have been things appearing on social media and other platforms … you'll have to excuse me if I go a bit jargony, it goes with the job, I suppose. Anyway, they haven't been overly outrageous, they don't use bad language; in fact, they have been carefully crafted not to alert any bots or anything and get the posts booted off. But they all say one thing. That although I appear to like women, I am actually gay. The person gives dates and details.'

'Is that it?' Megan didn't look up this time. Bells were beginning to go off in her head.

He leaned his cheek briefly on her head and gave her a squeeze. 'That's often enough,' he said. 'I'm always torn whether to tell or not to tell. Either way usually means my calls go to voicemail. No smoke without fire, that kind of thing.' He waited for a moment. 'But not with you, it seems.'

'No.' She struggled upright. 'Can we squash some other cushions?

This chair is really uncomfy.'

He laughed and got out of her way so she could get up. 'Isn't it? But the designer ... they were trendy at the time.'

'Designers?'

'Oversize chairs. I'll change it if you don't like it.'

They stood looking at each other as the words sank in. 'I ... it's no business of mine, is it?' she said at last.

'Perhaps not,' he muttered and sat on the settee, patting the next seat. 'Let's hear it, then.'

'I don't know ... I ...' She sat down and leaned back, arms folded across her chest, facing forward. And she told him everything. About Chris. About Louise. About how her life had suddenly unravelled and how now, having heard his story, she wasn't sure any more.

'Did you believe him?' he asked, simply. 'When he told you what had happened, did you believe him?'

'Yes.' And she had. She really had.

'Then why did you throw him out?'

'Well ... he'd ...' She had no answer.

'You threw him out,' Will said, 'because you didn't want him to be there any more. You didn't want his nightmares, his moods, his, well his lies, if that's what you thought they were. If you believed him, *truly* believed him and wanted him, wild horses on their bended knees couldn't have prised him from you.'

She sank her chin on her chest and let the tears flow down and soak into the silk of her shirt, chosen so carefully not so long before.

He reached out and stroked her arm. 'I'm not judging you, Megs,' he said, and she flinched at the endearment. 'I've had it done to me. I've done it. Life isn't simple. Sometimes, someone who you love to the moon and back is bad for you. Sometimes, someone you can just about tolerate is the best thing to keep your life on track and you well and happy.'

She nodded and sniffed. He was right. But that didn't make everything else right. Was her life a mess still, or was it turning a corner? She wriggled deeper into the cushions. She felt the settee move as he leaned back on the arm and she knew he was looking at her. She closed her eyes tighter. She had so messed this up.

'Megan. Listen to me. I'm older than you. I sometimes think I've seen it all. Nothing's perfect. Nothing's forever. Looking for a happy ever after is the best way never to find it. I think the happiest people are those who take things a step at a time. Shall we?'

'Shall we what?' Oh, God, now she sounded like Kyle.

'Take things a step at a time. Let's start from the point where I'm definitely not gay and you're not a heartless cow and go from there. Hmm?'

She smiled in spite of herself.

'Can we add one more thing?'

'Okay.' It was almost a question.

'Can we say that I am a hungry definitely not gay person and you are a hungry not heartless cow and order some bloody food before I die of starvation?'

She wiped her tears with the back of her hand and sat up, tucking her legs beneath her. 'Right,' she said, with a final sniff. 'Not Mongolian, though.'

'You're right,' he said. 'I think one helping of yak is ample for one lifetime. Shall we do Chinese?'

'Let's. And, Will …'

'Yup?' He was already scrolling down the menu on his tablet, ready to order before she changed her mind.

'Will you help me find Chris? Put things right?'

'If that's what you want, that's what we'll do. Shouldn't be hard. We'll go round the family, friends, at the weekend. Yes? Better face to face than phone, don't you think? I won't come in; I'll just be chauffeur.'

She reached out and pinched him on the arm.

'Ow.' He frowned. 'What was that for?'

She smiled and rubbed the place. 'Just checking,' she said. 'Just checking.

The End of the Affair

*

Chris sat across from his sister and looked at her in the soft light of the lamps. Her home may be closed to more or less everyone, but she had made it nice. It was calm and cosy, cluttered without being untidy; the home of a woman at ease in her skin. As she looked back at him, a smile playing on her lips, she did remind him very much of Cassie. He reminded himself to see if he could find her somehow; he missed her, now he understood what she was trying to do for him.

'So,' Claire said, suddenly. 'You don't think she'll have you back, then?'

'I never really thought it was an option,' he said. 'I was lucky she let me stay after … well, after that first thing, in the house I was showing. I don't know why she did.' He didn't tell her about the man he had seen her with. Perhaps he had misunderstood the whole situation and best said, soonest mended.

'Because she loves you,' Claire said, simply.

'Then, why throw me out when the only thing that happened was that that bitch went to her work and told her a load of lies?'

Claire smiled coldly. 'You can hear what you say, can you, Chris? You don't think it odd that you can say "only" in front of that remark? Of course it was the last straw. The woman confronted her. At her place of work. And if they were lies …'

'Of course they were lies!' He was on his feet now, the dog bouncing round the room, panting. Walkies!

'I repeat, *if* they were lies, they must have been damned convincing ones.'

Chris didn't sit back down. He stood there, in his mid-range shirt, jumper and trousers. Down to his skin, he was F&F; Claire had just bought the whole package. It wasn't actually sold as 'Dress Your Loser Brother Like A Mid-Range Exec' but it could have been; a marketing opportunity missed, he thought. 'They were lies,' he muttered and sat down again but on the very edge of the seat. 'I didn't ...'

'Yes you did.' She used the tone she had used to him all his life. 'You told me you did.'

'Only after the party and then again at the house.' His voice trailed away. He knew how it sounded.

'But you can see how it sounds, surely?' his sister said, exasperated. 'I'm your sister, Chris, I can say what I like and I'm going to, is that all right?'

The black dog leaned against his leg and waited. This was going to be good.

'My advice,' and of course by that she meant that it was her explicit order, 'is that you go and see this Louise woman. Ask her why she is telling these lies about you. I can't see what she is getting out of this. Why would she weave this incredible story if you only slept with her twice?'

He tensed and she held up a hand for silence.

'I'm sorry, Chris, but you are my brother and perhaps this is why I don't see it. You are a nice enough looking bloke, I suppose. I certainly had to beat a few of my friends off, back in the day. But you're nothing special. You're not exactly ...' she was stuck for the appropriate phrase and so just waved her hands vaguely between them, '... stacked, are you? For all I know, and let's leave it vague, you could be hung like a mule and have the technique of a porn star but somehow, I doubt it. I would have heard.'

He opened his eyes wide. 'Who from?'

'From whom,' she corrected, automatically. 'Don't tell me you've forgotten the one friend I didn't beat off with a stick?' She looked at him in mock sternness.

He blushed a little and looked down.

'Yes, that's right,' she said. 'Blush. Tanya was my best friend before you let her have her way with you.' She smiled.

'I thought that I had *my* way with *her*.'

'Bless your little heart,' she said. 'But that's a case in point and why you must go and see this woman.'

'And then I can go home?'

The yearning in his voice almost broke her heart, but she knew if she caved in now they would be growing old together, two weird old siblings in a strange and dependent mutual stranglehold. 'Well, it certainly won't happen if you don't, now will it?' It seemed the kindest way.

He looked at the clock. 'Now?' He was doubtful.

'A bit late. Go to where she works, if you know it.'

'Yes, I do know. She filled in the forms when she took on the let. It's that surgery in the High Street.'

'Perfect. Go there and face her down. It would be a lesson to her if nothing else. Now, what do you watch on telly these days?'

'I haven't been watching much, to be honest. I didn't really get the chance at Mum's. Mike …'

'… was off having a wank.'

'*Claire!*' She still shocked him when she talked like that. Like you didn't like to think of parents having sex, sisters also were out of bounds.

'Well, God, Chris. You were the one that shopped him to Mum. Don't go all mealy-mouthed on me now.'

'That wasn't what I was going to say,' he said, 'I was going to say …'

'He was off bonking the brains out of a hooker? Shagging the secretary of the Young Mums? Having a …'

'Are we going to have a reasonable conversation, or not?' His inner prude was showing.

'I am trying to make a point, here,' Claire said, with a smile. 'I just don't see you as a sex god, somehow. You won't even use rude words.'

'No, but I will have sex with a drunken woman up an alley.' The sentence was out before he heard it coming. He could hardly face it himself and her he was, telling his sister.

'Let's not go there,' she said. 'Perhaps another time. But, Chris, seriously, I don't know whether to tell you to stop drinking or start keeping it in your pants. Perhaps both would be a plan.'

He sat back, mouth set in a tight line.

'Drink. Sex. They only take your mind off the black dog, you know,' she said kindly, sounding more like Cassie than ever. 'They don't make it go away.'

The dog's tail thumped softly on the floor. This woman knew what she was talking about, alright.

Megan twisted her head around to look at the clock, glowing red by the bedside. She leaped up.

'God! Will! It's gone one in the morning. I must go!'

He draped a lazy arm over her and pulled her back down and under the quilt. 'No, you don't. Lily's staying, don't forget. Kyle's in bed. You don't need to be back until breakfast.'

'What if he wakes?'

'Lily's there.'

'But he'll want *me*.'

'Of course he will. But Lily will get him back to sleep. As long as you're there by breakfast. And anyway, *I* want you. Look.' He raised the quilt and in the dim light from outside filtering through the curtains she could see that he certainly did. And, as it turned out, she wanted him as well. But she had to be firm. She had been a slave to Chris's moods and nightmares. She couldn't let herself be slave to this man as well.

'No, I'm going.' She sounded firm, she thought, although clearly not firm enough, because his arm became heavier and she was pinned down.

'Go later,' he wheedled. 'I'll take you home myself. Just let me …' and he stifled her complaints with a kiss. And then some.

'As long as I get home for breakfast,' she murmured.

'Looking forward to it. Weetabix, is it?'

'Readybrek.'

'Mmm. Jam?'

'Of course.'

He rolled over onto her, taking the weight on his arms. 'Then it's a deal.'

After that, she stopped worrying about Kyle. In fact, she stopped worrying. Full stop.

Claire hadn't softened her stance on visitors the next morning and so Chris was out of there when she was, bag over his shoulder. The most she would do as a compromise was to offer him some money, to check in to a B&B or a cheap hotel while he got himself together. He refused it. She tucked it into his pocket nevertheless. And he didn't refuse again. He knew she loved him, but she was the cat that walked by itself and nothing would change that. On the pavement, they needed to go in separate directions but before they did, she cupped his face in a capable hand.

'Chris,' she said, gently, 'take care of yourself. Let me know how you're doing and … drop in whenever you like. For a meal. For a chat.'

'But not to stay.'

'I can't do that,' she said, with a shake of her head. 'You're not the only one in the family with problems, you know. I just can't share my space. Never could. Never will. Remember the arguments when Mum told me to share my toys?'

'Yes.' Many was the Christmas Day that had ended in storms of tears.

'Well, it's that. But bigger now, just like we are. And you're the same. Face your childhood, Chris. Face it and beat it. Or learn to live with it. Or it will kill you, for sure.' She patted his cheek then leaned up for a kiss. 'Take care. Don't be a stranger,' and she turned on her heel and walked away without a backward glance. That way, he wouldn't see she was crying. That was the secret, she told herself. Never let them see you cry.

The High Street GP practice was like a circle of Hell, one pretty near the centre, Chris guessed. There were howling children, coughing old men, shrill women and a belligerent early – or was it late? – drunk. Chris waited in line and finally reached the counter.

'Name?' the woman rapped out, not looking up.

'Louise Taylor.'

That got her attention and she stopped hammering on her keyboard and made eye contact. 'Gender reassignment clinics are on every third Wednesday, at the hospital.' She gave him another look; he was going to take a *lot* of work.

'No.' He knew he would have to be patient. Polite and patient, when he wanted to bounce her head off the counter. 'I would like to speak to Louise Taylor.'

She looked at him again, searchingly. 'Excuse me a moment,' and she ducked into a door behind her and disappeared into a brief snatch of office noise. Chris waited, drumming his fingers on the countertop and smiling every once in a while at the woman behind him, who was edging nearer and nearer so that her shopping bag was pressing into the sensitive spot behind his knee. He didn't move his leg, though – he knew if he did she would invade the space he left in an instant.

In another burst of conversation, the woman was back. 'I'm afraid Miss Taylor isn't available,' she said, with a frosty smile.

'Could you tell me when she will be available?' Still the politeness, still the urge to put one on her.

'I'm afraid not.' She moved in closer, as closely as she could with the width of the counter between them. 'I'm afraid she doesn't work here any more,' she mouthed. 'She … left.'

'Oh.' This was a bit of a facer. 'Oh. I see. Do you know where she works now?'

'I'm afraid not.' The words were unequivocal but the expression was not. It said that she could tell him rather a lot about what happened and where Louise Taylor now was, but confidentiality precluded it. 'I believe she is still in town, though. I saw her in Morrisons the other day.'

Was that a ghost of a wink?

'It was late.' She glanced from side to side. 'She was on a till,' she murmured and gave him a meaningful nod. 'Late shift.' Then, in a different voice, she spoke over his shoulder to the woman with the bag. 'Mrs Dunford,' she said, brightly. 'How can I help you?'

But before the woman could begin her litany of woe, Chris was out of there and striding off down the street, to the supermarket. If he had to buy a packet of crisps to get to speak to Louise Taylor, always and forever That Bitch in his head, then so be it.

'I'm afraid she isn't here,' the woman on Customer Service said. 'She works the late shift. Do you know where she lives? Or you could leave her a message.' She was looking Chris up and down. Not bad. Not bad at all. A bit dowdy as to the dress sense, but you couldn't have everything. He looked like someone dressed by his big sister. But Louise Taylor was no prize. Going over the hill and fast, in the opinion of the girls on the tills. Come down in the world, that was certain; she had been seen dressed to the nines going into the GP surgery up the road and now here she was, on the graveyard shift on a till. Something was up; could this guy be the answer? She would have loved to have taken him out for a drink, got the skinny on the Taylor cow, as she was universally known. But now was not the time. He was speaking.

'I do know her address, thank you. I won't leave a note for now – if I can't find her at home, I'll pop back later.' He gave her a smile which made her blush. If she had only known how rare it was, she would have treasured it more.

The staff room at the High Street Practice was small, but adequate for the numbers who worked there. This gave it an air of intimacy, well suited for the conversation that was taking place. Louise Taylor had started there not that many months ago, coming highly recommended by her previous employers and at first had been a breath of fresh air, improving systems, tidying frowsty cupboards, generally doing good. Everyone liked her. For about two weeks; then, the sidelong glances began and the covert gossip was not long behind. The GPs, on the whole, were an unexciting bunch. The usual mix of part-time returners from motherhood, those who were over retirement age but had stayed on because they couldn't leave their patients and just the one, eligible, make that *very* eligible thirty something. And he was a cracker, there was no doubt about it. Louise Taylor had set her sights on him within weeks and it was soon the talk of the office. Although she still did her job perfectly well, there was an air about her of smug complacency and although she didn't say anything, she managed to make it clear that he was definitely now Her Property.

Then the really juicy stories had started. No one knew quite where they had come from, but suddenly they were all over the place. Her smugness reached an almost critical level until, one day, every member of staff received an email. Most of them had kept it in the archive, to read at their leisure, because it really had been an eye-opener. It was from the Cracker.

'Dear Colleague,' it began, 'Please excuse this "round robin" but I am unable to speak to you all separately. I have discussed this with the senior partner and have his blessing to proceed. First of all, I want you to be aware that I have known for some time about the stories circulating about me, not just in this Practice, but also in certain sectors of my social circle. These involve me and Miss Louise Taylor and consist of some very personal details of our relationship.'

This first paragraph had raised some eyebrows but not as much as the second one did.

'As you all know, I am a very private person and I prefer to keep my home life to myself. It is therefore with some distaste that I find myself sharing with you all the fact that, last February, whilst on holiday with some close friends and my immediate family, I very happily became the husband of my long term partner, David. This is not the way I intended to share this news with anyone, but Miss Taylor has made it necessary. I hope this will make no difference to the excellent working partnership which our practice members have and I would appreciate your continuing friendship. Miss Taylor's position in this practice has been terminated with immediate effect and the partners and I would all be very pleased if you would undertake not to discuss the details either amongst yourselves or with others. Thank you very much.'

Needless to say, details were not only discussed, but picked over almost to exhaustion. And now, just when it was becoming old news, another man, not as gorgeous as the doctor, the receptionist would be the first to attest but she wouldn't kick him out of her bed either, was here, asking for Louise Taylor. Was she up to her old tricks? He didn't really look the type. She clearly went for power and position and he didn't look as if he had either of those. But … who knew? And the twittering and gossiping went on.

'So,' the Customer Service woman said to her colleague from Accounts when they met for their usual coffee in the staff canteen. 'He wasn't gorgeous, as such. A bit …' she sipped her drink and thought for a moment, '… vulnerable, that's it. A bit vulnerable. You wanted to mother him.'

'Well, that's not the bitch's usual target,' her friend said, snapping a bourbon biscuit between strong teeth. 'She goes for management, that's her hunting ground.'

'She getting anywhere?'

'Nah. Not as far as I can tell. Since she got moved to lates she hasn't really got much of a pool to fish in, tell the truth. There's only the pickers and the stackers; not much to choose from there. They're either students or retired and I don't think they fit her bill.'

The Customer Service woman laughed her hooting laugh. 'Fit her bill? Is it her bill they need to fit?'

The Accounts clerk opened her eyes wide and sprayed biscuit crumbs everywhere. 'You're terrible. No, really. You are!'

'Well, she has that look about her, don't you think? Kind of … desperate.'

'Well, I did hear she had a fling with one of them doctors up at the practice. Nearly broke up his marriage, they say. He's got a couple of little kids as well. Dreadful. She got the sack over it.'

'Can they do that?' The Customer Service woman was doing an online course in HR.

The other shrugged. 'I don't know. But the bottom line is she works here now on the late shift, so go figure.'

'True.' She drained her cup and brushed the pastry flakes off her front. 'Ah, well. Time to get back to work. We'll doubtless hear all about it. If there's one thing you can say about the bitch, it's that gossip about her goes the rounds quicker than a dose of the trots after the shepherd's pie in here.' She caught the eye of a woman wiping down tables with a grubby cloth. 'No offence.'

And they went back to their desks.

As Chris walked, he did some sums in his head. Because of the smell and other problems, forty-three didn't command a huge rent. But could she afford it on a supermarket salary? She had talked of having a housemate; perhaps she had gone ahead and done that and would still be living there. It was worth a punt, though and although it was out of town a way, it was a pleasant enough day, warm for the time of year and not a challenging walk at all. The last leaves were lying in drifts against the fences and to save a mile or so, he could cut through the park.

He closed his mind to memories of happier times here with Kyle and Megan, feeding the ducks and just watching the world go by. People out walking their dogs swung past him, older couples sauntered along hand in hand. All around him the world was getting on with its daily life, whether it was a grind or, quite literally, a walk in the park. He tried to feel part of it but it was as though there was a faint mist between him and everyone else. He hated the feeling and needed human contact to dispel it. In the distance, he thought he saw Cassie, walking her dog, the one he hadn't known she had. He quickened his pace but when he got to the gate, she had gone. He looked both ways but she was nowhere in sight. Although he really wanted to see her, to hear her warm voice, to get comfort from her smile, her soft cheek pressed against his in greeting, he was, for once, a man with a mission and so he turned resolutely towards forty-three.

She had added a doorbell. It was only a stick-on one; he had seen them on so many houses, linked to a wireless bell inside the house. He hoped she had asked permission, his inner letting agent thought. He pressed it and the Westminster chimes sounded from the rear of the house, followed by swift, sharp footsteps. She flung the door open with a sudsy hand.

'Yes?' she said.

'Louise. We have to talk.' He hadn't really thought this through. He had no idea how this conversation was going to go.

'Do I know you?' She was closing the door a little, putting it between him and her.

He instinctively put his foot in the lessening gap. 'What? Do you *know* me?' He pushed forward and was inside, slamming the door behind him. 'You've ruined my life and you ask if you know me?'

She backed away, hands to her chest clutching a teatowel but with no fear in her eyes. 'I shall call the police,' she said, too calmly.

'Why don't you? Yes, why don't you?' He snatched up the phone from the hall table and offered it to her. '999? Or is 101 enough? Shall I dial for you?'

She looked at him, at bay against the door of the cupboard under the stairs, a woman on the verge of a scream. Then, making up her mind, she dried her hands on her teatowel and relaxed, leading the way into the kitchen. 'You'll notice I've got rid of the smell,' she said over her shoulder, putting the towel neatly over the handle of the oven door to dry. 'It was, quite literally, an old sprout and a kipper skeleton, slipped down behind the cooker. Anyway, it's quite a nice house without it, so you should be grateful.' She looked at him hard. 'I assume you haven't come here to put up the rent or anything.'

'Why would I do that? You know as well as I do that I don't work there any more.'

'Really?' She raised her eyebrows and turned on a tap to fill the kettle. 'Coffee? Tea?'

'No. Neither. For God's sake, Louise, this isn't a social call.'

'Then, what is it?' She looked genuinely puzzled and he wondered just how sane, on a scale of one to ten, she actually was.

'It's to say, you've ruined my life. I hope you're happy now. What was it I did to you that was so terrible?'

'*I* ruined *your* life? I like that.' She was busy with mugs and coffee. 'Are you sure …?'

'Oh, all right, then. Coffee. No sugar. How can we be doing this? You lied to everyone, to Megan. You made up so much, I … I don't know where to begin.'

'You've gone a bit white, actually,' she remarked, as though he wasn't there for anything other than a friendly chat. 'Go through into the lounge and I'll bring the coffee in when it's plunged.'

He stood staring for a long minute, then with a shrug went through the hallway into the lounge. She had made that nice, too, all creams and browns, very restful, very calming. He needed all the calming he could get.

As he sat there, waiting, he realised how he missed his phone. He would be checking texts now, emails, Facebook. If the wait went on, he could play Cookie Jam. But as it was, all he could do was look around him, trying to find something in this room that would tell him something about the woman out there in the kitchen, humming quietly to herself and making him a cup of coffee.

Then, there she was, with a mug in each hand. 'You didn't say,' she said, 'but I've put milk. I couldn't remember how you took it.'

'What do you mean, can't remember?' he said snappily as he took the mug from her. 'We spent one night together and then you … well, I don't know what you did, but we apparently had sex here, no frills, no plumped pillows and a quick fag afterwards. How can you know how I take my coffee?'

She sat opposite him and curled her legs under her, in Megan's familiar pose. 'You are a silly,' she said, blowing on her drink. 'You've always been like this, playing games, pretending you don't know me. And how did it feel, eh, when I played it on you just now?' Her eyes narrowed. 'Not nice, is it?'

He put the mug down on the hearth and leaned forward. 'I. Don't. Know. You.' He jabbed the air between them with each word. 'Yes, I may have had sex with you …'

'Actually,' she broke in, shrilly, 'made love is the phrase I prefer. Animals have sex.'

'Then that's what we did. I don't care for you a jot, do you understand? I remember *nothing*, less than nothing of this famous one night stand we are supposed to have had. All I remember of the sex here was that I woke up with no clothes on and a sodding great love bite on my hip.'

'Don't forget the lipstick,' she said, sneering.

'Oh, yes, the lipstick. I won't pretend that my sex life has been varied or even very frequent,' he said, 'but one thing I am sure of is that, no matter how many blow jobs a person has, lipstick in a perfect circle on the underwear is not something you see that often. It was clearly a plant.'

'Little woman agree, did she?' she said, gulping her coffee.

'As a matter of fact, yes, in a way, she did. It was all the lies you told her when you stalked her at work that did the damage.'

'Stalked?' She was outraged. 'Stalked? I certainly did no such thing. We bumped into each other.'

'And you told her a load of lies.'

'I told her what we like to do when we're alone, yes. If she doesn't like that kind of thing, then perhaps she shouldn't be with you. Simple as that.'

'But we don't do anything, do we?' He was exasperated and also getting a little scared. He could feel the adrenalin beginning to course through his body and he was ready for flight. Because it wouldn't be right to fight with this woman who was so clearly, patently as mad as a tree. 'We're never alone.'

She spread an eloquent arm. 'I don't see anyone, do you?'

'This is hardly a tryst, is it?' Lord knows where he had dredged that word up from. It was the kind of thing Mike Green would use to describe his dodgy dealings to make them sound wholesome. 'I came to see you to … to …'

'Yes? To do what? To have some more of what you like to get from me? You know I can refuse you nothing.' She put her coffee down and stood up, facing him. 'I'm always ready for you, you know,' she said, licking her lips. 'I always make sure I'm good and ready.' She unzipped her jeans and began to peel them down but he was on his feet and grabbed her wrists, pulling her arms out to the sides. 'Oh,' she murmured, arching back. 'Rough. How I like it.'

He shook her and she went limp so he shook her some more then before he knew it she was back on the sofa and he was leaning over her, his hands around her throat. 'I don't care, right now,' he hissed, 'if I kill you. If you really want to know, I would quite welcome it. Handing myself over to the police,' he squeezed harder and her hands came up and grabbed his wrists, pulling frantically. 'I wouldn't need a trial. I would, what do they call it, allocute and just get a nice long sentence. In a nice warm cell, three square meals a day, some classes in how to clean toilets effectively.' He squeezed once more and then let go and stood back. 'But, on balance, I think not. Not today. I don't want my son to have a murderer for a father. But I do want you to tell me here, now, that you made it all up and that you'll tell Megan it was lies.'

She was massaging her neck and gagging, falling sideways on the sofa, her knees up in the foetal position.

He wanted to kick her, bite her, strangle her, anything to let the rage out of him. He had never hated anyone so much in his life. Then, she whispered something that he didn't catch.

'What? Speak up. I didn't hurt you that much. Come on.' He shook her.

She coughed and moistened her lips. Then, she looked up at him from where she lay. 'Yes,' she said, clearly. 'Yes, I made it up. It was all lies.'

He could hardly believe it. She had said it. She had actually said it. Now he could have his life back. 'And you'll tell Megan?'

'I'll tell anyone you like,' she said. 'I … I don't feel very well, Chris. I think you've hurt me.' She held her throat and he could see the bruises beginning to come out.

'You'll be fine,' he said, callously. 'I'm going now. Just make sure you tell Megan it was lies, now, won't you? Because if you don't, I'll be back.' He looked down at her and his adrenalin drained away. 'Look, Louise … I didn't mean to hurt you. I mean now and also the other times. You know, the times we … made love.' It was a big concession; he had always hated that phrase.

She looked up at him through hooded lids. 'Oh, *those* times. Yes, those times. Chris, you fool. You really are as dumb as shit. I never slept with you. You arrogant … piece of *shit*.' The vehemence made her cough and he watched as she retched, strings of bile tying her to the sofa. 'We never had sex, made love, bonked … call it what you like, you've never had me. Never.' She laughed hoarsely. 'But I had you, didn't I? Good and proper. Oh, yes.'

He grabbed her arm and hauled her upright. 'You mean … *never?*'

'I mean never,' she said, limp in his hands. 'Yes, you went home with me. But what makes you think I want to sleep with anyone who just puts it about where he fancies, with someone he's just met? But before I had to sling you out on your sorry, promiscuous arse, you passed out anyway. Very complimentary, I don't think. But, it turns out, you are very, *very* suggestible. I told you all the things I thought you might be into, whispered it in your pathetic, drunken, unconscious ear. And, it seems, it stuck. And so,' she shrugged as best she could, 'the rest is history.'

He didn't know what to do. He was pretty sure he had a court case, right there. But how would it look? She would win hands down, sure to. He wanted to drag her round to tell Megan, to shove her out of his front door and begin his life again. But instead, he just shoved her away from him, in the heat of his anger not hearing the dull thud as her head hit the corner of the fireplace.

He let himself out.

Who by Fire

*

'Claire?'

'Chris? Is everything all right?' Claire was at work and not best pleased to be getting a call so soon, but, as she tried to remind herself, blood is thicker than water. And she had worried about sending him to the lioness's den.

'I just wanted to tell you that I saw her. She said it was all lies. Even the times I thought I remembered.'

'What? Are you serious? How did she manage to convince you that you had …' she was conscious that people were beginning to stare, 'on the other times?'

'I don't know.' That was actually a very valid point she had there. 'I didn't ask.'

'Well, I seriously suggest you find out. If this woman is going around drugging people,' she had dropped her voice, 'as I think she must have done, it has to be stopped. Agree?'

'Yes. Yes, I suppose so. But … she said she would tell Megan that it was all lies. I don't want to report her to the police, if she says she'll do that. She might not …'

Claire loved her brother. She knew he wasn't stupid. But she could hardly believe her ears. 'Chris. Oh, Chris … have you been in touch with Megan at all since you split up?'

The phone line sounded strange, kind of echoing and dead.

'Chris? Chris? Are you there?' She looked at the phone in disgust. 'Bloody payphone. Where the hell did he manage to find one of those, these days?' She hit redial and with many whirrs and clicks, she got through. The phone rang and rang and rang and was eventually picked up.

'Hello?'

Oh, bugger. Little old lady voice. 'Hello. Can you tell me, is there a young man nearby? Wearing jeans and a shirt, jumper, jacket?'

There was a phlegmy chuckle at the other end. 'Any number of them, ducks,' said the voice. 'Do you want one in particular?'

'Just call out Chris.' Claire had no time for small talk.

In the distance, down the crackly line, the old dear called out as instructed, then came back to the receiver. 'No, ducks, nobody called that. Do you want someone else?'

'No,' Claire sighed. 'No one else. Just Chris. Thank you for your trouble.'

'No trouble, dear,' the woman said. 'I hope you find him all right.'

'Yes,' Claire said. 'Yes. Me too.'

Chris hadn't used a payphone for years and had forgotten how they could eat money, especially when the call was to a mobile. He had hardly started to tell Claire about his visit to Louise when the line went dead and he had no more change. He didn't want to buy anything so he thought he would leave the rest of the conversation for when he had some change. He wasn't going to do anything to scupper what might be his last chance to get his life on track, but he did see the wisdom in making sure Louise made good on her promise. He would find her at work tonight, keep badgering her until he knew she had done what she promised. As he mooched away, his head full of maybe, he thought he heard someone call his name. He stopped and listened. So did the dog. But there was nothing more and he walked on and for some reason, the tape that ran constantly in his head started playing 'Don't stop believing', stuck on the line about the midnight train. He just hated it when that happened but let his steps fall into time with it anyway.

Claire put the phone down and thought for a moment, then reached behind her for her coat. 'Just popping out,' she announced, to no one in particular and went out, leaving open mouths behind her. Claire Rowan *never* did the unexpected. They should have been expecting it, therefore, but somehow no one was.

Megan was enjoying a quiet few moments after a fraught lunch with Kyle. He had taken rather a shine to *Nerds and Monsters* and was engrossed, lying on his tummy on the carpet, thumb in his mouth and feet waving lazily in the air. Megan had a coffee and a book and was concentrating on neither; her head was full of maybes and she didn't want to spoil her daydream. It was in a very frail bubble which would take very little to go pop.

Kyle jumped slightly as the doorbell went but didn't take his eyes off the screen. Megan went reluctantly to answer it. It was bound to be Sam; she hadn't answered a single call or returned a PM or a text or an email either. It was about time she arrived in person. She opened the door, excuses at the ready.

'Claire! Hello. Umm … come in.'

Claire stepped over the threshold, but that was all. 'I can't stay. I've just popped out from work and they think it's weird enough as it is. If I'm not back soon, well … I need to be back soon. Have you seen Chris at all since he left?'

'No. What do you mean?' She didn't say that seeing him staggering around with a drunken woman in a dark alley perhaps didn't count. Perhaps it didn't.

'He's been to see Louise.'

Megan snorted and looked behind her to make sure the door into the lounge was shut. Kyle wouldn't understand this conversation but that was no reason why he should have to hear it.

'I don't mean like that,' Claire said. 'I mean, he went to confront her. To find out why she was lying about him.'

'So, you buy the lying story, do you?' Megan was surprised. Claire had no rose-tinted glasses where her brother was concerned, not as a rule.

Claire rocked her hand. 'Not sure, before today. But he's just rung me and said that she said it was all lies.'

'You said.' Megan folded her arms.

'No, I mean, *all* lies. Even the twice he thought happened. She just pretended it had all taken place, God knows why. He rang, but we were cut off.'

'Has he still got his mobile, then? I thought the office would cut that off, no problem. Dave Stanley has never been one to flash the cash.'

'It was a call box and when I called it back, he had gone. But he's planning to come round, Megan. He wants to come home. Can he?'

Megan's face said it all.

'As I thought. I saw you out on Saturday night and I happen to know the guy you were with.'

'You know Will?'

'Not well, but I know he is good pe. You know he's …'

'Gay. No, he isn't.'

'I was going to say older, but if you say gay, I wouldn't argue.' Claire gave her a funny look. 'But what I wondered was, how long has it been going on? Do you want Chris back, with all his hang-ups and the black dog and all that stuff? If you have Will. I mean, I *have* to love Chris and it isn't easy. I just wondered …'

Megan took a step forward and was suddenly crying over her almost-sister-in-law's shoulder. She had cried a lot in the past months, God alone knew how much she'd cried, but these tears seemed to come from somewhere else, somewhere that she hadn't plumbed as yet and for a while she thought they might never stop. But eventually, they did and she sniffed and let the other woman go.

Claire smiled. 'Better?' she asked.

'Much,' Megan said, wiping her eyes on her sleeve. 'Sorry. I know you don't really do the emotional stuff.'

'I do it,' Claire said, 'but on my own. Our parents may have seemed pretty normal to the casual glance, but they managed to bugger up me and my brother good and proper. Anyway, what I came to say was, if he turns up, best Will isn't here. But that said, don't let him find out from someone else. It could be the straw that breaks the camel's back, you know. He's very fragile.'

Megan smiled ruefully.

'Yes, I know you know that. But his depression is coming and going right now and every time he comes out of it, he seems to plunge deeper when he is on the downward swing. I know he's drinking too much. I know that … well, he's not being all that choosy at the moment is all I'll say.'

'I know. I saw.'

'Ah. Well, you know what I mean, then.'

'Yes.'

'Megan. This is serious. If you don't want to have him back, you need to tell him so. But don't shut the door in his face. Let him have his things. Let him see his son.'

'Kyle … well, he doesn't talk about his daddy any more.'

'Any more than Chris talks about him. They're the same animal, Megan. Don't meet trouble halfway. But they miss each other. They need each other. Sort something out.' She pulled her phone out of her pocket and shook her head. 'Look. I have to go. I've missed half a dozen meetings already and it can only get worse. I don't know where he's staying now, but he won't be hard to find. He'll be at Mum's I expect. We had a bit of … well, there was a bit of trouble, but Mum wouldn't turn him away. Or Mark. Try there. If he comes back to me, I'll let you know.'

Megan looked doubtful and began to shake her head. 'I was going to do it at the weekend. Will was going to drive me …'

'Leave Will out of this,' Claire said, 'if you'll take my advice. You need to do this on your own. Promise?'

'I can't do it tonight. I left Kyle with a sitter last night and I can't do it twice in a row.'

'Tomorrow, then.'

'I promise. I'll do it tomorrow.'

'Fine.' Claire gave her a peck on the cheek, her one concession. 'Let me know how you get on. It'll all be all right, you'll see.'

The day seemed very long. Chris had several cups of indifferent coffee and one spectacularly good one which cost the same as all the others combined, so perhaps no surprise there. He had a proper lunch as well and found to his delight he could still blend; that was becoming increasingly important to him, blending. The muzak in the bistro had finally beaten Journey into submission and that had to be a bonus. He let his spaghetti bolognaise last a long time and then had a pudding as well – it was a long time since he had eaten this well at lunchtime, but he couldn't believe that Claire would mind; his B&B would just have to be a bit cheaper than he had planned. He knew now how those killers in the US cop shows felt when they had a hearty meal before being executed. He perhaps wouldn't have chosen spag bol on such a momentous occasion, but even so; he felt full and content.

The bistro was full and noisy but it was impossible to dent his mood. A table way over to his left was more raucous than the rest and he turned his head lazily to watch what was going on and his blood froze, cold sweat breaking out on his forehead as a panic attack threatened to overwhelm him then and there. Megan's friend Sam was at the table, with a couple of other women, one of whom he thought he knew; it was the woman from the alley, for sure, much more elegantly dressed now and looking older, with a bit too much makeup. They were laughing and clinking glasses and it wasn't his imagination that Sam looked straight at him and sneered before carrying on with what was clearly gossip about him. He fumbled a couple of notes out of his wallet and left them with the tab on his table before stumbling out of the bistro, his perfect mood in tatters. Sam watched him go, as did her companions. The woman from the alley didn't recognize him at all. By the time she had woken up the next morning and staggered into the bath thoughtfully drawn for her by her very faithful and patient husband, all memory and all physical reminders of her little lapse had gone. Her pregnancy symptoms would take a while to kick in – and meanwhile, there were boozy lunches to be had. As Chris stumbled down the High Street, his blood singing in his ears, the women all clinked glasses together. The last thing he heard from them was a faint echo. 'Cheers!'

Finally, it was night. Chris had booked into a cheap hotel in the main drag of the town centre. It was cheap by hotel standards but he knew he couldn't stay long. But on the other hand, perhaps … no, not *perhaps*, he *definitely* wouldn't be there long. He would be home. In his own bed. Everything would be all right. He could get a job with a proper address. He found he was smiling. He cruised the aisles of the supermarket, picking things up – cheap things – and putting them back. Every now and again, he left something in his basket, just so it all looked a bit more normal. Not so shopliftery. Every time he got to the till end of an aisle, he scanned along for Louise, but no luck. Eventually, he took his haul of crisps, chocolate and newspaper to a till and unloaded it onto the conveyor.

'Is Louise here tonight?' he asked, trying to sound casual.

'No, she isn't,' the woman said, shortly. 'And that's why I'm here. She didn't show and I'm next on the roster. I could have done without this, to be honest. I was planning a night in, with the old man, no kids. Know what I mean.' She gave him an unpleasant leer and he smiled, paid and backed away.

What could this mean? Was she already at Megan's? Had she baled altogether and left town? He didn't know which was the most likely, but his innate sense of pessimism made his suspect it was the latter, or some option close to it. His mood had been going downhill ever since his lunch almost-encounter and he didn't know what to do now. He hesitated outside the shop, a plastic carrier dangling from his fingers.

'Hello.'

The voice was so close to him, he jumped. He looked down to see a smiling, rather grubby face smiling up at him.

'Hello.' He smiled back and edged away a step or two. She wasn't threatening but she was rather smelly. Perhaps a night with Claire had made him ultra-sensitive, but with his brand new clothes and a wallet of money, he had to be a bit careful.

'I know you, don't I?' The girl had moved too, so the distance between them stayed the same. 'I've seen you around town lately.'

'I live here.' It seemed easier to speak to her, but keep it simple. When he had exchanged a few words, she might go away.

She raised her eyebrows. 'Really. Where?'

He waved an arm. 'Here. Lived here all my life.'

'What?' She looked back and forth. 'Here? In the High Street?'

'Well, no,' he said. 'I've lived in this town all my life.'

'Oh, I see. Well, that's a bit different, isn't it?' she said. She seemed quite well spoken to be so grubby, so smelly and out so late at night on her own. She couldn't be more than eighteen, tops. 'So, where do you live?'

He smiled and walked away, the usual signal that this conversation is at an end, so goodbye.

'I only ask,' she said, 'because I really have seen you around a lot lately and since Friday in particular. I saw you out with that weird little pharmacy bloke at the weekend. I saw you giving that drunk cow one down the alley. I saw you yesterday …'

If there was one thing in the world Chris didn't want, it was another stalker. Not so soon after getting rid of one, at any rate. 'I stayed with my friend, the pharmacist,' he said, giving the words a lot of emphasis to try and make her feel bad, but she was impervious. 'Then I stayed with my sister.'

'And you live … where?'

He stared down at her. Funny how, though she was far from clean, she still managed to have smudgy eyeliner round her big blue eyes and her hair looked squeaky clean. 'At this very moment,' he said, with the definite air of someone giving just one last chance to the conversation, 'I am staying in the hotel behind Smith's. But I will be back home in the next day or so. I've … I've had a bit of a hiccup with the missus.' If ever there was an understatement, he thought to himself, that was surely it.

'Long hiccup,' she remarked, falling into step along with him and tucking her hand into the crook of his arm, in a companionable way. 'I've seen you mooching around for months. You've been dossing at the vicar's.'

'My mother is married to the vicar,' he said, loftily.

'Poor cow,' she said. 'We all know the vicar.' She laughed, a dirty, knowing laugh which was nonetheless catching. 'I'm lucky, though. He doesn't like them young. He likes them …' she let go of his arm to sketch a rather big and muscly lady in the air. 'Lesbians, for choice.'

'Yes … I did know that.'

'Really?' She spun round to face him. 'I'm surprised. I would have thought the old vic would have preferred to keep that kind of stuff to himself.'

Chris laughed to see her there, dancing on her toes, laughing at the thought of the silly old vicar sniffing around the big ladies. So he sat on a bench and patted the seat beside him and told her everything about his night out with Gavin's stag party, down to and including petuniacide. She laughed like a child, with her whole body and holding nothing back. He found it wasn't possible to stay miserable when she was there and laughing. He joined in and soon they were swapping stories like a couple of ancient mariners. Finally, after the same window above their heads had flown up for the umpteenth time, they moved on, arm in arm like old friends, old friends, sat on their park bench like bookends ... no, God no, not Simon and Garfunkel as well as Journey, all in one day. So he told her about the sound track in his head and she laughed some more. She said she had one too, but the one she had the most was the Pigeon Street theme song. So they sang it, in two part harmony, otherwise known as two people singing two different songs at the same time in the same place as they walked down the High Street, heading for the park.

'Wait a minute,' Chris said, suddenly realising he was the grown up here. 'Where do *you* live?' They were a way away from his hotel now and he didn't want to end up with a long hike back in the dark.

'No, don't let's start that again,' she said. 'I live here. Like you.'

'And what's your name?'

'What would you like it to be?'

He laughed. 'That's silly. I can't choose a name to call you.'

'I gave my name away long ago, to someone who needed it. I go by what I fancy now. But I like you; so you choose. What would you like to call me?'

Megan just sounded wrong. Claire likewise. 'Cassie,' he said. 'I'd like to call you Cassie, if you don't mind.'

She tasted the name, running it around on her tongue. 'I like it,' she announced. 'Is it short for Cassandra, do you think?'

'I don't think I've ever thought about it? Would you mind if it were?'

'No. It would be cool. Cassandra was the most beautiful of king Priam's daughters. She got the gift of prophecy from Apollo but she screwed him over in the end and so he fixed it so no one would believe her. It's a great story, floods and storms, Troy, Helen, all that. So let's say that's what it's short for.' She walked along beside him, bouncing in her tatty trainers, humming a tune that wasn't Pigeon Street or anything else he knew. 'But, who is she, Cassie? Is she your wife?'

'No. Just someone I like.'

She gave his arm a squeeze. 'I'm flattered,' she said and fell silent again. 'Have you got any money?'

'Oh, here it comes,' he said, flatly. 'Has this whole thing, this crazy chick thing just been for money?'

'Crazy chick thing?' She stood in front of him, arms folded, head on one side. 'What crazy chick thing?'

'Well, all this … all this.' It was the best he could do. He waved his arms around vaguely. 'These rather … gnomic remarks.'

'Ooh,' she mocked. 'Let's try the crazy chick with a difficult word, see if she knows what it means. The bottom line there, clever pants, is that yes, I do know what it means. But I wonder if you do. Look, sit with me here.' She plonked down on the nearest garden wall. 'Come on. I won't make a noise and frighten Mr and Mrs Suburbia. Sit.' She patted the wall. 'Sit.'

He sat down, gingerly. The bricks were cold and narrow. He was getting too old for this malarkey.

'How old am I?'

'Is this like the name?' He needed to check the parameters.

'Nope. This is a question. How old am I?'

'Eighteen?'

'Wrong. I'm twenty-three but I know I look young. I was like you, once. Boring, no offence, conventional. I went to uni, got a degree. A bloody good one, since you don't ask. But it didn't get me a job. It didn't get me a house. It got me a whole load of nothing, plus a bit of random touching up from time to time from my mum's old geezer boyfriend. So I split. I live where I can, now. Sometimes it's a house. Sometimes it's the park. Like now, for instance, it's the park, but I'll have to think about signing on soon, get somewhere warm. I don't take benefits if I don't need them. I work, sometimes. In general, my life consists of being as happy as I can. If I can make someone else happy for a while,' she mimed a slot machine, 'kerching. Bonus.'

He knew he should say something clever, something apologetic. Something. But he couldn't. Something about her simplicity and her basic joy had made the tears come that had been at bay for a while. He felt her grubby little hand on his arm.

'Look, don't worry. I don't want people to understand me. That's not what anyone needs. I am what I am and that's it. In my book, everyone gets in life exactly what they deserve. Same with death, too. Sometimes, you read in the news, someone dies too young, or in an accident that is so horrible you can't take it in. But me, I don't mourn. Not for anyone. If you die too young, as they say, it's so you can just get back on the bike again, have another turn, give it another go. No good hanging on if it's crap, is there?' She stood up and brushed the brick dust off her bum. 'That wall's not very comfy. Your nuts must be cold as charity. Want to warm them up?'

Chris was gobsmacked. This evening had been odd, he would be the first to admit, but the last five words were perhaps the oddest. 'I beg your pardon?'

'Come back to mine. Or go to yours, if it's that kind of hotel. I could do with a hot shower, if I'm honest. Then we can … what kind of word do you prefer? I know the vicar likes "congress" but that reminds me a bit of history lessons.'

'I … I …'

'We'll call that a yes, then, shall we?' she said, dancing in front of him. 'So. Your place or mine?'

He looked her up and down. She could still pass for respectable, in a dim light. And a quick tenner to the night porter should settle any problems on that score. And a shower for her might be nice … 'Mine,' he said with a smile, and took her hand.

Exit Music

*

The night porter was very happy with his tenner and Cassie II as Chris couldn't help calling her in his head was more than happy with her shower, which was followed, for some reason he couldn't fathom, by a bath. He had to go down to the lobby twice for more shampoo from the machine, but finally she was tucked up in bed, the crisp sheets under her, the quilt draped over her and she all but purred like a cat.

'Ooh,' she said, 'this is so lovely. When I win the lottery, I think I'll live in a hotel all the time.'

Chris called from the bathroom. 'Do you do the lottery?'

'Of course not. All property is theft.'

Chris looked around the bathroom door, startled but all was well. She hadn't changed into a Pugh. She just was quoting Pierre-Joseph Proudhon, though possibly of the two of them only she knew that. He went back just to wipe the toothpaste off his chin and found just one, low light on in the room. Her newly washed hair sprang around her head like a halo and he really did wonder whether perhaps he had died and gone to heaven. She didn't smell frowsty now, just sweetly of lemon and a hint of thyme, as advertised on the bodywash and shampoo. Her eyes sparkled in the little light there was and she lifted the quilt invitingly. He thought back to the sexual experiences he had

had lately and found to his chagrin it came down to one and that had hardly covered him in glory. The amazing creature in his bed read his mind.

'Never mind her,' she whispered. 'Tarts in an alley can happen to anyone. Come in.'

He didn't know what that might mean, but he climbed in under the cloud of quilt and very soon, hardly cared.

Megan was not looking forward to the evening at all. But she knew it was something that just had to be done. She needed to find Chris. She needed to put things right between them, sort out belongings, let him know there were no hard feelings but that it was never going to be the way it was again. She had thought it through and there was a way forward, one that might suit everyone. He could have the house. She could move in with Will; that she would be welcome was a given. Kyle could live with them both, turn and turn about. All would be hunky. All would be dory. She just needed to find him. And explain. And before she could explain to him, she had to explain to everyone else. She had turned down Will's chauffeuring offer. She had left her mother in charge of Kyle for once, silent disapproval dripping from every pore. And she had set off on her travels, like a heroine in a fable.

Easiest to find was Mark, if only because he lived above the shop. She turned up just as he was closing and although he clearly wasn't keen, he let her in.

He could tell her little. He knew that Chris had gone to the GP, because they had sent a digital scrip, as they always did. He hadn't collected it though, but it was only a few days ago, so he might still do so. Would Megan like Mark to tell Chris she was asking about him? He would be happy to do that.

There was a shadow behind his eyes that Megan understood. He knew what Chris had done the previous weekend. But he didn't know she knew. Perhaps telling him would remove the final barrier, but she didn't need that kind of pity. So she thanked Mark, jotted down her new mobile number and left, looking for her next quarry. It was sad that the list was so short.

The vicarage was lit up like a Christmas tree and there were several people heading towards it. Megan cursed under her breath. There always seemed to be something going on in the place; Young Mums, Old Mums, Fete Committee, for all she knew Fate Committee – she just hoped this wasn't one of the ones that Sarah had been co-opted onto. She tried to guess but it was impossible. Hope sprang when she saw Mike on his own in the hall, ushering people into the dining room. She took her place in the queue.

'If you'd just like …' he looked up and started in surprise. 'Megan! How … lovely. Kyle with you? No, I suppose it is a little late. Well, you catch me about to start a meeting, but Sarah is in the kitchen, if you would like to go through. Yes. Umm …' and he was already on to the next parishioner.

Sarah Green sat at the kitchen table, staring at the scum on the top of a cooling tea. Sometimes, she thought she had been doing that very thing every day of her life. The greasy layer split and rejoined, leaving lines which never quite went away. A bit like life. It looked all fixed, but it would never be the same again. She didn't look up as Megan went in. 'I'll do the drinks later,' she said. No endearment. Megan noticed that at once. Mike and Sarah had always been darlingers and now here she was, addressing him like a public meeting.

'Hello, Sarah,' she said, quietly.

Her not-really-mother-in-law-as-was jumped and splashed the cold tea on her jumper but didn't seem to mind. 'Megan! How lovely! Sit down, I'll make us a fresh cup, shall I? Or would you rather have coffee?'

'Tea is fine.' It was a little barb in Megan's heart that Sarah had already forgotten which she preferred when. 'Decaff if you have it. It doesn't matter if not.'

Sarah faffed and fussed making the tea and polite conversation. There wasn't really that much to tell. She told Megan about the petunias but not the pornography, about Chris staying and what fun it had been, but not his leaving. The whole monologue was just a series of snippets, with all the contentious bits left out. Finally, with a fresh mug in front of each woman, it was Megan's turn.

'I need to find Chris,' she said. 'Claire wondered if you might know where he is.'

Sarah looked at her with big eyes, not really following. 'Do you mean, you want him to go home?' The hope in her voice made Megan stifle a sob.

'No. I'm sorry, Sarah. I ... I've met someone.'

'That was quick.' Sarah Green in snap mode could beat Megan's own mother into a cocked hat.

'It was. But sometimes things are.' Megan gave her a long stare. 'Aren't they?' She had hardly let her husband get cold, as Megan had understood it, before she was shacked up with the vicar.

Sarah reached out a hand and spoke in level tones. 'Don't jump too fast, Megan. It doesn't work.' She waited for her words to sink in. 'Believe me.' Then she straightened and smiled her vicar's wife smile. 'But I'm sure you know what you're doing.'

'I think I do. I hope I do. But the main thing is, there is a way around this problem, a way where Chris can move into the house, share Kyle's care with me. We won't be a happy family like we were. But Kyle will have his daddy back and Chris won't be dependent on sofa surfing. It's time he was told. And apparently ... do you know about the woman?'

Sarah bowed her head. 'Apparently, she has admitted it was all lies. He is expecting her to come and tell me but I'm not holding my breath. Claire let me know. She persuaded me to come out tonight.'

'Claire can be very kind,' her mother said, in tones that implied that also, she could be just the opposite.

'I think she was right. I will rest easier when he knows what's on offer.'

'It's a shame that you can't ...'

Megan shook her head. That one had to be knocked on the head. 'It wasn't only the so-called affair,' she said. 'I was struggling before that. Chris was ... well, he was just wearing me out. Him and Kyle. Like two peas in a pod but relentless. I didn't sign up for two children.'

'The dog?'

'The dog, and the moods and the ... the everything, Sarah. I can't do it any more.'

'And now you've found someone perfect,' Sarah said. 'Someone with money, if you can let Chris have the house.' A son's mother is always like a tigress, when cornered.

'Yes, he has money. He isn't perfect. But he seems to like me ... more, perhaps, at least I hope so. He offers me comfort, Sarah. I need that for a while.'

'As the apple tree among the trees of the wood, so is my beloved among the sons,' Sarah said, with a faraway look on her face. 'I sat down under his shadow with great delight, and his fruit was sweet to my taste. He brought me to the banqueting house, and his banner over me was love. Stay me with flagons, comfort me with apples: for I am sick of love. His left hand is under my head, and his right hand doth embrace me.' She giggled. 'Song of Solomon,' she said. 'You have to read something in the sermons.'

Megan smiled but she also nodded. 'That Solomon knew a thing or two,' she said.

'He did, he did indeed.' The two women stared into their half-empty cups, heads full of thoughts they couldn't share.

'I don't know where Chris is, though,' Sarah said suddenly. 'Have you asked Mark?'

'Yes. He suggested I come here. Claire gave him money but didn't actually book him in anywhere. So I don't know where to begin ...'

'He won't have gone far out, not without a car. I think you could do worse than have a stroll up the High Street. Chris ... well, drink has become a bit of a prop.'

'I gathered that,' Megan said and drained her cup. 'Thanks for the chat, Sarah. I'll give you a call, arrange something with Kyle.'

'When you and Chris have everything settled.' Sarah smiled. Saying it could sometimes make it so.

'Yes. Then.' They bumped cheeks awkwardly and Megan let herself out, leaving Sarah watching the film on her tea break apart and reform, break apart and reform, endlessly different, always the same.

The morning had been such fun. The hotel was booked for a week and so there was no need to even get up, let alone get out. They had hung the do not disturb notice on the door and the chambermaid was more than happy to drop a room off her usually punishing schedule. They snoozed the morning away, breakfasting on digestive biscuits and instant coffee from the tray on the dressing table. But eventually,

Cassie II had stirred and stretched and said that time was a-wasting and she had to be away.

Chris leaned up on one elbow. 'Away? Where?'

'Hey,' she said, turning round from lacing her trainer. 'I didn't marry you last night, you know. I just ...'

'I know what you did,' he grinned, 'and there was no "just" about it. But I thought ...'

'Look,' she bounced up and down at the foot of the bed, eager to be off. 'I want to see you again, I really do. I like you. You've got ... layers. I like peeling you. But I have to see a man about a dog. I have some business to conduct. I need to ... I need to be out and about in the world. I'm like the devil, Pilgrim. I need to know what's going on.'

'Pilgrim?'

'Pilgrim. Christian. Pilgrim's Progress.'

'Chris is short for Christopher.'

'Not to me. Think yourself lucky I don't call you Bunyan.' She came round the side of the bed and kissed his nose. 'I'll see you tonight, shall I? But my place. Just go to the park before it gets dark. In that big bit of shrubbery in the middle, there's a tarpaulin, stretched between the trees. The back corner, right hand as you look at it with your back to the lake, that's mine. I'll see you there.'

'When?'

'Ah, ah, ah. Now, what did I tell you? I just will. Okay?'

'Okay.'

And she was gone.

The afternoon had dragged but finally it was late enough to go to the park without looking incredibly needy. He knew he just couldn't afford to be needy. To look needy that was; he would always *be* needy. He sussed out the shrubbery but there was no one there, just the tarpaulin as she had said. He would have recognized her corner anyway, from the beads, the fragments of feather, the lightness of touch. He kept going back, just to check and settled down against a tree as darkness began to fall, just to keep watch. It wasn't long before his eyelids drooped and he fell asleep, a smile on his lips for the first time in a long while.

The car was warm – he didn't remember getting in, but he was glad he had. The seat was big and squooshy, the seat belt wide and firm across his chest. He could just see the tops of trees and the upstairs windows of houses going by, then just sky. Over the sound of the engine, a bird was singing. He looked at the back of the driver's head and gave a puzzled frown. Why was the car so big? Why was he in the back?

'Where am I?' he asked. His voice was as small as he was, small and insignificant in a world suddenly built for giants. The head in front of him turned and his heart lurched to see a face he thought was gone for ever. 'Dad?' he said. 'Daddy?'

The man smiled and looked back at the road. 'So, you're awake. I thought you were taking a nap. We're out for a drive, remember? Going for a walk in the country, while Mummy and Claire do some shopping.'

Chris relaxed back into the enormous seat. Yes, he remembered now. A walk in the country. An ice cream from the van. The tarmac thrummed under the wheels and his father began to sing, under his breath, until his little boy fell asleep again.

In the silence, a black dog crept out from under the tarpaulin and lay alongside him, sharing body warmth and the same soft snore.

Cassie I and Cassie II were both out and about on errands of their own that night and they didn't know how near they were to one another. Cassie II was not a bad person, but had a living to earn, so she had a few customers who liked a bit of rather high-class weed especially when matched with some moderately high-class ass. She conducted her business with her customary discretion and had done well out of her afternoon so treated herself to a drink in the Bell. They had some pretty good live music there sometimes and she thought she would check it out. If it was anyone any good, she'd go and scoop up Pilgrim and bring him back. Cheer him up. But it was a folk duo tonight, one guy droning into the mic with one hand over his ear and the other playing the fiddle. Sadly, they hadn't agreed the set list, so things weren't going well. She downed her gin and turned to go, bumping into a middle aged woman with a sweet smile, who was coming in with a man who had to be her husband. They were cut from the same cloth, those two, Cassie II thought. How nice. And Cassie I, seeing the pretty girl jinking off on the balls of her feet, smiled even wider.

'Now, that's the kind of girl young Chris could have done with,' she said to her husband. 'Someone to let him be who he wants to be, not try and make him someone he's not.'

Her husband kissed her hand, clasped in his own. 'My love,' he said, 'Don't ever change.'

'I'm not sure I can,' she said, sliding into a corner seat by the window. 'Even if you wanted me to. Especially if you wanted me to. I think tonight, I'll have a gin.'

'And tonic?'

'Yes, and tonic. I need a few bubbles tonight, somehow.' She turned and watched the night street, the procession of the harried, the hurried, the strolling, the stalling, the lost souls. She sighed.

Megan didn't really know what she was doing there. Walking up and down the street wasn't going to do her any good, not when it came down to it. She did a couple of circuits and couldn't find Chris and she was damned if she was going to go up to strange barmen and ask. She did have a photo of him in her purse, as it just so happened but still – this wasn't *CSI*. She decided to walk around to Sam's. She could phone but she needed somewhere warm about now and anyway, after dipping her calls for days, perhaps the face to face, the chilled friend on the doormat might work better. It would certainly be harder to ignore. And she might even then get a lift home. She started off, skirting the park.

Chris woke up finally, chilly and stiff. He had been lying awkwardly, on the cold ground and it hadn't done his joints much good. He tried to move his left leg and found it pinned down; a scary thing to happen in a dark strange place. He looked down, almost afraid to look, but he needn't have worried. It was just a dog, its head pillowed on its paws which in turn were across his ankles. He gave it a gentle nudge and it growled before lifting its head and looking at him with dark, unfathomable eyes. He stumbled to his feet and stamped, trying to bring some life into them. He looked around. There was a dim light under the tarpaulin and he made his way there across the damp grass. Several men were grouped in one corner, opposite to Cassie's little nest. They turned to stare, stopping their conversation as he walked over to where she had told him to go and pulled back the cover to her bed.

What happened next was over in a winking of an eye. The boy sleeping in the bed was awake almost before Chris bent down to take up a corner of the bedding. His knife was in his hand even faster. And it slid between Chris's ribs as if it belonged there, nicking the artery that carried his blood to where it needed to go. There were no words, just a gasp from Chris as his last breath left his body. The boy sprang back and was gone into the darkness before anyone could stop him, had they cared to. Chris hadn't quite hit the ground when Cassie's flying feet had brought her to his side.

Megan, walking fast as women do when out alone after dark, stifled a cry as a black dog streaked out of the park as if hounds of hell were after him. In the silence that followed, she heard a wail, a howl of visceral sorrow from over by the trees, one dark mass against the soda-orange sky.

'Pilgrim!'

But it meant nothing to Megan, so she walked on.

Author's Note

*

While writing *Downward* I had, like Chris, tunes playing in my head from time to time. Some are chapter titles, some simply referenced but if you would like to share my playlist, some links appear below. Please note that these links were live at the time of publication and availability at later dates is not guaranteed.

Bethan White, 2016

Live – Lightning Crashes
https://www.youtube.com/watch?v=xsJ4O-nSveg

Hootie & The Blowfish – Let Her Cry
https://www.youtube.com/watch?v=1aVHLL5egRY

Tears For Fears – Mad World
https://www.youtube.com/watch?v=u1ZvPSpLxCg

Simon and Garfunkel – Sound of Silence
https://www.youtube.com/watch?v=4zLfCnGVeL4

Bill Withers – Ain't No Sunshine
https://www.youtube.com/watch?v=YuKfiH0Scao

Phil Collins – In the Air Tonight
https://www.youtube.com/watch?v=YkADj0TPrJA

Justin Hayward – Forever Autumn
https://www.youtube.com/watch?v=hsCdlX-5UjE

Radiohead – How To Disappear Completely
https://www.youtube.com/watch?v=lAF8D0ugyVk

Bob Dylan – Ain't No Man Righteous
https://www.youtube.com/watch?v=jlnzQbs3Tuo

Seldom Scene – Through the Bottom of the Glass
https://www.youtube.com/watch?v=l-sD4PahUME

Crawler – Stone Cold Sober
http://tinyurl.com/stonecoldsober

Joni Mitchell – Chelsea Morning
https://www.youtube.com/watch?v=F_y7O06z77Q

The Mamas and the Papas – Monday, Monday
https://www.youtube.com/watch?v=h81Ojd3d2rY

Foreigner – I Want to Know What Love Is
https://www.youtube.com/watch?v=raNGeq3_DtM

Tom Waits – God's Away on Business
https://www.youtube.com/watch?v=W9mhsW5aWJM

Michael McDonald – I Can Let Go Now
https://www.youtube.com/watch?v=xirq2kdcZkc

Ben Howard – The End of the Affair
https://www.youtube.com/watch?v=Unz9gWteR1s

Leonard Cohen – Who by Fire
https://www.youtube.com/watch?v=EQTRX23EMNk

Journey – Don't Stop Believing
https://www.youtube.com/watch?v=1k8craCGpgs

Pigeon Street Theme
https://www.youtube.com/watch?v=lav92tfPNBg

Radiohead – Exit Music (For a Film)
https://www.youtube.com/watch?v=RByvzmmEFiQ